The Santanapping

A South Pole Santa Adventure

Book 3

BY

JINGLEBELLE JACKSON

ISBN: 1500895296
ISBN 13: 9781500895297

For the young, and the young at heart,
who love Christmas too

And for my brother-in-law, Jeff,
one of Sandra's biggest fans

Choose Kindness

Character List:

- **Santa** – The main man, the big guy, the elf in the red suit
- **Cassandra Penelope Clausmonetsiamlydelaterra...** (**Sandra Claus...**) -- An 18-year-old girl selected (*The Search for South Pole Santa*) to be the South Pole Santa
- **Cappie** – Also known as Captain Margaret Richmond is Sandra's legal guardian since her parents disappeared when she was eleven
- **Squawk** – Sandra's beloved talking macaw
- **Rio** – An emerald-colored dolphin that is loved by, and travels with, Sandra and Cappie
- **Ambyrdena "Birdie" Snow** – Sandra's best friend; daughter of a water wizard and African princess mother. Birdie can talk to birds
- **Spencer Mantle** – Sandra's super smart other best friend; son of two humans
- **Sanderson "Sandy" Claus...** -- Sandra's dad, of elf and human descent; tragically lost at sea
- **Cassiopola "Cassie" Claus...** -- Sandra's mom, of royal elfin and human descent; tragically lost at sea
- **Christina Annalise** – Headmistress of St. Annalise Academy and mother of Jason Annalise
- **Jason Annalise** – Adopted son of Christina; Sandra's boyfriend and unexpected King of Fairies
- **Thomas Jackson** – A retired St. Annalise Academy professor living on the island and a friend of Sandra and Cappie's

- **Gunderson "Gunny" Holiday** – A runner-up for South Pole Santa from the great state of Texas. Now assists Santa
- **Major & Josephina Holiday** – Gunny's parents
- **Chance, Crow & Ghost Holiday** – Gunny's brothers
- **Blue & Glory Holiday** – Gunny's sisters
- **Zinga**– An elf who is the executive assistant to Santa
- **Breezy** – An elf in charge of weather reporting and friend to Sandra. She, like many elves, can read thoughts.
- **Emaralda "Em"** – A bright green "delgin elf" with special talents who assists Sandra
- **Dear Lovey** – A North Pole elf who writes an advice column
- **Wistle** – A Shan fairy
- **Reesa**-- The Shan fairy ruler apparent
- **Nicholas Navidad, Redson O'Brien, Klondike Tannenbaum, Rollo Kringle** – Runner-up competitors for South Pole Santa
- **Beatrice Carol** – A World Wide News TV reporter from London, England
- **Calivon** – A royal elfin, head of the Esteemed High Council of Magical Beings
- **Zeentar** – Water wizard and Birdie's dad; serves on the High Council of Magical Beings
- **Grosson** – A granite, on the Esteemed High Council of Magical Beings
- **Laile** – A moonraker serving on the Esteemed High Council of Magical Beings

- **Goldie, Periwinkle, Rudy, Violet, Emaralda** – Colorful elves that can shine as the Northern Lights
- **The Mistletoe** – The tugboat Sandra and Cappie call home
- **St. Annalise** – A remote island in the Caribbean Sea that is home to St. Annalise Academy where Sandra attended school

PROLOGUE

Cappie was standing on the *Mistletoe's* deck, looking at the clear Christmas sky, wondering what had delayed Sandra and Em. *Had their Christmas Eve deliveries gone long?* she wondered. *Was that even possible? Didn't all gifts all around the world have to be delivered by midnight on Christmas Eve?* The sun would be rising on a beautiful Christmas day in the tropics soon. She placed her last gift for Sandra under their merry tree set on the tugboat's big deck and turned to go back inside. As she did, she realized someone was standing on her deck.

"Thomas," she said. "You surprised me."

Thomas Jackson said nothing in return. He simply reached out and handed her a note.

CHAPTER 1

Santanapped!

Location: Somewhere very secret

"Are they awake?"

"They should be."

"Oh, we're awake, aren't we, Em?"

"Grrrrrrrrrrrrrr."

"And when we get loose, you two, and Thomas, and anyone else involved in this Santanapping are going to be so sorry." Sandra meant it. Every word. And so did Em. Every growl.

"Fine then, if you're going to threaten us like that, we'll just keep you tied up. Don't you agree, Christina?"

"Well, now, Gunny." The headmistress of St. Annalise Academy, Christina Annalise, actually sounded a little sorry about this, thought Sandra.

"Gunny, you lying, no good, slithering, slimy, snake in the grass," Sandra said loudly so she could be heard over Em's growls. "And Christina! I trusted you. And Thomas. How could you? Cappie is going to be so heartbroken."

Sandra struggled mightily against the ties that bound her hands and feet. She hated the vulnerability of being tied down and blindfolded, but if they were hoping it would make her compliant so she would do whatever they wanted, they were sadly mistaken. In fact, thinking of Cappie increased her anger.

"What have you done to Cappie?" She was shouting now. "Have you hurt her? Where is she? It's Christmas! How could you all do this on Christmas?"

Her toughness now melted into despair as she realized that everything she thought she knew about these three people had turned into dust. Fairy dust, she decided. All sparkly in the air but almost always best to avoid.

Her mind flashed on all the things that had happened in the past month. She had turned eighteen, and despite the huge concerns everyone had expressed for her safety, and the many close calls that seemed to put her in peril, her birthday had passed by without any threat to her. She knew she had her parents to thank for that. They had provided her with the protective locket and chain she always wore. Besides providing protection, it had the magical ability to take her places, but her three kidnappers had made sure her hands were bound so she couldn't reach it.

They had also tied up her fingers. She knew why. Gunny was one of the people she had confided in that the ring she wore, when twisted just right, could make her go invisible.

Both gifts were invaluable for delivering gifts to children on Christmas Eve. The locket got her into homes quickly and the ring kept her presence secret from any children who might have stayed up late.

Not that many children were used to her being South Pole Santa yet. The selection had been made right before last Christmas. After a chaotic year of touring the world, trying to quell people's fears about having a second Santa, and the fact that she was a girl, well, there was really no time for her to learn all she needed to know and go out on her own as South Pole Santa. So she and Em had ridden along with Santa and the reindeer to assist again this year. Next Christmas was to be their big "coming out party", so-to-speak. If they made it till then.

She knew Em wasn't scared. Em was never scared. She might look like an elf, aside from her bright green coloring, but Emaralda - her given full name - was in reality a delgin. A fine, beautiful, huge delgin. Sandra knew Em was all tied up or she would have been on her feet spinning into her big dragon size. While delgins are far kinder than their fire-breathing cousins the dragons, when mad like this, you would never want to face one. You would lose. Honestly, as mad as Sandra was at her "friends" that were now her kidnappers, she was worried for what Em would do to them when she and Em finally got loose.

"Sandra? Sandra?" She heard Christina talking to her again. "Sandra, are you okay? Did you hear what Gunny asked?"

"I'm listening," she said sullenly. "Ask me again."

"Okay, if you like," said the voice Sandra knew so well as Gunny's. He was the guy who came in second to be South Pole Santa. She was sure that was what this was all about. But why did Christina and Thomas have to help him? The whole thing made her shudder.

"Sandra, are you cold?" Gunny asked with concern in his voice. "Christina, grab that horse blanket from over there in the corner."

"Please, you surely must know, that under the circumstances, and for the rest of our lives, I really want nothing from you." Sandra's voice dripped with sarcasm. "I'm not cold. Just disgusted. Keep your old horse blanket."

"Suit yourself," Gunny said as he set the blanket down next to Sandra. "Now listen--"

"No, Gunny, you listen! And you too, Christina and Thomas, who I know is there but just isn't speaking right now. You all listen. This is wrong. You may think because I'm just the new Santa, that no one knows me or Em and won't come looking for us, but you're wrong! Some children already know us and like us. And Santa cares. And the elves. And Cappie, if you haven't hurt her. And Birdie and Spence. Oh, my gosh! Have you hurt them? And what about Squawk? You better not have so much as ruffled a single red feather--"

"ENOUGH!" This time it was Christina who spoke up. "Let Gunny speak, Sandra. Please."

Sandra was quiet for a minute but couldn't help herself from continuing. "What about Jason, Christina? Your own son? Is he okay? Please tell me he's not in on this too." She really couldn't bear it if her boyfriend had conspired on this Santanapping as well. It would just be too much.

"He's fine, Sandra," Christina said. "In fact, every person you named, including your beloved bird, Squawk, and Rio, your pretty dolphin friend, are all unharmed."

Sandra didn't know whether to believe her or not, but stayed quiet. For a moment. Emaralda continued to move next to her, trying to get loose from her binds.

"Okay, done for a minute?" Gunny asked. "So I can explain what's going on here?"

She said nothing but glared in his direction through her blindfold.

"When I get big again, Gunny, you better run," Em said in a quiet voice that was actually horribly frightening. Sandra felt scared for Gunny.

"I know, Em, I know. But first, a story," he said.

## CHAPTER 2

A Whopper of a Story

Location: Somewhere Secret on Christmas Day

"Alright, here's the thing." Sandra could tell Gunny was nervous because he was pacing as he talked. His voice was coming from different directions. It actually made her happy to know he was uncomfortable. Why should this be a good Christmas for him? He created this mess.

He started again. "The thing is. Well, the thing is--"

Gunny took so long to get started that Christina jumped in. "Oh, for the sake of all things Christmas, let's get to the point already!" she exclaimed. "The thing is that nothing is what it seems. There. It's out. So stop shouting and accusing when really and truly all we've done is try to save you and Em, Sandra. That's the real thing."

"Save us?" Sandra's voice still smacked of sarcasm, but it was mingled with confusion now.

"Yeah, that's right. Like it or not, we did this for you."

Now Gunny was back up to full speed and plunged in, talking fast. "You remember when I left you that note after you won the South Pole Santa competition and I didn't? The one that despite me scribbling it out, you were able to read, *'You should know that'* and you've wanted to know what 'that' was ever since? Remember that?"

"Of course," Sandra responded. "And I also remember that you left without any other good-bye, and that you wouldn't tell me what 'that' was when I asked." If she could have folded her arms in front of herself she would have.

"Because I couldn't. Or at least I wasn't supposed to," Gunny said. "I wanted to, but it was better for you if I didn't. At least others thought so, and I let them decide, but I should have followed my own heart, uh, reasoning, on that and just told you."

"Told me what?" Sandra practically screamed at him. "Just tell me!"

"That I'm a guardian," Gunny said. "There you go. To be perfectly clear about it, I'm *your* guardian. So are Christina and Thomas."

CHAPTER 3

Guardians!

Location: Somewhere Super Secret

"A guardian! You mean, you all spy on me?" Sandra reeled, taking in this unexpected information. If Gunny and Christina had hoped this would calm Sandra, they were getting a good sense now of how wrong they were. "Who gave you that role? Or did you all just decide it for yourselves?"

"How about, before we go any further, we take your blindfolds off so we can talk face-to-face? That way you can see we're telling the truth," Christina said.

"Fine," Sandra said. "But you do it, Christina. I don't want Gunny near me."

She couldn't see it, but Gunny winced at her words.

"Me neither," Em added. "I'm mad at you too, Christina."

"I know, Em, I know, but won't it be nice to get to see again?"

The sullen delgin said nothing.

As the blindfold came off, Sandra blinked, prepared for the adjustment her eyes would need to make to daylight but instead she realized right away they were in a shadowed area that was easy on her eyes. She looked around to see where they were. It appeared to be a huge hay loft. Gunny stood right in front of her, a big cowboy hat on his head, with a look on his face she couldn't quite make out. Concern? Sadness? Affection maybe? That couldn't possibly be it, she thought.

She put those thoughts aside and asked, "Where are we? Where've you brought us?"

"Why this here, Madam Santa," he said in his best Texan drawl, sweeping his hat in his hand all around. "Is one of the big barns on the Happy Holiday Ranch in Holiday, Texas."

"Your ranch?" Sandra repeated in a questioning voice. Gunny was just full of surprises on this Christmas Day. "Does your mom know we're here?" Sandra had liked Gunny's mom and couldn't believe she would approve of this.

"I sort of mentioned to her that I thought she'd have some extra people for Christmas dinner. You'll get to formally meet all the brothers again, and my sisters and dad. It's going to be a big ole Holiday Christmas party later," Gunny said, smiling, trying hard to get a smile from her. Without success.

Sandra ignored him, in fact, and turned her attention instead to Em. "Good your blindfold is off too. Can you see now, Em?" she asked with concern. "Are you hurt at all?"

"I want untied," Em said in response, still pushing on her bindings.

"I do, too. What do you say, Gunny? Christina? How about as a sign of trust between friends? Or wait, how did you put that? As a sign of trust between "guardians" and the person they are guarding, you untie the two of us?" Sandra asked directly, expecting the answer she got.

"Yeah, that's not happening yet," Gunny said. "C'mon, you and I and Em and Christina all know exactly how that would go right now. Em would spin. You would hop on and use the locket to get out of here. And that would probably only be after Em thrashed us a bunch and broke us up real good. I'll untie you. I promise." He added that as they both looked at him skeptically. "After you have heard our whole story. Then if you both want to go, neither of us will stop you." He looked over at Christina for agreement and she nodded her head. "Agreed?" he said to Sandra.

"Talk," was all Sandra said.

CHAPTER 4

Much More to the Story

Location: The Happy Holiday Ranch

"I'm going to be straight up front with you, Sandra," Gunny said. "Even before you knew who you were, Christina and Thomas already knew. I didn't find out until shortly after the competition, but since then I've known who you are."

"And just what do you mean by 'who I am?'" Sandra asked, not wanting to assume they meant the same thing as she thought they meant, lest they didn't and she told them more than she cared to say.

"You're a Leezle," Gunny said, leaving no room for misunderstanding this time. "In fact, you are very likely the one and only Leezle left, and therefore, of the royal line and a clear heir to the elfin crown. That birthright makes you not just the whispered about possibility that has been the subject of hopes and dreams of many in the magic realm for years, but also the target of those who would prefer to see you gone. That would be so they, and their heirs, can take the rule from the elfins. You may or may not realize this, but it was long ago established that the nature and fairness of the elfins' race made them the best and chosen species to rule all of the unseen world. This is the case unless, or until, there are no more Leezles left. At that point, the unseen world, made up of creatures you have yet to even know exist, and others you are well familiar with like the leprechauns, fairies, wizards, moonrakers, brownies, wood sprites – you know how long the list is – would then decide the next ruling party."

Sandra sat silent, taking it all in, while Gunny paused. Even Em had stopped wrestling about and was listening now.

"I guess it shouldn't be all that surprising to learn that many magical kinds want to take the rule of the realm, but probably none more than three particular groups. Those three would be the Shan fairies, other royal elfin families, and the granites who you likely do not know but as their name suggests, they are beings largely made of rock. A very powerful, strong family." Gunny said, now pacing again.

"I know you feel you need not be concerned about any of them or any of this, Sandra, but I assure you there are many people who are and have worked to assure your safety." It was Christina who picked up the story and was speaking now. "Your mother was the Crown Princess and her brother was the Crown Prince. When your grandfather died and your uncle inherited the crown, your wise and insightful parents chose to step away from the magic realm, leaving all of its privileges and responsibilities behind for others to sort out. They did not want any children they might someday have – for at that time, you were just a hope and dream they held for the future -- to be part of that world of power and politics, suspicion and greed. They wanted instead for their children to be able to lead simpler lives focused on contribution, kindness and, well, love for all creatures and all kind. She was happy to leave the royal title and politics behind for her brother and others.

"Sadly, though, your mother's concerns were prophetic and her brother died just two years after taking the monarchy. He was a very good swimmer, actually, but he drowned. You can imagine how the accusations flew as to what had actually happened, but it was eventually ruled that it was an accidental drowning. Immediately, the search went out for your mother to step into the royal role."

"But she, and your father, were nowhere to be found." It was Gunny who said this, taking up the storyteller role again, looking as serious as Sandra had ever seen him. "A rigorous search commenced on the top of the planet and in the unseen world, as well, for years, looking for your mother. She and your father knew it was happening but they also knew something else. They had had you. And you, Sandra, meant more to them than any possible chance of them going back and putting not just Cassiopola – your mother -- in grave danger, but more importantly to them, putting you in the direct line of the royal throne and assured danger. So they worked to become as 'invisible' as possible."

It was now Sandra who spoke up. "That's why we lived on the *Mistletoe* and moved around from country to country, I'm sure." Christina and Gunny nodded their heads. "And why when I was little my mother taught me how to hide the sparkle in my hair with a special shampoo so only we would know how shiny it really was. And why she used her magic to enable Squawk to talk and be my very best friend." She looked over at Em after she said it to apologize, but even Em couldn't object after hearing the story so far.

"All of those things, Sandra," Gunny said. "It's also why you have your locket and chain for protection. There were a few trusted people in your mother's inner circle who always knew where the three of you were. But there were hundreds of others always searching – some to do her harm, some to bring her back, and some because they wanted to confirm for themselves whether or not you existed."

"They found her, didn't they? They found her and my dad, and they hurt them that day they disappeared, didn't they?" Sandra asked quietly, voicing the worries she and Cappie had always wondered about.

"Probably, Sandra, probably." It was the last thing Gunny wanted to say to her because he knew that, even though she suspected it, to hear it would still hurt. He knelt in front of her so she could see the pain in his eyes and know he didn't want to tell her this.

"Can you take off our binds now, please?" she said. "We won't leave. Right, Em? We won't run away?"

Em nodded and Gunny moved over to untie Sandra's feet and hands. Sandra stretched out while he moved to Em.

"It feels so good to move. I--"

"Whoa there, girl! Whoa! You said you wouldn't run!" Gunny actually sounded a little scared as he tried to slow Em down from the spinning she had started the minute he had set her free.

"I won't leave," said the spinning delgin. "But I'll be listening to the rest of this story full size."

CHAPTER 5

Lots More to Know

Location: The Happy Holiday Ranch

"Alright then, where was I?" Gunny asked as he nervously eyed Emaralda at her full dragon-sized self. He was hoping his story wouldn't make her mad because he was pretty sure he would lose that fight. Sandra wanted to move around but was too entranced with all she was learning about her own family history to fuss about much.

"Here's the thing, even if the evildoers found your parents, they still didn't know for sure about you. By putting that protective spell on your necklace to keep you safe till you turned eighteen, your mother assured that even if they wondered if you were a Leezle, they couldn't possibly confirm it. That gave you time to grow up and to have the happy childhood they wanted you to have."

"It was happy. We all had so much fun living around the world. Mom and dad and me and Squawk and Cappie. Hey, did Cappie know about all of this?" Sandra asked.

"She did," said Christina. "She does. She took care of your mother as a child and voluntarily went with them when they left. She is not a guardian as a role she's been assigned, but she is your beloved guardian in the most important sense of the word. She loves you truly and deeply and would give her own life for yours if she ever needed to do so."

"And I would do the same for her," Sandra added. Gunny and Christina both nodded with understanding. Em though, gave a big delgin huff at the very idea of Sandra being in harm's way.

"It was at about that time that I came into the picture," Christina continued. "Before they disappeared, your parents had been looking for a place to put down anchor and stay for a while. They wanted a quiet spot where they could stay and let you go through school with friends besides just the two of them and Cappie and Squawk. It needed to be a private and safe place where you could have a more traditional childhood experience. They had reached out to me through a mutual, trusted acquaintance whom I shall not name, and I flew to the Polynesian area to meet with your parents about what St. Annalise had to offer. So, when, long ago, you asked if I knew your parents, it was because of that meeting I was able to say I had met them. I felt the meeting had gone well and we had agreed on you coming to St. Annalise. Unfortunately, it was shortly after that they went missing. Somehow though, you and Cappie still managed to make it to the island and the academy."

"We got there because mom sent me a note in a bottle. Or at least I was pretty sure it was mom,' said Sandra. They all looked at her quizzically but she dismissed them, not wanting to go into it. She hadn't really meant to talk out loud. "Please, Christina, go on."

"Well, you know most of it from there since you have lived at St. Annalise now since you were eleven. It's been a privilege for me to have you there. Before you arrived, one of the highly trusted elfin council members reached out to me and to Thomas and had us swear an oath to take care of you. I don't know if they actually knew you were Leezle, or just suspected, but, either way, there were those who wanted you protected. It was really all for naught, though. In all your years at St. Annalise, nothing even remotely peculiar ever happened. Nonetheless, we were ever on the alert. I believe there are others as well who serve in this guardian role, but it's on a need-to-know basis. I suspect who they are, and Thomas and I did not need to know. We were sworn to secrecy from even telling you."

"As was I," Gunny said, now picking the story back up. "Fairies and elfins and magical beings in general don't mean much to the working stiffs on a cattle ranch. Until, that is, I made it as a finalist for the South Pole Santa competition. Out of the blue one day, three fine fellows — and I use that description as code really for intimidating and somber — showed up while I was flushing out some strays in the far back land of the ranch. They needed a guardian for a part elfin young woman who was also in the competition to be South Pole Santa. They wanted to know if I'd be willing to do it. They said the need would be short while she did her best at trying for a part she wasn't really right for. And before you even say anything, Sandra, those were their words, not mine. Though, at the time, you being a girl and all, and me being me, the perfect person to be second Santa, I quite naturally thought they were right."

He smiled one of his charming Gunny smiles while Sandra struggled not to grin back. Em huffed at him and he continued.

"I'm not sure what they even would have done if I'd said 'no', but I knew it was something I needed to do. It was more than just appealing to my chivalrous side, it was a gut feeling inside that said I needed to step up. As it turned out, I believe they were right to look for someone to keep a watch on you."

"I will never forget your quick actions that saved me from drowning in that deep vat of blue paint, Gunny," Sandra said sincerely.

Gunny nodded, thinking back on the close call. "I think that's everything. You pretty much know the whole story now."

"Not really. None of that explains why we're here and why you Santanapped us," Sandra said to him firmly. The history was interesting but, guardian or not, none of them had any right just to snap her and Em out of the air.

"Okay, yeah, there still is that," Gunny said, now with deep reluctance in his voice again. "That actually is the most disturbing part of the story. Yes, we did, I confess, take you and

Em, rather roughly and without any notice, but it couldn't be helped."

"Couldn't be helped? We were doing just fine! We had just finished our rounds, waved good-bye to Santa, and were headed back to St. Annalise. We were less than an hour away from home only to wake up rudely – in Texas of all places!"

"Hey now, there's not a doggone thing wrong with Texas!" Gunny objected.

"Enough!" Christina intervened with her best headmistress voice. "Just tell her why, Gunny."

"Yeah, why am I here in this hay barn?"

"Because, as your guardians we did our job, even if you end up hating us. We did what we had to do. We didn't want you to go missing, too."

"Missing?" Sandra asked confused. "Why would I be missing?"

"Because," Gunny said with a heavy sigh. "Someone, or something, took Santa."

## CHAPTER 6

The Big Guy is Gone

Location: The Happy Holiday Ranch

"WHAT? You've kept this from us this whole time? Santa is missing and you just now are telling us? Who took him? How do I even know you're telling the truth? That any of this is even true? In fact, where's Thomas if he's one of my 'so-called guardians?' And why aren't you all out looking for Santa?" Sandra was livid and panicked now, full of questions and not sure what to think or even believe.

"I'm here," said a tired-looking Thomas, walking through the barn door with the sun behind him, putting him and his companion in silhouette.

"And it's all true, Sandra, I'm afraid, every word," said his companion.

"Cappie! Oh thank goodness, Cappie!" As soon as she heard the voice, Sandra jumped up from her spot and ran the length of the barn to the one person she did call her guardian. The person in her life she trusted most. The two hugged each other hard.

" . . . *squawk* . . .What about me? . . . *squawk* . . . I count, too."

"Squawk! Hooray! Oh, Squawk, I'm so happy to see you! Come over here and love me up," said Sandra. reaching out her arm. The big bird promptly landed on it and started rubbing his head on her head and shoulder.

"Are you all right, Sandra? Where's Em?" Cappie asked, concerned for the delgin she had come to love already as another member of their unconventional family.

"Well, she's right there." Sandra pointed to the back of the barn behind her, wondering how on earth Cappie could not see the big, dragon-sized, elf, only to realize Em was no longer there. Instead, she had converted to her normal small elf size and was hugging on Cappie's leg.

"Here I am, Cappie. I'm so happy to see you," said the little elf, being unusually affectionate, but clearly feeling the same affection for Cappie as Cappie did for her. "We're not happy about any of this, but we're okay. They tied us up, Cappie!"

"I heard," said Cappie. "Thomas assures me that they didn't know what else to do. They were so afraid that whoever took Santa was about to take you both, too, that they had to act fast, and hastily, with no time for explanations. They needed to buy time by making the Santanappers think that you both had been Santanapped too, if that makes any sense."

"We figured that if they thought you had been snapped up too, they might think it was one of their own that did it. And if they thought that, then they would head on back to wherever they were from instead of trying to follow whoever took you and overtake us," said Gunny. "The plan seems to have worked, except we had to decide between getting you both to safety or trying to trail who took Santa. Since our prime directive as guardians assigned to you was to keep you safe, we had to leave solving the mystery on the other Santanapping for someone else. Except it seems, no one ever thinks anyone would be so bold as to take Santa on his biggest night of the year – or ever, really – so no one was watching him. He has security assigned to him, but obviously something went very wrong. They feel terrible. They had joined the Christmas celebration at the Pole and were there when they received the news."

"Well, of course, they were," said Sandra. "You three should have been at your family celebrations too, instead of worrying about the two of us. I'm glad you weren't, though." After hearing the whole story, she had to acknowledge that they had done a good thing for her and Em. "So is Santa's security team out looking for him?"

"Well, that's another story," Gunny said. "But please, can we eat first? It's Christmas, we've been up for more than 24 hours, and even though I'm tired, there's nothing that can keep me away from my mom's Christmas dinner. It's the best and I'm hungry!"

"Me, too!" said everyone else gathered in the big barn all at once.

CHAPTER 7

Catching a Ride Home

Location: Happy Holiday Ranch and St. Annalise

The hungry group piled onto the back of one of the flatbed trucks the ranch used to haul hay around. Em had offered to fly everyone to the ranch house, but not everyone, it seemed, was keen on riding on the back of a delgin. Besides, Gunny would have to drive the big truck back anyway, and riding together gave them all a bit of a chance to catch up and exchange Christmas greetings.

"Can we agree not to talk about Santa missing with my family?" Gunny said loudly so he could be heard out the back window. Christina was riding up front with him but otherwise, everyone else had piled in the back. "I mean, it's Christmas and I don't want to put a damper on their happy day. Not to mention, there's a real good chance he's already been found." The last part sounded more like he was trying to convince himself than the others.

"*squawk* . . . Not a word . . . Just wanna eat! . . . *squawk*"

"Me too," said a famished Em. "Hope we're having some kind of bird for dinner."

"*squawk! squawk!* . . . Bird eater!. . . Told you! . . . *squawk!*" Squawk fluttered all around and settled on top of the roof of the truck cab, glaring at Em.

"Emaralda! What a thing to say on Christmas," Sandra admonished. "You apologize to Squawk this instant. I know you didn't mean it."

"I did too mean it. I did. I didn't mean parrot. I like chicken. Lots of people do, not just me," said Em.

"My whole family does, Em," Gunny said, laughing. "There's a good chance there'll be chicken on the menu and Cornish hens and prime rib and a big ole ham. This is a ranch and we eat ranch kinds of food. Seeing's how I told ma that I thought you islanders might be joining us, I bet she'll throw in some good seafood and non-meat choices too. I know those are your preferences, Sandra."

"Thanks, Gunny. Right about now I would likely eat anything you put in front of me. I'm hoping she has a plate of those great cinnamon rolls she makes. Wait till you taste them, Cappie. They are almost as good as yours!" said Sandra, reminiscing on a meal Gunny's mom had made them when they had visited the ranch last summer.

"All I can say is, thank goodness you let her know we were coming," said Cappie. "I've been worrying about that since we all piled into the truck. We're way too many to just spring on a person."

"Not on my mama, Cappie. She's been cooking for a mess of people ever since I can remember. My two sisters help, even one of my brothers lends a hand and the Major – which is what we call my dad – who makes sure she has hired help for the kitchen whenever she wants it. I love it when Bonita is helping 'cause we get the very best tortillas anyone has ever tasted. But being's it's Christmas Day, I'm figuring it's going to just be ma and the rest of everyone putting this big dinner together.

"Alright, here we are, everyone. Get ready to meet my wild and crazy bunch of family. Sandra, this time it's going to be all my brothers and my sisters too, but none of the ranch hands, so I'm not sure who all you'll recognize."

"Gunny!" The happy voice of Gunny's mom rang out as they parked in front of the front door of the big main house. "Merry Christmas, everyone! What a way to get to the house, on the back of a hay truck. My word, Gunny!"

"Merry Christmas, Mrs. Holiday," said Sandra, happy to see their host again. "I'd like you to meet my family. This is Cappie and this is Squawk. And, of course, you already know Em."

"*squawk* . . .! Pleased to meet you! . . . *squawk*!"

"Likewise, Squawk, and, Cappie, what a true pleasure. Please call me Josie, short for Josephina. And this is my husband Crenshaw, Gunny's father."

"How do you do?" said the tall man who looked to be just an older version of Gunny as he tipped his hat to the little group. "Please call me Major. Everybody does, even my kids."

"Hey, Major, this lovely lady over here is Christina Annalise, the headmistress of the Annalise Academy," Gunny said as he helped Christina out of the front of the truck. The two of them had been in deep conversation for much of the ride back, and as Christina spoke, Sandra understood what it must have been about.

"It is such a pleasure to meet you both," Christina said, shaking their hands. "I would so love to stay and meet your whole family, but really I must be going. I have a son, you see, and I don't want him to spend all of Christmas Day without me."

Jason! Sandra couldn't believe she hadn't thought about that earlier. She had been so caught up in her own world she had completely forgotten about her boyfriend being alone on Christmas.

It wasn't entirely her fault. Since their birthdays – on the same day no less – when he had found out that he was king of the fairies, he had been in no mood to talk with Sandra or anybody else for that matter. She had been so busy on Christmas countdown with Santa at the North Pole, that not talking had been okay. As Christina had reminded her, Jason was the kind of guy who needed time to think about things. Now that Christmas was here, though, Sandra had been looking forward to the two of them having time together to catch up and sort out Jason's new role as fairy king.

"I can take you, Christina!" Sandra said as the group looked at her. Most, including Christina, did not yet know about the magic of her locket. "That is to say, why don't the rest of you go in and get started and let me talk to Christina about some of her options for getting home."

They all looked at her a little puzzled, but hunger overruled talking about it for all but Gunny, who hung back.

"Listen, Sandra, I don't want you running off with Chris--"

But that lecture was too late! Sandra looked at Gunny as she grabbed Christina's hand with one of her own, held her locket with the other and wished them both to St. Annalise. She hadn't been sure it would work with two, but when they opened their eyes, they were standing right outside Christina's front door.

"Sandra! How did you do that?" Christina exclaimed, truly surprised but pleased. "Never mind, just thank you. Would you like to say hello to my son?"

Sandra nodded. She was so anxious to see him.

"You go on in. I'll join you both soon," Christina said.

Sandra opened the door with a combination of wanting to excitedly shout out and reservation, not knowing if she would be welcome.

"Is that you, mom, finally?" She heard Jason call out as he heard the front door close. "Where'd you go for so long on Christmas? You're making me wait to--"

Jason stood there with his mouth open, staring at his girlfriend. "Sandra," was all he said.

"Jason, I, that is, your mom said I could come on in, but," her voice drifted off as he just stared at her and she didn't know what else to say. "But I can't stay," she finally added, thinking to herself that it was lame but true.

"Why not? You got somewhere better to be on Christmas, than with me, your boyfriend who has been missing you like mad?" He grinned at her, not caring about all the challenges in front of them and just so happy to see her.

She grinned too, and walked toward him while he walked backwards. When she got close, he stepped two steps sideways and then said, "Now." pointing to the ceiling where mistletoe was hanging.

She just rolled her eyes while he grabbed her up in a big hug and a giant size kiss. "Hmmmmm, that was a very nice hello," said Sandra happily.

"It was the mistletoe, really," Jason said, grinning. "It really gives it a little extra something."

She laughed and punched him this time as Christina came in the door.

"Mom," he said, holding onto Sandra. "You got me just what I wanted this year." Sandra knew she had a dopey grin on her face but she didn't care. It was the very best she had felt all day, maybe the best she had felt in a month. Besides, he had a dopey smile too.

"Now those two faces make this mom really happy," said Christina, feeling the exhaustion that having been up for too many hours without sleep brings on. "Jason, I'm afraid

Sandra can't stay." Her son's face shadowed immediately but she continued firmly. "I promised Cappie that if I let her bring me home and say hi to you, we wouldn't keep her. That's how it is on Christmas when your girlfriend happens to be South Pole Santa and just got home from the biggest gig on the planet."

Jason looked from her to Sandra and realized how tired his beautiful girlfriend looked too. Six months ago, having her go so fast would have sent him in to a sullen spin, but he realized he was indeed growing up and he could wait to catch up with her until she got some rest too.

He held her face gently in both hands and looked into her Christmas green eyes. "Come see me as soon as you are rested up," he whispered to her and then leaned closer into her ear. "I've missed you so much." Then he lightly kissed her on the lips and said brightly, "Now away with you! I'd walk you home but my mother here has left me alone all day long on Christmas and we have gifts to unwrap. Right, mom?"

"Right, my handsome son," Christina said, feeling relieved he was in such a good mood on this special day. "Sandra, let me see you out."

"Thanks, Christina. Bye, my guy!" She gave a little wave to Jason at the door as he moved into the other room. As they stepped back outside, Christina quickly said in a low voice, "Sandra, I don't like to keep things from my son, but my guardian status cannot be shared even with him." Sandra nodded, understanding. "So we need to agree not to share anything about this night, at least for now, with Jason, or any others. Do you feel the same?"

"Yes. Agreed," said Sandra, nodding her head and reaching for her locket to go.

Christina turned to go inside as Sandra disappeared to return to the ranch. Wistle, the always annoying fairy who could never mind her own business, flew off from her hiding place behind the front porch light to tell what she had just heard to fairies who would want to know.

CHAPTER 8

Back at the Ranch

Location: Happy Holiday Ranch

Gunny was waiting for her, eyes a blazing when she returned.

"That," he said, "was not cool."

"She had to get back," Sandra said, not looking at him and heading for the door. "How else was she going to get there?"

"You're not the only one with some magic ways, missy. We could've got her there. Maybe not as fast as you did, but in a reasonable amount of time. That was all about seeing your island boy and we both know it," Gunny said, sounding very annoyed but less annoyed then he felt.

"So what if it was?" Sandra challenged him. "He's my boyfriend. I miss him. I haven't seen him in a month and it's Christmas. I'm eighteen and nothing happened to me, even though everyone was sure something would. I am grown up and can now choose to do what I want. For all those reasons, of course I want to see him!"

"He's a fairy! The king of fairies! You are very likely the queen of elfins. Don't you get it? You two cannot make that work! The two are longtime adversaries," said Gunny, flinging his arms around animatedly as he talked.

"Well, Gunny, here's something I do 'get,'" she made finger marks in the air around the word he had used. "We didn't get the memo and we don't care. Those are old feuding rules of some kind of order that has nothing to do with us. We don't want to be rulers and we don't care about the differences. We just care about being together. That's it."

"I wish it were that easy," Gunny said quieter now.

"Well it is, and you know what?" Sandra asked with her back to him and her hand on the front door. "I am sooooo hungry that you'll just have to forgive me and let us in to go eat." She turned and smiled her most charming smile ever at him.

He was caught off guard but happy for the change of subject too. It was Christmas Day. Worry and fighting were for another time. "Yes'm, your royal highness of Christmas town," he grinned, putting on the charm now too. "Just you wait till you try my mom's chili relleno casserole. Killer, I tell you, killer."

CHAPTER 9

What's in a Name?

Location: Happy Holiday Ranch

Mrs. Holiday's Christmas dinner was everything the hungry bunch had hoped for and more. There were mighty piles of magnificent, endless food. Sandra had sat down on the far end of the long table with the rest of her friends. The table was in the Holidays large great room and right next to a gorgeous, 20-foot-tall Christmas tree decorated in the same kind of ranch theme Gunny had used at the South Pole Santa competition. They were all so hungry and the dinner was in danger of getting cold by the time Gunny and Sandra sat down, so there had been no time for actual formal introductions before dinner. Afterward, though, and before dessert, the Major pulled them all together around the Christmas tree and made family introductions. Josephina had run around and given the youngsters and elves tall cups of steaming cocoa and small glasses of after-dinner port to the adults.

"I'd like to propose a toast to our guests," Major said, lifting his small glass of port high. "No one who passes through our door is ever a stranger but a family member waiting to be welcomed in. Here's to our newest family members."

"Here, here!" sang out the rest of the family. For Cappie, Sandra, Thomas, and even Em and Squawk, it was touching and so sincere they couldn't help but feel warmly welcomed. It was a completely unexpected way to spend Christmas but surprisingly special, Sandra found herself thinking.

"Thank you so much," Cappie said, speaking for them all. "Now it would be really nice to know the names of all our new family members."

The Major grinned. "Good point, Cappie, good point," he said. "Yes, let's get to it. Well you met my beautiful wife Josephina – Josie to her friends -- the center of this family and the presenter of our delicious Christmas dinner." With that, the whole of the group broke out in cheers and applause. Josie blushed and bowed with a great flourish, playing along.

"That brings us to our kids, and we got a bunch of em," the Major continued in his booming voice. "I'm going to introduce them to you in birth order, which means the first one up in the line-up is Gunther, who you all know well. We, of course, all call him Gunny. A fine boy he is, fine boy. Shame he didn't get picked up for that Santa Claus gig, but he tells me you were the best choice." The Major said the last part talking right to

Sandra, who wasn't sure how to respond. He was clearly disappointed in Sandra's selection.

"Ah, Major, c'mon. Don't go embarrassing us all every time you introduce us. Go on and talk about Chance. He likes being talked about," Gunny said, grinning over at a brother and trying to get his dad to move on.

"I sure do," said the brother Gunny was talking to as he played along. "Go on ahead, dad, tell em all about me."

"Alright, alright. Just one last bit on Gunny. He used to work the ranch regularly but, these days, he's become more of the 'public relations' director for us. I could say more about his shenanigans and charming ways with the girls, but I'm getting too old to outrun him," the Major grinned as Gunny grimaced. "Alright then, as Gunny said, next up is Chance! Where are you, son? Did you move? Give me a wave."

"I moved over here by mom, pop," said the good-looking brother Gunny had been teasing, waving his arm in the air at the Major.

"Ah, yes. There you are, Chanceller, who is Chance to us. Chance is the one that got away. He went and got a big degree in law and moved out to Houston. Good to have you home, son."

"Good to be home, Major. You forgot to mention that I'm not just the smartest, but the best looking, too," said son number two, grinning as three pillows out of nowhere landed on him.

"Okay, boys, save it for later. Now we move on to my pride and joy as a parent, my girls." That statement resulted in all sorts of hooting and hollering and objections from the boys, who all made one sort of noise or another – albeit still full of clear affection for them.

Two very pretty girls had moved in on both sides of the major, but neither of them looked like Gunny. Nor did they look like each other. "This blondie with springy curls the color of bleached sand in the summer is Blue, short for Bluebonnet, one of Josie's favorite Texan flowers."

She grinned at everyone and waved. "Blue does a lot of things here at the ranch, but one of her main responsibilities is helping Josie run the main house and feed the ranch hands. That has made one of my main responsibilities, as her father, glowering at cowboys who come a courting."

"Daaaaaaddddd!" Blue said to him in protest.

"And then we got my Glory here." The Major affectionately rustled his other daughter's jet black straight hair with his big hand. "Hard to believe the two are sisters, huh?" He saw nods, not just from the guests, but from the family members too, which made the girls laugh. "Glory here's full name is Morning Glory after another of Josie's favorite Texan flowers. She's all about animals and loves nothing more than working with the horses. If you're looking for our Glory, you'll likely find her in the stables. Oh, and I took Glory out of order. She's really our youngest and the only one still in school."

The girls both smiled, curtsied for fun, and gave their dad a light peck on the cheek before sitting down again. "Now next up and the last of the bunch, at least let's hope." He glanced impishly at Josie, who went bright red. "Major, really! It's Christmas!" she exclaimed. "My thought exactly," he mischievously teased back to a bunch of grinning grown boys and a bright-red wife.

"Ok, last up, we've got the twins, Crowder and Casper. Or as we call them around here, Crow and Ghost. Crow, I see you but where has Ghost got off to? He was late to dinner and now gone again. Has he picked up a girlfriend I don't know about or something?"

"Or something, Major. Not sure what he's been up to but he's been gone most the day. Still, hi, everyone," said a young version of Gunny with a deep bow all around to the crowd. "I'm Crow and my brother Ghost pretty much looks just like me except he's got hair that's a little bit longer and a uni-brow." The group all laughed. Sandra thought Crow's personality seemed the most like Gunny's.

"Crow and Ghost are a couple of our all-around ranch hands helping out wherever they are needed. That is everyone. I warned you there was a bunch of us on this big ole ranch!"

"It's nice to formally meet you all, and thanks for opening your home to us today. You certainly have interesting names," said Thomas, speaking for the whole of the small group. "I've been Thomas my whole life and not even really called Tom, just Thomas. I have to say, your names are a true inspiration."

Everyone gave a chuckle to that. "Well, sir," Major said. "It's a Texan way to be big and original. I like to think we're just doing our part. Big ranch, big names, big ole family!"

Gunny laughed with the rest of them, partly because he had heard the line many times, and partly because the Major really had no idea what a truly "big and original" not-to-mention, long, name could look like.

"Major, I know I introduced our guests quickly at dinner but I wasn't as clear as I should have been about them," Gunny said, plunging into a break in the conversation. "Yes, this is Captain Margaret Richmond – Cappie for short – and this is Thomas Jackson, always Thomas not Tom. Oh and over here, the bravest elf I know," he said with true affection, and Em puffed up. "This is Emaralda, Em for short." He paused as everyone in the room did another round of smiles and nods at each other. Gunny made his way over to Sandra.

"This beautiful person here, absolutely stunning, really, on this day of days, even as tired as she must be," Gunny said, looking directly at Sandra. "This is the one of us with the long and original name. I introduced her as Sandra Claus but truly her name is, well, let me let her tell you."

"Truly my name is long and, I think, wonderful," Sandra said with appreciation to Gunny for letting her share it. "My parents named me Cassandra Penelope and our last name is Clausmonetsiamlydelaterra dot dot dot." She stopped and smiled, knowing there would be questions. There were always questions when one carried such a name. The room buzzed with noise.

"Well, I'll be," the Major said. "And just how does one get such a long name? Especially a name that ends with dot dot dot?" He said the dot's with pauses in between each.

"I know," said Sandra smiling. "Seems crazy, right? My parents loved the world. They called themselves 'worldologists' since they loved to study each place we visited. We lived on our home, the *Mistletoe,* a big ocean-going tugboat. Cappie and I still live there." Cappie reached over and squeezed her hand. "It was the best childhood anyone could ever have. Each time we left a country, my parents added on to our name. So, in honor of France--"

"You added Monet!" said Glory, smiling.

"Right!" said Sandra. "And where do you think 'Siam' came from?"

"My turn," said Josie. "I'm going to guess Thailand. Am I right?"

"You are!" said Sandra, pleased with the fun her name had created. "The next piece is Ly. Any guesses?"

"I'll go," said Chance. "I'm going to take a chance, get it? Take a chance? From me? Chance?"

The room groaned as he grinned.

"Okay, okay," he continued. "I'll take a chance that it was added for General Lee from the civil war and therefore, the United States."

The room burst out in moans as Sandra just looked at him puzzled. She'd never heard of General Lee. Her United States history knowledge was lacking. Before she could ask though, Blue spoke up.

"Chance, that is crazy," she said, shaking her head at her smart brother, while he grinned and she realized he was just having some fun. "Sandra, I'm going with Vietnam."

"Yes!" said Sandra smiling. "If we had prizes, it would go to you." She smiled at both Blue and Chance, who just shrugged his shoulders good-naturedly.

"Lastly then, we have the De La Terra part of my name. Who would like to take the final guess? Anyone?" This being a family with Mexican and Hispanic roots, the room was filled with answers.

"Mexico!"

"Cuba!"

"Panama!"

"Guatemala!"

"Okay, stop, stop!" Sandra said with her hands up and smiling. "I give up! Those are all great answers and none of them really are wrong. The De La Terra part of my name came as a nod to several Latin America countries, including those you named - except Cuba, though, whoever called out that one. I don't think we ever had a chance to live there. At least not yet."

"And the dots at the end?" the Major asked.

"The dots at the end I think are the most important part," Sandra said in a quieter tone. "While my parents were here, they wanted people to know our name wasn't finished so they added the three dots at the end to indicate 'more to come.' I love the dots most of all.

"You can call me, like almost everyone, including myself most often, Sandra Claus dot dot dot."

The room burst into spontaneous applause while Sandra blushed and then played along and took a deep bow all around. It was a true bunch of unexpected Christmas fun.

"Well, well," said the Major. "I see your point, Gunny, on what a really long name can be. Let me lift my glass to all of us no matter our name's length. Merry Christmas to our old and our new family members!"

"Merry Christmas!" rang around the room from all.

After that, some of the group opted for the dessert table but after the wildest twenty four hours she could ever remember, Sandra felt exhausted and headed straight to the guest quarters where Josie had graciously set them all up for the night. The room was down a long hall with just a sliver of light coming out from below the shut door showing the way. She didn't know where the hall switch was so she just made her way in the very dim light and promptly ran smack into Gunny.

"Gunny," she said, feeling surprised and a little annoyed. The day had ended well but she was ready for a break from the tall cowboy. Her wrists were still sore from being tied up. "I'm sorry. I'm just really tired and not paying any attention to where I'm going. I thought you were still back with the rest."

He looked at her strangely in the dim light before he leaned down and kissed her on the lips. "Miss Claus, you may have missed it in this light, but there's mistletoe hanging off this ceiling right where we're standing. Oh, and maybe you guessed by now, but, if not, I'm not Gunny, I'm Ghost. It's a real pleasure to meet you."

And with that he disappeared as quickly as he had come, living fully up to his name, while Sandra stood there trying to remember her name after a rather spectacular, completely unexpected, Christmas kiss! Oh. Oh. Ooooooh.

CHAPTER 10

Wake up Call

Location: Happy Holiday Ranch

Despite being exhausted, Sandra slept restlessly that night. She tossed and turned with worry over Santa since they had received no word. She pined for Jason and berated herself for enjoying the kiss from Ghost. *What kind of girl was she*, she wondered, *that she could be crazy about one boy and enjoy a kiss from another?* "Not a very nice one," she muttered.

"Not a very nice what?" Em asked.

"Em, what time is it? Sandra asked, surprised the little delgin was awake.

"It's 5:20 a.m."

"Why are you awake? We need to sleep in."

"I can't. The yelling woke me up and now I'm awake."

"The yelling? What are you talking about?" Sandra said as she realized she could hear a mumbled shouting going on.

"See for yourself," Em said as she pulled back the curtain so Sandra could see Gunny out away from the house, with Ghost, both of them shouting and waving their arms. From there, Gunny looked more like Ghost's twin than Crow did.

"Well whatever is wrong is none of our business, so back to sleep for at least another hour, please," Sandra said firmly. "And if you choose to stay awake, please don't move around. You'll wake up Cappie, Thomas, and Squawk." They were all sleeping in one big bunk room that the cowboys usually used. If anyone woke up, they could easily wake everyone up.

"Okay," whispered the little quirky elf as she curled up on the floor rug next to Sandra's bunk. There were plenty of beds available, she just preferred the floor. "Oh wait," she said, still whispering. "One more thing. I found this." She held out her hand, and in it she had the gift Santa had given Sandra. In all the chaos of being captured, Sandra had completely forgotten about it. "This year your gift really is from me," he had said, chuckling, since the year before he had given her something that was really, somehow, delightfully, from her parents.

"I'd forgotten about it," Sandra whispered to Em, reaching for it. "I'm glad you found it. What do you think? Should I open it now?" She smiled at her, already knowing the answer as the little delgin nodded yes.

Sandra quickly unwrapped it to find an exquisite watch inside. It was like no watch that she had ever seen except for the one Santa himself wore. It looked very old. It had the time listed for multiple time zones on it, as well as an arrow pointing north like a compass. Sandra knew it was a very special gift, and under the circumstances with Santa now missing, it made it even more special.

Em sensed her feelings about the gift. "It'll be okay, Sandra," she said. "We'll find him."

"I know, Em," Sandra whispered back, feeling oddly calm about it too. Something kept tugging on her to believe that all was well. "Now, back to sleep for both of us for just a little bit longer. Just because the Holiday boys are up early doesn't mean we have to be."

Em curled up below for more sleep, but Sandra couldn't resist taking one more peek out at the two brothers before sliding back under the covers. She looked out but they had moved away and were no longer in her view. She lay back on her bunk hoping she could get a little more rest, but guessing it was unlikely - until two hours later when she woke up to the smell of bacon and a whiff of cinnamon. From her bunk, lying there with just one eye open, it seemed she was alone in the bunk-room. So much for the idea that if one person woke up, it would wake everyone else, she thought, surprised she was the last one still in bed. She lay there and stretched, thinking about the day ahead. It was the day after Christmas and there was work to be done.

"Even the tantalizing smell of bacon doesn't get your highness out of bed?" She heard the question and knew the voice before she actually saw the tall cowboy leaning against the end of the bunk.

"Gunny! Are you spying on me? And please don't call me 'your highness.' Or 'your princess' or any of that royalty stuff. My mom didn't like it, and I don't either."

Just another thing he liked about her, Gunny thought to himself. "I'm not spying. Just admiring you sleeping," he said, smiling. She was conscientious of the mess her hair must be in and tried to pat it into some kind of early morning order. Truth was, without a brush or comb, that was very likely impossible.

She gave up on trying to constrain her wild tangles and focused instead on a big idea she had been thinking. "I'm actually glad you're here," she said, sitting up in bed as his face brightened.

"Really? So what is clicking around in that smart head of yours?" he asked.

"I was thinking," she said, "that I could use the locket to find Santa. I mean, it can take me almost anywhere."

"Sandra, that is a Texas-sized great idea! Let's do it, and don't even give me that look. If you are going to find him, I'm going with you. No argument on it. We have no idea where he is or who has him. We go together."

"You're right, so c'mon then, take my hand," Sandra said.

"You look good, really good," Gunny said, grinning at her. "But I'm not sure showing up in shorty pajamas and tangled hair is really the image you want to give Santa or the kidnappers or any press we'd need to talk to as well. How 'bout after you've had a chance to have breakfast and get dressed?"

Sandra nodded reluctantly. He had a point. She knew he was right, but now that she had thought of how to find Santa she wanted to get going.

"Really it was ma's fault that I came looking for you," Gunny added. "She's cooking breakfast for everyone and wants to know what you'd like. You're the last one up."

"The last one up! It's only 7:15. Are there cinnamon rolls?" she asked with an elf-like innocence.

"Of course. That is if Em and Squawk haven't eaten them all," he teased her.

"What? They're horrible! Out of my way, Mr. Holiday, I have a breakfast to eat," she smiled as she jumped to her feet.

"Sandra, one quick thing." Gunny sounded serious as he held her back with his hand on her arm as she went walking past him. "Ghost told me about last night. I'm sorry you had to meet my little brother in a full-on-the-lips kind of way."

Well this is uncomfortable, she thought. Now she at least suspected she knew what they were shouting about earlier that morning.

Despite being caught off-guard on an uncomfortable topic, she tried to play it cool. "Hey, it was the mistletoe," she said, pointing to the criminal plant hanging from the ceiling down the long hall just where Ghost had said it was last night. "Already forgotten."

"Not by me it isn't," Gunny muttered as she hurried down the hall to breakfast. "And not by him."

CHAPTER 11

Making Plans to Rescue Santa

Location: Happy Holiday Ranch

"Alright, here's what we know about Santa." Gunny was speaking to Sandra, Cappie, Thomas, Em, and Squawk, plus his brother, Chance. The rest of his family he was hoping to protect by not sharing the news or next steps. The twins needed to be working the ranch that day anyway. He had included Chance in case they would need any legal advice.

"Santa, and the reindeer, who are all missing too, were heading north after the last stop with the two of you," he said with a nod to Sandra and Em. "We estimate he had made it just off the coast of Texas ironically, not all that far from here. That's when he reported being engulfed in some very dark clouds that even Rudolph was having trouble seeing his way through, and then we lost all contact."

"Excuse me for even asking this," Thomas said, "but how do we know it wasn't just a horrible accident and they went down at sea?"

"Good question, Thomas," said Gunny, nodding his head. "Of course, it's a possibility but very doubtful. First of all, there are all sorts of safeguards built into Santa's sleigh, and in the many hundreds of years we've had Santa delivering, there has never once been even a close call. Second, he could have sent out a distress message that they were going down. Third, we've found absolutely no wreckage at all in the area. And lastly, there is an emergency beacon located on the sleigh that would have triggered on impact. All of those reasons lead us to believe we are dealing with a 'Santanapping' rather than a crash."

"Good to know," said Thomas, "and somewhat a relief as well. At least, if someone took them, we can assume they're alive."

"Don't even think the other way, Thomas!" Sandra said, jumping up in clear distress and reaching over to calm Em, who had hopped up and started to spin. "Em, it's okay. We don't have room for you to be full size in this room. I know this is all upsetting, but Santa needs us to stay calm as we think it through."

"It's much more likely that this was a well-thought-out, well-timed take of Santa and the reindeer. The tracking device was dismantled immediately, which is how his team knew he was missing so quickly. Santa had not indicated any sense of danger or concern other than the dark clouds. The only thing we actually know for sure from the Santa Tracking Center at the South Pole outpost is that, for just the briefest of minutes, some kind of plane or flying object came right over the top of Santa's sleigh and then it too disappeared. The outpost notified us immediately, and it was then that we zoned in on Sandra and Em's coordinates which, thankfully, were not far out from St. Annalise. We moved in on you as fast as possible to try and thwart any further Santanappings that night."

"Yeah, on behalf of Em and me and our many sore muscles this morning, we still think you could have handled that a whole lot different," Sandra said while Em gave out a little growl of agreement.

"Okay, yes, I admit we, I, panicked a little when I heard Santa was taken. You have to admit, though, that you are not always open to ideas without discussion, and you ride a really big delgin. I didn't feel like we had time to convince you of the danger or take on Em if she didn't feel like cooperating. Not to mention, you two had also reported having to move through some ominous dark clouds as well."

Reluctantly, Sandra could see a little bit of the crazy logic in his thinking.

"Just don't do it again," she said firmly.

"Never!" said Thomas and Gunny at the same time. It sounded like they really had learned their lesson.

"So, if you know it wasn't an accident, have you heard yet who they think did do it?" Chance, who had been quietly listening and taking it all in, asked the question everyone was wondering.

"Well there aren't many people yet who even know he's missing," Gunny said. "Actually it's pretty much limited to all of us here and Santa's crackerjack, highly trained for all kinds of emergencies, Elf Security Team. They were the ones on duty that night. They are known as the 'Sherlocks' actually. Apparently, the team was originally formed during the height of interest in Sherlock Holmes detective stories, and you know how elves love good stories. I've actually met many of them as they briefed Thomas, Christina and me on keeping you secure. They aren't like most of the elves who are easy going, cocoa-drinkers. This team is full of very intelligent, highly trained, very somber, elf 'thugs', which I mean in a good way. They take their work seriously and are very unhappy that Santa has been taken under their watch. I kind of feel sorry for whoever took Santa and the reindeer team in a way. It won't be pretty when these guys find them!

"I actually had a briefing with the Sherlocks this morning." He turned to talk directly to Sandra. "They don't want you to go anywhere right now since we don't know for sure that the Santanappers won't still be after you. For now, you need to plan to stay here on the ranch. I hope that won't be a problem. The Sherlocks are coming here to work with us since they don't want you travelling at all."

Stuck at the ranch. That's how it felt to Sandra. It was a great place and it was easier having Cappie and Squawk with her, but she hadn't been home to St. Annalise in a month and she missed Jason and her best friends, Birdie and

Spence. Not to mention, January is always Slumber Month at the North Pole where the elves all tuck in for a long, very deserved sleep right after Christmas – almost like the way bears hibernate. Virtually all activity at the Pole comes to a halt and Sandra gets to have the month off for fun. She had been completely looking forward to it after the very busy Christmas season.

None of that mattered at all now with Santa missing. She was kind of mad at herself for even thinking it.

"It's okay, Sandra. Don't be mad at yourself. You deserve to have some fun too," Em said to her in a comforting way for the little, usually tough elf. Sandra realized her little friend had read her thoughts like some elves – including Em – had the ability to do.

"Thanks, Em. I love you, my little friend," Sandra said, appreciating the kindness.

"I know," said the little delgin with a smile. Sandra couldn't help but smile back.

"*squawk* . . . me too! . . . *squawk* . . ." Sandra knew she had not been paying nearly enough attention to her beloved bird – and he knew it too.

" . . . *squawk*! . . . where's my love? . . . *squawk* . . . "

"Of course I love you, Squawk," Sandra said. "A huge amount."

". . . *squawk* . . . love you more . . . *squawk* . . ."

"Okay, okay, either let me in on this little love fest," Gunny said in his teasing manner, smiling. "Or let's get busy."

"Staying at the ranch will be fine," Sandra said, knowing he was right. There was so much to do. "Finding Santa is our top priority."

"Good. The Sherlocks will be here tomorrow and brief us then. Until that time, Sandra, you need to be with me or Chance or anyone from the ranch at all times. Understood?" Gunny asked her sternly.

She nodded her head knowing he was right – for now.

"One more thing for everyone here," Gunny continued. "Until we hear differently from the security team, nothing about Santa missing leaves this room. Not a word. Now, how about a horse ride around the ranch? Anyone?"

CHAPTER 12

The News Isn't Good

Location: North Pole Village

It had been the bleakest moment that Mrs. Claus could ever remember having. She had dozed off in her rocking chair waiting
for Santa to return from his big deliveries and had awakened to
knocking on her door. *Oh goodness*, she thought, *had she locked
the door?* She almost never did. She hurried to let in her tired
husband.

Instead, she had found three of the members of the Sherlocks
standing on her front porch looking solemn, along with Zinga
and Breezy, both crying – as elves do – and she had immediately feared what she was about to hear.

They had given her a full report on what they knew, which
hadn't been much. They didn't have any answers for the questions she was asking. They only knew that Santa was missing.
The reindeer were missing. Sandra and Em too were missing.

Missing. Despite the dire news, the word brought joy to her heart and allowed her to breathe again. She had feared worse when she saw them all at her door. Missing was not dead and hope lived.

## CHAPTER 13

A Jumbled Up Rescue

Location: Happy Holiday Ranch

By "anyone" wanting to go horseback riding, Gunny had really meant just Sandra since he knew she wanted to use her locket to try to rescue Santa. Sandra had never actually ridden a horse so when it got right down to it, as the two walked out to the stables they skipped the horse ride and walked to an out-of-sight spot behind the stables. A place they could plot and plan and disappear from unnoticed.

"Okay," said Gunny, noting to himself that he felt a surprising amount of concern over what he was about to do. Not the rescuing part – the disappearing part. "Just how does this disappearing thing work?'

"It's really pretty easy," said Sandra. "I just hold on to my locket and wish out loud – or even just think sincerely – on where I want to be and I go there. It has to be about something important, though, or I don't go anywhere. So if I wanted to use it to get groceries or something like that, it would never work. But this is totally important so I feel certain it will."

"Sounds simple enough. Are you sure it can take both of us?"

"It worked when I took Christina home last night so it should work now, too. I think if you hold on to my hand, I should be able to take us both."

"And then what? I mean, what happens when we get there? Do we 'land' nearby? Or right next to the person?"

"I always seem to land nearby. Somewhere close, but not in direct view, if you know what I mean."

"Good. That should give us a minute to size up where we are and what we need. Here's what I'm thinking. We pop in on whoever is holding Santa and the reindeer, we get a look around and we pop right back so we can figure out what we need and how we can get them free. Can the locket get us back that fast?"

"I think so. I've never tried." Sandra felt sure and unsure all at the same time. The locket always served her well but this was a major mission they were about to try.

"Well," Gunny said. "There's no real way to find out except by trying. I'm willing if you're willing." He reached out and held her hand. She used her other hand to grab onto the locket.

"I wish to be taken to Santa Claus and the reindeer," she said. For anyone watching, they would have seen them there and then not there. Holding hands had indeed worked for taking both of them.

But where were they going? For the briefest instance, they had seemed to arrive at their destination because Sandra saw Santa's red coat hanging on a rack and one of the reindeer –Dasher maybe? – had looked up in surprise from the hay he was eating. Like he had seen them. But just as fast, it felt like some kind of pulsing wave had hit them and they went tumbling end over end, landing in a big desert with nothing around for miles except scruffy cacti, tumbleweeds, and some rock piles likely full of resting rattlesnakes.

"What in the world was that?" Gunny sputtered as he picked himself up off the ground. "Where are we? Is it always this rough of a landing? Where'd my hat go?"

"Did you see that?" Sandra asked, confused by it all as well. "Did you see Santa's coat and Dasher there? At least I think it was Dasher."

"I didn't see anything till we landed here. Wherever here is," Gunny said, dusting himself off and looking around. "Actually, now that I look around, I think you've landed us back on the ranch -- a really remote part of the ranch anyway. That building way over there you can just make out is one of the old hay buildings. From the looks of things, I'm thinking that maybe you need to work a little more on being more specific about our return destination. Ah, there it is," he said as he spied his hat hanging off a nearby cactus and set off for it. Sandra pulled him back.

"I don't need to be anything." she said. "I didn't have time to think about coming back. Nothing like this has ever happened. I wished for us to get taken to Santa, we got there and then somehow something kicked us out. Maybe Santa is here. Did you think of that? I told you it doesn't take you directly to the location most of the time."

"Are you kidding? Look around here, Sandra. There's nothing here! This is Texas scrub. Even the cattle don't like to roam around back in this area much. There's nothing any direction you look."

She knew he was right with just a glance. "Okay, so let's try again." He nodded his agreement. "Just let me get my hat."

Hat back in place, the two stood holding hands and Sandra wished again to go to Santa. This time the two could feel themselves whirling and tumbling. Every other time, Sandra just appeared where she had wished to go, but this time they were tossed about until they finally landed. Exactly where they had been.

"This is getting to be really frustrating," Gunny said, going after his hat again.

"I'm going on my own this time, Gunny," Sandra said as the cowboy ran back.

"Oh no you're not!" But it was too late; Sandra had wished herself away and was gone. Even without Gunny though, she was being battered about. She got another glimpse of the reindeer but just couldn't break through to the location. She landed smack in front of a very frustrated Gunny.

"Look it, Locket Lady," he said storming about. "You may be South Pole Santa, and you may be the one with all the 'tricks' and the magic and the big royal title. And I may just be a cowboy from Texas, but I happen to be your guardian and a guy who cares about you and you can't just keep leaving me in the dust this way. I'm not going to go for it. You want another guardian then let's get you one, but--"

"Gunny –"

"Don't be interrupting me yet."

"Gunny," she was insistent, now pointing her finger to something behind him.

"I mean it, Sandra," Gunny said, realizing at last she was pointing at something behind him. His eyes opened wide when he turned and saw what it was.

"Mountain lion," he said quietly, seeing what Sandra was pointing at and knowing there was nowhere they could run.

"He's running awfully fast," Sandra said urgently. "Where'd he come from?"

"They can come out of nowhere and this one looks hungry. Or just mean," Gunny said. "It's not unusual to see them in the back country, but usually I've got a gun to scare them off and a truck to hop into and go.

"Okay, Sandra, we need to be going now. So if you wouldn't mind, I'm going to take your hand and then you get us out of here, okay? Let's go on home to the ranch house." Sandra reached out for Gunny's hand as the racing mountain lion closed in on them and Sandra wished them away.

They landed right where they had left from originally – behind the stables. Only it wasn't they. It was just her! She hadn't grabbed Gunny's hand completely in her fright of the big cat.

"Locket, take me back now to Gunny!" she said, frantically grasping it, never wanting to be anywhere more than she did now.

Fortunately she was accurate this time. She landed right next to him as he stood there in a state of shock. There was little he could do to fight off the cat that was about to make him dinner. He wasted no time when she appeared, grabbed on to her tight and yelled, "Go! Anywhere! Go!"

They landed hard with Gunny flat out across Sandra this time, both of them relieved to be alive. "I gotta thank you for saving my life. I believe I was about to be a cowboy burger for that mad cat."

Sandra was so glad he was in one piece she squeezed him hard.

"eeeeeeee, eee, eeeeeeee"

"Rio!" she exclaimed, pushing the big cowboy aside.

"The *Mistletoe?*" he said, surprised that he was surprised. "I say 'go anywhere' and you take us here?"

"Gunny," Sandra said, a little surprised but not surprised with herself. "I'm always thinking of home." She pulled off her borrowed cowboy boots and dove into the clear water for playtime with her favorite dolphin.

CHAPTER 14

Home Sweet Home

Location: St. Annalise

After she had showered and cleaned up, she was back on the *Mistletoe* deck waiting for Gunny to finish with his shower too. He came back on the deck in a pair of baggy surfer shorts and no shirt. Sandra couldn't blame him. It was way too warm on St. Annalise for a long-sleeved cowboy shirt and boots.

"Found these shorts in the guestroom closet and figured it'd be okay to borrow them," he said, checking to see if he was right.

"Cappie tries to keep extras of all kinds of island wear in there for guests," Sandra said. "She even added some choices that fit elves, which cracks me up. She's always thinking of everybody else." It made her smile thinking about it.

"Like you," said Gunny, toweling his hair dry. "You do the same thing and I'm thankful you do."

Sandra went to protest but he stopped her.

"I mean it, Sandra," he said, sitting down next to her. "You didn't have to come back for me. In fact, you shouldn't have come back for me. It was dangerous! Don't get me wrong though. I'm totally glad you did. And there's certainly a whole bunch of worse places we could have landed than here on this little island paradise of yours. I'm really grateful."

"Gunny, what do you think happened?" Sandra said, voicing what she had spent the last hour thinking on. "Why couldn't I get us to Santa?"

"I wish I knew," he replied. "I know you tried hard, but we have to try another way. I need your word that you won't try the locket again, Sandra. With or without me. I don't think it's meant to be used that way. We'll figure out a way to find him."

She knew he was right. For whatever reason, the locket was not the way. "I promise," she said. "We'll find another way."

"Now, I know you're not going to like this," he added, "but we have to get back to the ranch."

She was already shaking her head, which he had anticipated. "I'm not going without seeing Jason."

"Sandra--"

"Save it, Gunny," she said. "I know the Sherlocks are coming to the ranch, and I know people are going to wonder where we've gone. I don't care. I mean, I do care, but they have to understand I'm not just South Pole Santa. I'm a teenage girl with a life and a boyfriend who I have barely seen in more than a month, and I'm here now."

"Go."

She looked at him. That was too easy.

"No, I mean it. Go. You're right. Everyone needs a life. Go."

She smiled big at him, which made him happy just looking at her. If only the smile wasn't because of the fairy king guy. He just was not a big fan.

"But Sandra, you can't be gone long, and you can't tell him anything. Not even him, Sandra."

"I won't be, and all this stuff is the last thing I want to talk to him about. I promise to be back by this evening and then 'locket' us back to the ranch. This time to the ranch house." She grinned, already hopping onto the dock. "Bye!"

"Yeah, yeah, bye," he said, waving her away. "Hey, wait a minute, is there anything to eat around here?"

Sandra didn't hear the last part since she was already down the dock and headed to Jason's. She took the shortest route there, and while she would have liked to have seen one of her best friends Spencer, who had spent Christmas on the island with his parents, she only had time for one visit and that visit was going to be with Jason.

"Where you going?"

Oh Christmas crackers. Wistle. Truly the very last fairy she would like to see on this day or any day really. She ignored her. So the fairy buzzed up in her annoying way even closer.

"Hello? Santa girl? Are you hard of hearing?"

"No, Wistle, I'm just full of joy about seeing my boyfriend and not wanting to spoil my mood talking with you."

"Your boyfriend? Oh you must mean His Highness."

Sandra ignored her.

"You really need to stop calling him your boyfriend. He's way out of your league."

Okay, now she was mad.

"Way out of my league? You don't know anything about us, Wistle." Sandra tried to hurry but the annoying ball of light always kept up.

"I know stuff. One thing I know is that he's not at home. He's not on the island at all."

Finally she said something that mattered to Sandra. "What does that mean? Where is he?" Sandra asked in spite of herself.

"Well I'm sure you'd like to know, but I'm sure if he wanted you to know, he would have told you," the smug little fairy said.

"Well he didn't know I was coming or I'm sure he would have, so if you could just be so kind and share his location, I would very much appreciate it," Sandra said, truly meaning it. She missed Jason enough to be nice to Wistle even.

"I can't say," Wistle said, zooming off. "Guess you better not surprise him next time."

CHAPTER 15

Not Happy

Location: St. Annalise

It had turned out that Wistle was telling the truth this time. Christina was at the house but Jason wasn't, and Christina didn't know where he'd gone.

"He just said he needed to do some 'fairy' business off island and he'd be gone a few days," Christina had told her. "When I asked him about it, he said he couldn't share more. I don't know if that's because he doesn't know more, or he's not allowed to share more. This is a complicated time for us. I want to keep him close and I know that to keep him close I have to let him go."

Sandra just stood there for a minute taking the news in. She and Jason seemed to have the worst luck.

"I'm sure if he had known you were coming he never would have left," she heard Christina saying but it didn't help. Then

Christina wanted to know what was going on with the Santa search but Sandra was too impatient to share and had waved her off. "Honestly there's not much yet to tell, Christina," she said. "I'll make sure we catch you up on everything as soon as we know something."

"Should I tell Jason you came by?" Christina called after her as she hurried away.

"No thanks," she called back. "I'll tell him myself." Like in a few minutes, she thought to herself. This was what the locket was made for as far as she was concerned as she ran the whole way back to her big tugboat home.

"Gunny! Gunny! Where you at?" she called out as she jumped on the deck of the *Mistletoe*.

"In here," he called from the galley with his mouthful of pecan pie. "Did you know Cappie baked two pies? There's this pecan here and what looks like some kind of fruit pie. Hey, you're back early. What's going on?"

"Jason's off the island and I just came back to tell you that I'm going to use the locket to go see him so I might be a little longer than I planned," she blurted it out while reaching for a sweater to take along. She couldn't be sure where she was going.

"Wait a minute. Just slow down for a minute," Gunny said, setting the pie aside. "Let me understand this. Island boy is off the island and you want to use the locket to see him? Yeah, that's not a good idea."

"How did I just know you would say that?" said Sandra.

"Think what you want, but I'm trying to do you a favor here. This is not because I'm not crazy about the fairy ruler." Sandra looked at him skeptically,

"No, hear me out. This is a boyfriend/girlfriend thing. Did you ever stop to think that maybe if he had wanted you to know where he was going he would have told you? Even being far away you know he could have sent word. Or he could have told his mom to tell you. Or Spence even."

She was listening.

"I'm just trying to tell you that if I was your boyfriend, as crazy as I would likely be about you," he paused and grinned, "I would not appreciate you being able to 'locket' your way to finding me all the time. In fact, I'd really resent it after a while."

She knew Jason would hate it too. He'd be glad to see her and not glad at the same time and that's not what she wanted. What she did want, though, was a boyfriend who told her where he was going.

# # #

And what Jason wanted was a girlfriend who was around more often and didn't just surprise him with a visit, he thought to himself, as he re-read the note Wistle had sent by Fairy Express. Dang it! Well it didn't matter now. Their meeting would have to wait. Right now he was prepping for a more pressing meeting. A meeting he hadn't sought or expected but had been summoned for. He was to appear before the Supreme Esteemed High Council of the Fairies. The claim that he was the King of Fairies, though he had not made it, had been challenged and an order to appear at once had been issued. While Jason did not care a bit about what they thought, he had been briefed as he travelled to the meeting, that the stakes were high. Only royalty could meet with this Council. If he was not who everyone was saying he was, then it was likely he could not return to being who he had been. In fact, it seemed, he likely would not return at all.

CHAPTER 16

The Fairy Council

Location: Unknown to All Humans

In the world of magic, fairies often chose to stand apart. There was a recognized "Esteemed High Council of All Magical Beings" that, by mutual agreement from all but a very few species, was the ruling body over the magical realm. At the top of that Council, the elfins ruled and had for many centuries. The fairies, while having a place on the Council, did not recognize the elfins as the top rulers and instead felt that the head Council position should be held by the royal fairy line. A Shan fairy line, to be more specific. In protest of that not change occurring, the fairies had changed the name of their own fairy council to the very long and presumptuous "*Supreme* Esteemed High Council of Fairies" and pronounced it a higher council than the one ruling all of the magical realm. The only problem was that only fairies felt it was the highest of the high. No other magical beings paid any attention to the fairy council or what they called it or that it even existed. Fairies being fairies, however, had no care that others chose not to recognize their true superiority. It was to this council that Jason had been ordered to appear. Many fairies feared it.

Jason, however, did not. He had been ordered to report without notice, blindfolded and whisked away to this "top secret" spot of fairies, delivered a message about a visit from his girlfriend, and made to get dressed in clothes deemed "appropriate" enough for a Council visit (but highly fussy by his standards. As he told his mother later, "they were like something I would have worn to prom, which is one of the reasons I never went to prom.") Now, as he stood there waiting to go in, he was not in the least bit "nervous" as one of the fairies accompanying him indicated he "should be" and much closer to resentful and angry. This meeting held no interest for him and his patience was at its limit. A glowing lavender colored orb – a rare color for fairies – floated up to him just as he had decided he wasn't waiting any longer. "The Council will see you now."

"Lucky me," he said under his breath.

"Indeed," said the fairy orb in return, choosing to take him at his word.

The door to the Council chamber opened to a very bright room full of glittering and glowing fairies. Fairies as a species were always spectacularly beautiful and these were some of the most stunning of all. Most were appearing in full size as Jason was but there were a few glowing orbs in the room as well.

"You are Jason Annalise?" said a fairy at full size in the center of the curved table where they were all seated. Jason's quick count showed nine seated, two orbs and two empty seats.

"I am," Jason replied. "And you are?"

The fairy smiled, bemused by his insolence. *Very fairy like*, she thought, before responding to him directly.

"Juna of the Shans, daughter of the royals, Jinkara and Tochar. I am the acting head of the Council." She said all of that in ancient fairy. Jason ignored it and chose to respond in English.

"For what purpose have you summoned me here, Juna of the Shans?" Several of the fairies whispered to each other in response to him understanding what Juna had said. Only fairies could understand ancient fairy. She raised her hand and all fell silent again.

"Why, Jason of St. Annalise, I believe we simply wanted to meet the one who has presented himself as our King of Fairies. As you can imagine, this is news that is of great interest to us for we have not had a king in many ages but instead have been ruled by a magnificent line of queens. Her Highness Reesa of the Shans is our heir-apparent."

The most stunning of the fairies at the table stepped forward to stand close to Jason. "I am Reesa. While I do not know if I believe you are who you state, I do see you are as handsome as the fairy reports have indicated."

Jason completely ignored that. "I have never stated I was anything more than a regular guy. It's your fairies on our island who have insisted I was more."

"Tell me, Jason," she said his name as if it was distasteful in her mouth, "such a non-fairy like name, can you orb?"

"I can."

"Let us see."

"No thanks."

The Council members whispered again. Jason wasn't sure if it was because they didn't believe him or because he refused.

"Can you read the paper on the wall posted there?" She pointed to the farthest point in the room to a small piece of paper that appeared to have nothing on it.

"The one that says 'Only Those of Royal Blood will Claim a Council Place and Live Another Day?' Is that the one? Not very friendly of you all, I might add."

Now the whole of the Council was not to be hushed. The words were so small that it was impossible for anyone other than a fairy to read. Juna indicated that an aghast Reesa should be seated again and hushed the other members before she proceeded.

"Tell us your story, Jason of St. Annalise. Please."

"Well, since you asked so nicely," he smiled, knowing the "please" had just been for him, not out of any true kindness. "Okay, my story. There's not a lot to tell. Basically, I showed up in a dinghy one day adrift off the shores of St. Annalise Island. Christina Annalise, the headmistress of the school there, conducted a search to find my parents, and after no one came forward to claim me, she adopted me - for which I will always be grateful. I've never been that big on school, like to surf, and for whatever reason on my eighteenth birthday a crown tattoo appeared on my arm and the fairies on the island all went crazy. That's my story."

There was just silence.

"What? No round of applause?" Jason added to fill the awkwardness. "I told you it wasn't that interesting."

"May we see the 'crown tattoo' as you call it?" Juna asked.

"Sure." Jason rolled up the sleeve on his right arm to reveal the tattoo and the whole of the Council bowed except Reesa and Juna.

"Please step closer for my review," Juna said. He stepped up and held out his arm. She looked at it and then she too stood and bowed. Only Reesa now stayed seated.

"Reesa of the Shans, you too must stand and bow for our King," Juna said to her with firm direction.

"I will not," was her reply.

This was getting good, Jason thought. He didn't care one way or another, but if it bugged the great-looking fairy chick with the bad attitude, he was game on.

"Well it seems like you better," Jason said, holding out his arm and moving her way. "It seems in the fairy realm of things, this tattoo--"

"Please, Your Highness, we call it the Divine Mark," Juna said, interrupting him briefly.

"Okay," Jason said, not wanting to insult them in any cultural way, really, and aware that he very likely was one of them as well. "This Divine Mark indicates you must."

Reesa looked at it closely and Jason was not sure if it was pain or hatred that flashed across her face, but he knew for certain it was not affection.

"Juna," her voice now had a plaintive tone to it. "Juna, surely you do not recognize this, this, *human* as one of us. At best he is a masquerader. He has learned some tricks. He cannot be the lost one of our lore. He cannot."

She looked at him again and any sense of despair left her and she spoke more surely and direct again. "Even if he is who he appears to be, I will not bow to a Shanelle."

What did she just say? thought Jason. *A Shanelle? It wasn't enough to find out he was a fairy but he had to be from the nice line of fairies?* He grinned at the irony that he couldn't even be a tough guy fairy. And he realized something else. He knew just enough about fairy history to know that the Shans had pretty much always ruled the species and his discovery very likely just ended a long reign, whether this Reesa of the Shans liked it or not.

This just got worse and worse.

CHAPTER 17

Alive!

Location: North Pole Village

Time seemed to fly and a month had passed already since Santa had been taken. Every one of those days had been tense with frustration. The Sherlocks had uncovered nothing. No amount of magic had produced any results either. At the Pole, the only saving grace was that they managed to get the elves tucked into Slumber Month before any of them caught on to Santa being gone. To do so had required Mrs. Claus implying that he had swung by St. Annalise for a bit and would see them after they woke up. She had refused to outright lie, even, or especially, with something this important. "We tell children all the time they cannot lie, I won't either," she stated in a tone that left no room for arguing. In the elves exhausted state, none of them were awake enough really to wonder about it and the whole pile of tired elves tucked in for their long winter's nap.

Mrs. Claus, though, had paced for the entire month. She had been relieved beyond words to have received the news that Sandra and Em were safe, but distraught that it hadn't been all of the missing who had been found. Zinga and Breezy, and a handful of others who knew the news and could not think about sleeping all month, were all still up as well. Even though they were all exhausted, none of them managed to get more than a few hours of rest each night.

Exactly a month from when they had last seen Santa, a clue finally came in. A letter addressed to Mrs. Claus with the words "OPEN ME NOW!" in large letters written on the front, in red ink, arrived. Inside was a photo of Santa with the London Times newspaper, dated January 24th. He was alive! Her husband, probably the most beloved man in the world, was alive! And he looked well. Despite the circumstances, he even appeared to be smiling a bit and there behind him was Rudolph. In a small white space, was a handwritten note in red ink, "Ho Ho Hoo!" There was nothing else. No postmark. No signature. Just this proof that Santa was alive and the misspelled ho ho's.

Mrs. Claus sat down and set pen to paper. When she was finished, she handed it to Zinga, "Please have this delivered to Sandra. I know she's been working on finding Santa with her team at the ranch with Gunny and the Sherlocks and she was hoping to go home to St. Annalise. The elves will be waking up soon, though, and Santa isn't home. We need her here."

CHAPTER 18

Family Dynamics

Location: Happy Holiday Ranch

It was ironic, Sandra thought again, that all of this was happening while they were working from Happy Holiday Ranch when nothing about their mission was happy.

Despite not making any real progress on finding Santa, it had not been for lack of trying. The team had been busy chasing down even the most remote clue. The Sherlocks had been to places near and far around the globe. They had made the ranch their center point for the search not only because it was more central to the world than the North Pole, it was close to where Santa and the reindeer had gone missing. Plus, they were able to come and go in this remote part of Texas without almost anyone noticing. Not to mention, despite its remote location in the low country of Texas, the ranch was more connected by modern technology than the North Pole. The Pole was beginning to change, even over Santa's continued objections, but it would take time.

Despite keeping a low profile, there was still plenty of buzz at the ranch and the nearby town about what was happening there. The Santa rescue teams' days were filled with meetings held in a rundown outbuilding that Gunny had commandeered. It was perfect for their work since it wasn't being used by the ranch for anything; it had no windows, and was hidden away from most of the world, but it wasn't so great if you didn't want people wondering about your business. Their mission was top secret so none of them could even tell the other members of Gunny's family about it. Gunny and Sandra wanted to, of course, but it was agreed that it was safer for the family and ranch hands if they didn't know. Gunny had only shared it with the Major. He had to. The Major was his dad and it was his ranch. Naturally, the Major had been shocked to hear what their mission was, but proud the ranch could be part of helping to get Santa back. While some of Gunny's family members – like his mom and Blue – didn't seem to care that they didn't know what was going on, his brothers and Glory definitely did. It wasn't going over well with the twins at all, who were used to being part of whatever Gunny was scheming on.

"Seriously, Gunny," Crow was saying to him. "Day in and day out, you go in to the old tool house for hours and hours with those little itty-bitty elves going in and out. Hey, and by the way, they do not act like you described them. You kept telling us elves were funny and happy and just plain silly. That pile of elves you got there look and act, well, they look kind of tough. They never even smile."

Gunny held back his own smile. Crow was right. These were not the nice guy elves of common lore. These were elves with belts. Black belts. These were the "we-know-karate-and-tai-kwon-do-and-kickboxing-and-we'll-use-it-on-you-if-we-need-to" kind of elves. They were elves ready to slap you down and ask questions later. You messed with one of their own and they were coming for you.

"Ah, it's just that they've had to stay up through Slumber Month," Gunny said, trying to quell some of the curiosity. "It's a top secret elf project, brother, and that's all I can tell you."

"Well, Ghost and I don't like it. Chance isn't around or I'm sure he'd hate it too. None of us really believe you, and we don't like it when you leave us out."

"Where's Ghost been anyway lately?" Gunny asked, realizing he hadn't seen his little brother that much, and when he did it seemed like Sandra was always somewhere nearby. His brother was many things, but shy and unsure were not two of those qualities. He seemed to have fallen hard for Sandra, and while Gunny understood it, he wanted none of it. "I want to tell him that he needs to quit being all googly over Sandra. I'm sure it's making her uncomfortable."

"Googly, huh? That's a new one. You're sure she's the one who's uncomfortable? Has she actually said so, brother, or is it that maybe she's not the one who's uncomfortable? We get a pretty girl here at the ranch and suddenly all of us Holiday boys are standing up straighter and shining our boots, if you know what I mean."

"Exactly how old are you?" Gunny asked, again surprised at the insight of his younger brother. He often seemed older to him. Like Sandra, the twins were eighteen, and all three of them – Sandra, Crow and Ghost -- seemed older than their given number. Well, not really Ghost so much, Gunny thought. He could act more like he was ten at times still, but the other two for sure. Crow just shrugged at the brother he looked up to in response to his question. Gunny and Josie were like the two center points the Holiday family revolved around. Just by either of them entering a room, the energy could change for the better. The Major had always held the respect of the family, but it was usually their mom and Gunny who brought in the most fun and lifted their spirits the highest. Crow and Ghost especially, would do anything for Gunny.

That's part of why they all supported him so much when he got the hare-brained idea to enter the competition for South Pole Santa. They knew he had the biggest heart of all of them and they knew he would bring his best to the job. They also knew he had the advantage of having all of them to help him succeed once he got the job and that the whole world would absolutely love him, like they did, once they got to know him.

It was for all of those same reasons that none of them could believe it when he came home as a runner-up. Runner-up? Impossible, the Major had said. No Holiday would come in second on a role he was so clearly born to fill.

Crow and Ghost had felt similar and were outraged he hadn't been selected. When they found out a girl had won, they just about couldn't take it. Gunny had been struggling with his conflicting feelings as well. He knew, by then, that Sandra was an excellent choice but he had been so sure he was just a little bit better of a choice. Yes, there had been the business of him being one of her "guardians" so she needed him, but a new guardian could have been recruited if he'd become South Pole Santa. And why would she have even needed a guardian if she wasn't selected? That was the kind of thing he asked himself. The whole thing had weighed heavily on his mind. Not the least of which was his own behavior toward Sandra after her selection. He had felt like there were some feelings for each other possibly growing between them as they progressed through the competition. He knew about Jason, even then but the guy wasn't even her boyfriend. He was just some lame guy who was letting a great girl with a teenage crush on him slip through his fingers.

Just like Gunny had done. He had blown it with her big time at the Christmas Cotillion, and then afterwards when he took off without so much as a goodbye. Just a note. He thought back on it and winced. He'd left a super lame note. He had no idea how he would ever make it right with her again. Even thinking about it now made him feel surprised that he had ended up working for Santa. He recalled the day again, in his mind, that Santa had visited him and convinced him to come back to the Pole to help.

It was days after his sorry departure from the North Pole. His behavior at the South Pole Santa competition with Sandra just proved he wasn't right for the part from the start, he remembered thinking, as he tossed another hay bale off the big truck full of them. This was his life. This was his place in the world, and honestly, the ranch was a real good place to be. He had been kidding himself to go after more. He slung another hay bale, this time, high in the air.

"Ho Ho Ho, what did that hay bale ever do to deserve that big toss?" Gunny had whipped around from his sour thoughts and hay bale throwing to find the big guy himself that windy Texas afternoon right after Christmas the previous year.

"Santa?" he asked, totally puzzled to see him there. He had been fairly sure he would never see Santa again. Not with his bad behavior.

Santa dispensed with the small pleasantries and got right to the point.

"We need you, Gunny. She needs you," Santa had said and Gunny knew without asking that the "she" was Sandra.

"Well now, that, Santa, with all due respect, is pretty hard to believe considering everything," he said as he went back to tossing hay but without quite as much vigor. "I mean, you had your shot at my help and you chose another direction. Now it's up to me to accept that and move on graciously. I'm the first to say, that hasn't been my strong point here, but I'm working on it. I truly am."

"I know this is hard to hear, but I'm glad you've struggled with accepting the news," Santa said to Gunny's complete puzzlement. He guffawed at the idea and Santa continued. "Gunny, the other contestants all accepted my decision quite easily, with the exception of Rollo,

but Hotshot made that choice impossible." Gunny thought back on how the misguided elf had tried to help by hurting and understood what Santa was saying. "If for any reason Sandra hadn't worked out or for some reason doesn't work out, it is a comfort to know there is someone out there who really wanted it as much as she did.

"I understand second place isn't easy when you're a competitor, and especially for a once in a lifetime position like South Pole Santa," Santa had said.

"Sir, I'm not sure of your point, but I gotta tell you you're not helping right now," Gunny said, being very honest with him.

"My point is this. Just because you weren't selected doesn't mean there's not an important role still for you. Did you know that I had my own guardians? When I was younger and just starting out, I had five as Sandra does now." Five, Gunny noted. He had thought he was the only one. "Now, instead, over the hundreds of years, that has changed into the services of the Sherlocks and I am grateful for them. But my gratitude toward the five will never be matched. They saved me many a time — sometimes from some real danger and sometimes by just being a safe shoulder to lean on. Sandra is going to need both.

"She is more than you have yet been told, Gunny. Few know she is of the Leezle elfin family and if that were more widely known, there are those who would stop at nothing to do her harm," Santa had continued. As someone who had a bit of elfin in his own family history, Gunny had actually heard the 'lore of the Leezles' as he thought of it. But to a working cowboy from Texas it was all just some kind of mumbo jumbo. "The role of Santa is a tremendous honor, as you know, but it is always also a job, and one of the biggest anyone can carry. Sandra is willing

and right for this evolving world of ours but she is also in need of a strong team. She needs you for that team, Gunny."

"She'll never accept me, Santa. I blew that," Gunny had said, embarrassed again by his behavior.

"Nonsense! We all have our moments. You think I put anyone on the naughty list for one or two bad decisions? Absolutely not. It takes a commitment to bad behavior to get on the list. Besides, Sandra's the new Santa, she is kind by nature, and being kind means forgiving," he said the last part smiling.

"I promise to consider it, Santa," Gunny had said, feeling like maybe he would be able to smile again after all.

"Ho Ho Ho, Gunny! Do more than that. There's trouble brewing around my choice and I need you at the Pole. Next week. Make everything right here and then come on back to your second home. Ho Ho Ho!" And just like he had come, he had left.

The one-on-one with Santa had helped restore Gunny's good nature, and for the first time in weeks he had been his old self that night at dinner. Laughing and teasing with the rest of his family members and the ranch hands. Fun and laughter had been restored in the Holiday house. Right up till a few days later, when he shared he was headed back to the North Pole to assist the two Santas.

"What?" just about every member of the family had said at the same time, except his mom and Blue. They always accepted him no matter what he wanted or did. Crow and Ghost were the maddest. They just couldn't believe he would be willing to help out the new Santa. "If she's so good that Santa picked her over you, then she needs to be able to do it alone," Ghost had said while Crow nodded in agreement. Gunny knew it was a tough thing to understand – he barely understood it himself. But something inside him woke up after his talk with Santa, and he knew the jolly ole elf was right. Gunny still could make a difference in the world, even as a runner-up.

No amount of explaining had helped his family to accept his choice during the past year. Crow had softened a bit, but Ghost seemed to just dig in more in his opposition to Gunny's choice to return to the North Pole and help. Ghost didn't like his brother being gone all the time and especially since he'd been overlooked. That was Ghost's view on it. Pretty much all the brothers felt the same but just weren't quite as obstinate about it. Gunny had kept trying to win them over but he knew his decision had changed their relationship. He knew it wasn't as close as it used to be.

For that reason particularly, Gunny had been sort of pleased that Sandra and the others had ended up at the ranch on Christmas. It had given all of the Holiday family a chance to see for themselves why he was willing to accept being second and carve out a way to still be involved and serve the children of the world. Like Gunny did, Sandra had a special "magnetism" around her that drew people in. She reflected a genuine kindness (most of the time - even she had her off moments) that surpassed even Santa's, and once you had met her, it was hard to argue that she was not the right choice. It was as if being named South Pole Santa had lit a glowing flame inside of her.

Gunny could tell right away that his family was happy to have her there, and more accepting of Santa's decision now than they had been before in their misplaced loyalty to him.

It was only Ghost who continued to worry him. On the one hand, he seemed the most drawn to Sandra and yet, on the other, he also seemed drawn to her for all the wrong reasons. He seemed to want to charm her as a conquest rather than like her as a friend. Gunny had stepped fully into his role as one of her guardians but he never expected he'd need to be in that role around one of his own family members. Not to mention that he also had to make sure that what he was feeling, was real concern for real actions, and not just some kind of weird jealousy because Sandra clearly enjoyed Ghost as well. She seemed to laugh louder and smile more when he was around. Or did she? Gunny was having trouble sorting it all out and he hated confusion of that sort. *First, she's drawn to a fairy king and now to his most immature family member*, he thought. *Oh, brother.*

Ultimately, truth be told, while some of his family members were suspicious about what was really happening with the Sherlocks coming and going at the ranch, other than they didn't know that Santa was missing, there really wasn't anything else to tell. There had been no Santanapping note, no demands from the Santanappers, and no sightings from anyone. A lot of the tension being experienced by the team came from none of them having any answers and arguing about what they should do next. Some of them wanted to go to the general public and the rest wanted to keep it Pole business. For now.

"If we take it out to the whole world, then we'll have everyone in the world helping to look for Santa and the reindeer and we'll be able to find them faster," said Sandra, not for the first time. She was on the side of calling Beatrice Carol, the World Wide News reporter based in London, and breaking the story.

"Maybe," said Gunny, who didn't feel it was the way to go. "But it seems to me that if Santa was spotted today, there would already be news out about that. Instead of clues about where he is, I think we would just get worldwide chaos. Santa is likely the most beloved figure by children everywhere and to share that he's been taken is to invite despair. Do we really want to be the instigators of that? Can't we just keep this under wraps for a little bit longer and let the Sherlocks work it through their channels? If they really can't find him, then we could agree to go to the world press."

Sandra saw his point. She wanted as many people as possible looking for him, but knowing Santa was missing was something that came with great amounts of anxiety. Until they knew more – until they knew something at all – it was probably better to keep it as Pole business only.

But each day turned into the next at the ranch without any progress. Cappie and Thomas had gone back to St. Annalise to keep things appearing as regular as possible, and Em was getting in some fun giving delgin rides to the ranch hands. Gunny had spread the word that Sandra had selected their remote ranch as her January vacation spot, and the family, ranch hands, and townfolk were gracious enough to accept that explanation.

They sort of had to. No one would even think to guess the real truth, and even if they had, they wouldn't have wanted to know. Santa was gone. How would the world ever be the same if he never was found? No one on the team dared to even consider the thought, let alone ask the question out loud.

CHAPTER 19

Road, er, Air Trip

Location: In the Sky/North Pole Village

As soon as Mrs. Claus' letter had arrived, Sandra and the others headed for the Pole. Sandra watched the land speed by below, but despite how fast the Reindeer Express was flying, it felt to her like they would never arrive at the Pole. It had been a month since Santa had disappeared, and Sandra had not felt so low since the year when she was eleven and her parents disappeared. She knew most people believed they were dead but she felt, in fact she would say, she knew, they were not. In her heart, she could feel them still around, and she believed they had found small ways through the years of letting her know that and making sure she knew they loved her. A tear ran down her cheek thinking about them and she hurried to wipe it away. This was not the time for sentimentality and explanations. The coach was far too full for crying.

She would have welcomed the time on the flight for some rare time alone, but Gunny and the Sherlocks would have none of it, and Em and Squawk almost never left her side. So they were all there, stuffed in what was normally a four person maximum coach. Fortunately, what Gunny needed in space, being tall with long legs, the diminutive elf size provided, and somehow they had all managed to fit. Elves, though, even disciplined ones like the Sherlocks, really hated a few things, and two of those were flying and sitting still, so the trip was a lot like flying coach class on a plane with three toddlers and a parrot who wouldn't quit talking, all sitting in the same row.

". . . *squawk* . . . she's crowding me . . . *squawk* . . ."

"Am not," Em said, crowding him a little more.

". . . delgins can fly . . . jump out the window . . . *squawk* . . ."

"Delgins like to eat birds too," Em said smugly.

". . .*SQUAWK!* . . . told you . . . *SQUAWK!* . . . bird eater! . . . "

"ENOUGH, you two!" It was Gunny who had lost patience this time on the trip that seemed would never end. Sandra was wishing she had just used the locket to get to the Pole but she didn't want to become "locket dependent" and she really wanted to keep a limit on who all knew what it could do. She checked the watch Santa had given her again. Four minutes had passed since the last time she looked. Four of the longest minutes ever.

When they finally landed, they all practically burst out of the coach. Before doing even one more thing, Sandra had to be firm with her friends.

"Em, we haven't been home here for more than a month. Take some time for yourself and get a nap. You too, Squawk. Go on into the hotel, please, and get us checked in so you can have a room to rest in. And both of you, stay apart, no fighting, and be quiet so you don't wake the rest of the elves. Am I clear here?" She looked at them both for confirmation. Truth be told, they both looked as tired as can be and welcomed the chance to rest. They nodded their agreement.

"Okay, good," she said as they headed off in the opposite direction. "Now, Gunny, as for you and the Sherlocks, I am in one of the safest places on the planet. I do not need or want your constant care and oversight. Please, I am begging you, give me a little room." Gunny gave a quick nod of agreement. He was devoted to her, but the guardian thing was wearing thin for him, too. It had been a very long month. A break sounded great.

"Yes, Your Clausness!" The two Sherlocks stood at alert and saluted. She had come to understand that it was an unusual relationship between Santa – now her too – and the Sherlocks. It was one of both being ordered to do things by them for her own apparent safety as well as being the governor over them and addressed with this funny "Clausness" they all used. None of the Sherlocks called her Sandra. They all called her, as they did with Santa, "Your Clausness."

"Mrs. Claus!" *Well that was a surprise,* Sandra thought, turning to greet who the Sherlocks had called out to in delight. Mrs. Claus? No "Clausness" for her? The Sherlocks were another surprising piece of the Pole, she thought wryly. She set the thought aside to greet the favorite mom to everyone. "Mrs. Claus! I am so happy to see you!" Sandra exclaimed, hugging her tight and getting warmly hugged in return. "I am so sorry we haven't been able to find Santa yet. But we will never stop looking."

"Of course, dear. I know that, and I believe truly that you all will bring him home. For now, we know he is being held but is alive, and by the appearance of things, the reindeer too," Mrs. Claus said to Sandra before turning to the "at-attention" elves next to her. "Sherlocks, your work has been impeccable as always but elves need their rest. As a Claus, I am relieving you of duty for twenty-seven hours (one day in North Pole time.) Sandra relieves you as well, isn't that right, dear?"

"Of course," Sandra said as the two elves saluted and ran elf-like down the street. Even Sherlocks were gleeful elves at heart.

"Come join me, Sandra, for some cocoa. You too, Gunny," she said to the cowboy who was trying to be nonchalant about hanging around. He looked quickly at Sandra for the okay and then quickly accepted the offer. "Cocoa sounds like exactly what I need after that long ride, ma'am," Gunny said, smiling. He always called Mrs. Claus "ma'am." It was a Texas thing. "You got any cookies to go with it?"

"Would I be Mrs. Claus if I didn't?" she replied as he held out his arm for her to take, and the three walked to the Claus home.

It was good to be back, Sandra thought, as they made their way down the streets, still quiet from the elf slumber. She knew Santa would feel the same way if he were walking with them.

# # #

Far away, Santa was indeed lonesome for home. But he had the reindeer and none of them had been hurt. For now, that was enough. He believed in the good in everyone. Even in the Santanappers.

CHAPTER 20

A Little Chat with Mrs. Claus

Location: North Pole Village

So often things are not what they appear to be at first glance, thought Sandra as she listened to what Mrs. Claus was saying, slurped on her hot cocoa, and looked at the paper she had received. The "ho ho hoo" message on the paper was in Santa's writing. Mrs. Claus was sure of that and it hadn't been misspelled after all. It seems that long ago, with Santa having such a high profile job, the couple had come up with a code to share so they could pass messages between them if anything like this ever happened. The code for "everything is fine, don't worry" was two o's on the end of the last "ho" which is what had been written. Four o's would have been a call for alarm – and a message to say "I love you" in case they never met again. Mrs. Claus, while still very worried about where Santa and the reindeer had been taken and how they were being treated, felt calmer. She had shared this news with the Sherlocks, who were less impressed and still very set on catching the perpetrators, but for her, she would trust it was all going to be fine.

"Until they find him, Sandra, you will need to be North *and* South Pole Santa. I'm sure you can do it," Mrs. Claus was saying as Sandra considered this news. Her thinking was more like the Sherlocks' than Mrs. Claus' – not at all certain that things were okay.

North and South Pole Santa! Was Mrs. Claus crazy? Sandra thought, as this obvious need hit her full on. Of course, she would be expected to do that, but she hadn't even fully become to understand everything about being South Pole Santa yet. To be both seemed impossible. But she had been selected to be South Pole Santa, proving nothing was impossible.

"Well, Mrs. Claus, to be honest, I thought we could just wait for some time still and see if Santa returns. After all, if they can locate him quickly, there'll be no real need for me, or anyone, to step into his role," said Sandra hesitantly.

"Nonsense, dear," said Mrs. Claus dismissively. "There are many things Santa does every single month but Slumber month. They must be done, and you are the person he chose to do them."

"For the South Pole, Mrs. Claus! Never ever have I wanted to take on Santa's role," Sandra said with distress.

"Of course not, dear, but we don't get to choose each challenge and opportunity presented to us in life. We only get to choose which direction we will go and whether we will step up or not. That is the choice before you now," said Mrs. Claus, offering Sandra wise counsel with compassion and understanding. "Santa believes in you, and I do too. And, Gunny, surely you do as well?"

"I do," he said. "Like Sandra, though, I hope to get Santa back soon. It seems like a mighty big role for her to fill on her own otherwise."

I wonder who he thinks should fill it? Sandra thought, still feeling a little grumpy about him Santanapping her. *Oh yeah, that's right, him. Yeah, that's not happening.*

"I can do it, Mrs. Claus," she said, feeling stronger and with a full conviction to making it happen.

"I know, dear, that's what I've been saying."

CHAPTER 21

Waking from a Long Winter's Nap

Location: North Pole Village

They actually made it to the fourth day of February before the elves woke up. Not surprisingly, Sandra thought later, it was due to a loud argument between Em and Squawk, but she knew they all would need to wake up soon anyway. By the time they did, her best friends Birdie and Spence had arrived at the Pole too, so she felt more ready to take on what was ahead. She had asked Cappie and Jason to join them too. Cappie was assisting Christina at the academy and couldn't get away and, in his typical fashion, Jason had given no specific reason for why he had turned her down. At least she had finally been able to talk with him for a change. Yes, it had been by phone, but thanks to Spence and his new Pole to Pole system, including the "Equator Pole" as they had taken to calling the barge building site at St. Annalise, they had more choices for communications.

The call had been better than nothing, but it had left Sandra with a feeling of wanting more. She wasn't sure afterwards if it was a feeling of wanting more time with her boyfriend or simply more from her boyfriend. She felt, as Gunny had pointed out in their talk on the *Mistletoe* the day she had last tried to visit Jason, that she seemed to always be the one seeking him out, going to him, looking for him. She knew it was frustrating to have a girlfriend who was South Pole Santa, but he added to their problems instead of helping to make it easier. He could, for instance, take a little interest in her job and come check it out at the North Pole. He was insistent that "I will, I will," but his actions were that "he didn't he didn't."

Having her very best friends in the world with her now, though, helped make everything better, despite Jason not joining them. The team had worked together to put up signs all around the Pole, directing the wakening elves into Happiness Hall in the center of the village. There, Mrs. Claus, Sandra, and Gunny sat on the stage ready to talk to the happy, chattering elves. It had been a nice, long sleep this year – not short like last year – and they were ready to be awake and busy. Laughter filled the hall, which tugged at Sandra's heart. She loved seeing them so joyful and hated that she and the others were about to impact that in such a negative way. But it couldn't be helped. They would all find out and they had to know. She saw Periwinkle in the crowd with her pretty blue color and gave her a quick wave. She was glad the South Pole team of elves were here too so they wouldn't hear the news about Santa second-hand. They always came home for Slumber Month. When the hall was full, Mrs. Claus stepped up to the podium and the crowd broke out in cheers.

"Mrs. Claus! Love you!"

"Hi, Mrs. Claus!"

"Hope you slept good, too!"

"Well good February morning, my dear elves," Mrs. Claus said, trying to sound as positive as she could. "How much I always love this day when I see your happy, smiling, well-rested faces after our month of slumber." If possible, the whole room seemed to look even happier in response to her kind words.

"I have an announcement today," she was sounding less sure and more hesitant and paused just long enough for one of the elves to call out, "Mrs. Claus, where's Santa?" The room then broke out in typical elf behavior with all of them chanting in believed support of their very favorite elf in the world:

"Where's Santa? Where's Santa? Where's Santa?"

And then just:

"Santa! Santa! Santa! Santa!"

That caused Mrs. Claus to burst out in tears and the chants quickly changed to wailing by the whole room. And they didn't even know what they were crying about. The trio had expected tears but not before they even got to tell them what they should be crying about! Zinga, Breezy, and Birdie went through the room handing out tissues as first Gunny and then Sandra tried to restore order.

"Elves, hello, elves! Please can you get quiet for another moment? Please. I know I'm not Santa Claus, but I am Sandra Claus… and I'm so happy to be here with you all today." The crowd began to quiet, and after a round of what seemed to be every one of them - judging by the noise level - blowing their noses at the same time, it finally was calm again.

"Now, it is very important that you try very, very hard to stay brave and quiet while I tell you this story. I know that is hard, but it's important news that we must share with you today," Sandra said as thoughtfully as she could. To her surprise, they all stayed quiet with just a sniffle here and there. Elves were highly emotional but they were also very curious, some would call it nosy even, so hearing the story topped continuing to cry.

"First of all, while Santa isn't here this morning to be with us, we want you to know that he is okay." Still the room was calm. All was well so far. *Maybe this will go better than we worried about,* Sandra dared to think as she pressed on. She remembered that later as being such a funny thought. Of course it wasn't going to go well.

"But we don't exactly know where he is. Our Santa, well, there's no easy way to say this so I'll just be honest with you all. Our dear Santa has been Santanapped. And the reindeer too."

The room was eerily quiet and the trio on stage braced themselves for the crying and sobbing that was about to occur. Zinga and Breezy had tall stacks of tissues at the ready. Birdie and Spence were standing nearby ready to offer comfort.

Life, however, rarely goes just the way you plan. The team had worked through all kinds of scenarios, thinking they had all the outcomes considered. They had planned for pep talks and ways to keep the elves feeling emotionally secure and safe. They had insured there was plenty of boxes of tissues and counselors available for afterward. They had been sure the elves all found out together so they could ask questions. But, as it turned out, despite their attentions to it, they hadn't planned for *every* possible scenario. Sandra, Gunny, and Mrs. Claus stood on the podium fully realizing their oversight as they looked at their beloved bunch of elves - every single one of them lying flat out on the floor. The news had been too much, and they had all simply fainted where they stood.

CHAPTER 22

Dear Lovey

Location: North Pole Village

Slowly, each one of the elves began to regain consciousness from their fainted state and then the crying and sobbing, wailing, and questions the team had expected from the start began in full. They were inconsolable, and the team could do nothing but let them cry it out. Eventually, the room of elves wore themselves out and started to calm. Sandra was able to take to the stage and address them all again.

"Hello to all you wonderful, waking elves who love Santa so much," she said, starting again. The elves showed the first signs of smiles since they had woke from their faints. "We must join together at this time for Santa's sake and be as strong as we've ever been. I know the feeling of wanting to curl up and just wait for it to all be over or simply sit and cry, but Santa would not want that from us. You know it and I know it.

"What he would want is for us to set sadness aside, put on our happiest faces, and get things done. The Sherlocks are working around the clock to discover who has taken Santa and the reindeer and where they are holding them. We know, for sure, that he is alive and looking well, actually, and we will get him home. We will! Plus, remember that Santa is not alone. He has all of the reindeer with him to keep him company." Sandra paused there and looked at her friends for some quiet support. They were there smiling and cheering her on.

"So here's the thing. I need your help. First of all, we need to keep this news a secret held by only all of us. I know you all love to tell a secret but this secret, if the world found out, would scare children everywhere – much like it did with all of you – and none of us want to do that now, do we?" She paused so the elves could rally around her words and to be sure they were grasping the importance of the request.

"Nooooo!!" she heard from all around the room and cries of "never" as well.

"Good, good, I knew you would feel that way. And the other thing I need your help with is that, as your new South Pole Santa, it falls to me to keep Christmas production on track and I could never do that without all of you. Can I count on you to help me keep Christmas on track and protect the children from this news of Santa?"

The elves began to murmur and nod their heads and Sandra heard welcome words of support.

"We can help."

"You can count on us, Sandra."

"We'll do it for Santa."

"Mrs. Claus, are there cookies?"

Thank goodness, Sandra thought, they are getting hungry!

"I have all sorts of cookies and I made cupcakes too as a special treat," Mrs. Claus said, smiling with true affection for the elves she loved and counted on for their quirky, loyal ways. "Before we go, however, I have a very special surprise guest for you all today.

"We all love the *North Pole Times* for its thorough coverage of everything Christmas and all the latest news of everything happening at the Pole. Although, as Sandra just explained, don't expect to see this news about Santa in the Times. But besides the comics, I happen to know the feature you like the most in the *North Pole Times* is the Dear Lovey column and, with all of this going on, I suspect you are going to be wanting a lot of advice from the wonderful Dear Lovey. So, without any more chatter, we have here, for you, with her excellent advice, one of your very favorite elves and the Pole's most popular newspaper columnist . . . . Dear Lovey!"

With that Mrs. Claus waved her hands to the side of the stage and Gunny pushed in a lovely elf seated in a wheelchair. Dear Lovey was beloved by all for her wise advice in her newspaper column. That advice came in spite of, or maybe because, she had been born with some unique challenges. She was an elf born without legs and also with a shorter than normal left arm.

You hardly noticed, though, as she came on stage with Gunny, a huge smile in place and waving brightly to all of her many fans. Though it was the first time Sandra had met her, she had often read the Dear Lovey column in the *North Pole Times* and found her advice exactly right. It was easy to see too how loved she was by all the elves gathered in Happiness Hall. Including Dear Lovey was a smart move by Mrs. Claus as the bad news seemed to fall away and even thoughts of cocoa, cookies and cupcakes had faded for the moment. All thanks to an appearance by Dear Lovey.

Gunny adjusted the microphone to her height.

"Hello, everybody!" Dear Lovey shouted out to them all. "Isn't it great to be awake again? We're alive at this challenging time in our history, but we live here at the North Pole where all of us know that absolutely anything is possible.

"When I heard the news about our missing Santa, like all of you, I was stunned. It seemed impossible and I knew I would be getting lots of letters about it. Right away I started considering what advice I might have for dealing with a problem like this that is fraught with so much anxiety. So, for the first time ever, I wrote myself a letter and I replied to it as well. Would it be okay if I shared that question and answer with you right now?" She paused as the elves applauded her on.

"Thank you. Then here is what I wrote:

Dear Lovey,

Santa Claus has gone missing and I'm feeling worried and helpless. I just want to cry, curl up, and not talk to anyone until he gets back. I don't think that's what he would want me to do, though. I think he would want me to still be happy. How can I be happy when he's in trouble?

Sincerely,

Very Worried About Santa

"Does that sound like a letter some of you might have written to Dear Lovey?"

"It does, Dear Lovey, it does."

"Yes!"

"What's the answer? What can we do?"

"Well, I didn't write out my answer, although I will for my next column, but I am going to give you two suggestions, and Sandra, Mrs. Claus, and others are going to help us carry it out." The elves all were very quiet now, wanting to hear about anything that would help them at this difficult time.

"First thing, we all need to stay active. We've got to go to work and concentrate on doing our best job, and in your off-hours I want to encourage you all to get in some exercise."

There were some moans from the crowd. Elves were notorious at trying to avoid exercise.

"Now wait. I know that exercise, like running and working out in a gym for instance, isn't for everyone, but there is something for everyone. If you don't like to run, then try walking. If you don't like exercising by yourself, try a group class or team sport. Keep trying things until you find something just right for you. Lots of you like the wild team sport of Pole Pong which might be your choice. Whatever you choose, working out will keep you feeling better and help keep you from sitting around feeling sorry for yourself and worrying about Santa.

"For me, I plan to keep swimming. How I do enjoy it! I'm going to get in some extra laps in the pool just to stay especially busy and wear off some of my energy. I sure would welcome having any of you join me that would like to get wet. The rec pool offers open swim every night. They also offer classes and lap time where you can go back and forth, back and forth, swimming away your cares and woes for just a bit. The water lets us all feel free.

"Okay, that's idea one. Now idea two has a little more fun added to it. We are going to exchange names and each have a secret pal!"

The room got noisy really fast and Dear Lovey had to speak up to continue.

"I am so excited about this! I can tell already that you all like the idea too! Later this week, we'll all get to draw a name and you will be the secret pal for that person. Let's call them our 'secret person.' Then, until Christmastime, we will all be thinking of fun, thoughtful, kind things we can do for our secret person, much like a random act of kindness each month. But we must not tell anyone else who our secret person is, and most especially not your secret person.

"So what do you think? Do you like my ideas on ways we can stay happy while Santa is gone? We can work hard, we can work out hard, and we can put extra attention to kindness."

The entire room of elves, who had been crying for more than an hour earlier, was now jumping up and down, smiling and cheering. Dear Lovey took it all in, smiling and laughing herself, happy to know she was helping in the way she knew best.

This from an elf who had every right to feel life was unfair and too challenging. Instead, there she was, front and center, sharing her experience and wisdom, rising above any of her physical limitations and encouraging them all to embrace the good things in life as well.

She was a rock star, Sandra thought. Despite the bleak news the elves had just all received, Dear Lovey had helped to turn this into a really good day. If Santa were there, she knew he would be pleased.

CHAPTER 23

Being Proud of Who You Are

Location: St. Annalise

Could the last few months have been any worse? That was the question constantly in Jason's mind since he had got back from the meeting with the "fairy top dogs" as he had described it to his mother. He made a checklist in his head of all the things that he considered totally sucked, that had happened most recently in his life.

He turned eighteen and gained an unwanted tattoo. "Check," he said out loud.

He got the unbelievable news that he was apparently the king of fairies and, oh by the way, he could turn into a fairy orb just by thinking about it making that news seem too real. "Check again."

He got all moody with his girlfriend at their birthday party, she took off for her giant job and pretty much never returned.

He had only seen her one time and talked to her one time in more than three months. Could they even really call themselves girlfriend and boyfriend anymore? "Triple quadruple check,' he said with a voice dripping in irony.

Then, as if being a fairy king wasn't bad enough, he finds out he's a good guy fairy instead of being a "tough guy" fairy and had turned the whole fairy world upside down with Shanelles now being the ruling party. "Big giant check mate, Mango," he said to no one but his trusty dog sitting in front of him on the sand, hoping he would throw the stick she had plopped there for him again.

"Next, I'll be sprouting some flippin' pink fairy wings," he said as he picked up the drooly stick and gave it a toss. Mango didn't run after it, though. Instead she stood there and barked. "I appreciate the support, Mango, but you can go after the stick." Still she stood barking until he understood why. It wasn't out of support, it was out of alarm.

"The men in our world never have wings," said Wistle, buzzing over closer before changing to full size and sitting next to him on the beach log. He should have known she was nearby. It seemed like she always was nearby these days. "Good girl, Mango," he said, ignoring Wistle. "Way to bark at the bad fairy."

The two fairies sat there for a minute before Jason spoke up. "I don't get it, Wistle. Why do you keep hanging around me? Especially now when you know I'm a Shanelle, not a Shan like you? You crushing on me, is that it?" He knew she wasn't. He just added it to make her mad. *I might be a Shanelle,* he thought, *but I'm definitely not the nicest one.*

Wistle didn't take the bait this time. For once, she seemed almost reasonable. "Yeah that's it. Fairy or not, I can't resist those surfer boy muscles of yours.

"I'd like to talk seriously with you, for once, Your Highness," she said. She never called him Jason anymore. "As soon as I saw the Divine Mark, I suspected you were a Shanelle not a Shan. It doesn't matter in our world. Whoever bears the mark, rules the realm."

Jason thought about this and his meeting with the Council.

"That didn't seem to be the way they all felt," he said. "That Reesa chick definitely didn't feel that way. What's the deal with her anyway?"

"It is not for me to say," Wistle said, fussing with the sand with her hands and not looking at him.

"Okay then, let's try this. I command you to share with me what you know about the Reesa chick." To his surprise, Jason rather liked the feel of that and, also to his surprise, it seemed to work on Wistle.

"Well, King," she said with just an edge of attitude that he could see she was working to keep in check. "When you put it that way, I can tell you what I know as someone not on the official royal court, although, naturally, all fairies are superior beings to all others. You do understand that, right?"

"At least in your own minds," said Jason. "I definitely do get that."

Wistle ignored him and continued. "Reesa is a descendant of the ruling family of Shan fairies who have been in power for more years than a present-day calendar can count. By birthright, she has been set to take the throne when she turns two thousand by our count and approximately twenty years old by a human calendar. That occasion is approaching."

"Alright I'm with you. Basically she's a little older than us. I'm cool with the rule being hers. You know this isn't something I want."

"That's because you are a Shanelle. It's not that simple, Sire."

"You can cool it with the 'sire' stuff. I can tolerate the 'your highnesses' but you move into the 'sire' stuff and I feel like you're talking to my great grandfather or something. C'mon, I'm eighteen here."

"Yes, of course, Si-, that is, Your Highness."

"Seriously, Wistle, as long as no other fairy folk are around, like at least for right now, call me Jason. I really think I liked you better when you were being awful to me."

"Please, Your Highness, don't remind me. Fairies rarely feel shame and it is a black spot on my wings."

"Let's just get back to the story. So, I can't simply let Reesa rule?"

"Reesa was next in line as long as no one else came forward with a larger claim to rule. You see, the Shans took the reign by force from the Shanelles long, long ago. It was for the best."

Jason rolled his eyes, making it clear he thought that, of course, a Shan would say that.

"No really," Wistle continued. "You can even ask most Shanelles – if you can find one. Shanelles don't seek the limelight or relish turmoil. If you are honest with yourself, you know this is true, for even you look for a way not to rule."

Jason conceded that he could see her point.

"So both parties have accepted the way it, is but that does not mean it always feels safe for either really," Wistle continued. "The Shans know the Shanelles could make a rightful claim and the Shanelles worry that, because of that, members of the Shans could step up and lock away, or even do something worse, to the Shanelles. Or at least to the royal lineage line of the Shanelles."

"Whoa, you fairies are way more complicated than the human stories that you're featured in."

"We are. We know those stories, of course. They are mostly told of Shanelles. Nice little stories about sweet Shanelle fairies but they don't speak to the real grandness of the fairy line. We Shans are proud of who we are and choose not to be so sweet and subservient to beings such as humans who are less than we are. We see the destiny and rightful place of fairies in a different light than the Shanelles do."

"So if everyone is cool with it all – Shans ruling, Shanelles being in stories – why does it have to change now with me?" Jason asked.

"Because we know of you this time. Each time a new Ruler is to be crowned, the Shans must wait to see if any Shanelle will step forward before the Shan heir apparent can be crowned. There are always rumors of a Shanelle being out there as a possible challenger but, century after century, since the time of the overthrow, no Shanelle has chosen to step forward. It has been believed it is because no Shanelle royalty is still alive. More likely though, most Shanelles, as I have said, live quiet lives, far out of the limelight, and those in line for the throne perhaps choose that path more than others. They do not wish for the fairy realm to know of them. Though if any of them had worn the divine mark, it would be hard for them to hide."

Jason didn't know it, because Sandra had not had time to share it with him yet, but his story was turning out to be a lot like Sandra's. Only in his case, it seemed, it was his fairy family hiding, and in her case it was the Royal Leezle elfin family, ruler of all of the Magical Realm, who had fled for the sake of their own safety.

"You, though, Jason Annalise, are more complicated still," Wistle said in almost a whisper, reluctant to say more but under commandment.

"Why does that not surprise me?" Jason quipped, waiting to hear what was coming next.

"Your Divine Mark, while seen as a Shanelle by the Shans, is really not that simple. Your mark is the mark of a combined house. Do you see this line here?" she asked as she traced a rambling line in the crown tattoo that wrapped around the arm. "It proves you are the son of a Royal Shanelle and a Royal Shan. This is a combination only rumored at, and frankly, dismissed as impossible, and yet here you stand with proof of such a union. That is why all bowed so quickly to your claim and also why Reesa did not. You are a Shanelle and a Shan with a clear claim and birthright to the fairies, the greatest of all species. Surely, Jason," she deliberately used his name this time, "even with your stubborn ways, you can see this is a grandness you must embrace and not turn from?"

He never thought he would get anything but sheer annoyance from Wistle, but in that moment, she had given him something more. Was it a stirring of pride perhaps? He could feel the first real tugs in his being of stepping into his role and, more importantly, stepping into the grandness of who he really was. Royal or not, he had been adopted and raised as a human named Jason Annalise, but he was a fairy with a proud heritage and, very likely, even a different name. Wistle, of all people, had awoken an urgency to find out who he really was.

"Wistle," he said after a very long pause of contemplation. "As your King, I thank you for sharing this knowledge that I needed to know."

"You are welcome, Siiiiire." She drew the last word out, bowed quickly, and orbed away.

Mango barked again.

"Good girl, Mango, good girl," Jason said with a begrudging bit of rare respect for the feisty Shan fairy.

CHAPTER 24

Secret Pals

Location: North Pole Village

Like most things with the elves, even simple things can get complicated. Dear Lovey's idea on launching a Secret Pal program was brilliant! Sandra, Birdie, and the rest were so excited to get it going and the elves were all abuzz about how it would work. It took about a week for the team that Sandra assigned, which included both Birdie and Dear Lovey and some elf volunteers, to come up with the "rules" for the Secret Pal and how it would work. Sandra was happy to see that Rollo's name was on the list of elves who had volunteered to be part of it. Since not being selected as South Pole Santa, he had kept a pretty low profile at the Pole, but it seemed he was ready to be more involved again. Sandra made reviewing their drafted rules a top priority.

Secret Pal Rules

Rule 1: Everyone at the North Pole and the South Pole, and the elves currently assigned to Equator Pole, could participate in the Secret Pal program but each had to exchange with their same groups. Otherwise they were often too far away from each other to be able to be a successful Secret Pal.

Rule 2: No one was required to be in the Secret Pal program. Sandra thought perhaps some of the more seriously inclined elves would opt out. (In the end, not a single one did. At heart, all elves loved fun.)

Rule 3: Secret Pal meant keeping it secret! This would be hard for the elves.

Rule 4: Secret Pal activities included, but were not limited to: doing nice things for your secret person without them knowing, sending them cards, making them something special, and saying nice things about them. Any act of kindness was encouraged.

Rule 5: You cannot tell someone else who his or her Secret Pal is if you know.

Rule 6: Only one Secret Pal action would be allowed per day at maximum, and no less than one action per month.

Rule 6: No trading Secret Pals.

Rule 7: All Secret Pals would be revealed in December before Christmas. The date would be determined later. (They wanted Santa to help select.)

Rule 8: Have Fun!

The day of the drawing arrived, and the elves had all day to come by and draw a name out of Dear Lovey's Magic Secret

Pal Hats, as the team had chosen to call them. There were three hats for all three Poles. Each elf would draw a name out of their proper hat while Rollo held it and then showed the name to Dear Lovey, who would be the only one to know all names. At that time, they would also receive a copy of the rules.

Naturally, elves being elves, they all came at once, first thing in the morning, before the drawing time even began, making the line very long. Elves can be quite patient. Things like long lines never bother them. Being very social, they simply talk and laugh while they wait for their turn. Rollo opened the doors early so the elves didn't waste their whole day in line. Diva was first through the door. She moved to the stage quickly and reached into the North Pole hat with much fuss, handling nearly every slip of paper. Rollo felt that was silly since she could see none of them, but she *finally*, very dramatically, pulled out a name from the bottom of the hat. Only to look at it and toss it back in much to Rollo's complete duress!

"What?" he cried out. "Only one drawing per person and you must take the name drawn."

"Oh no," said Diva very dramatically. "That name didn't suit me at all! I wish to have a girl as my Secret Pal. That was one of the boy elves."

"Boy or girl, elf or human, fairy or other, all picks count," Rollo said, trying to keep some order in the day.

Diva was once again digging away in the hat and once again dramatically drew out a name. "LuLu!" she announced. "This one I'll keep!'

"You can't keep it now!" exclaimed Rollo, almost beside himself and it was only the first elf to select. "You told everyone. The name is supposed to be secret. That's why it's called the *Secret Pal* program."

"Yes, I see," said Diva. "Well I'll keep it anyway. I'm sure she didn't hear."

"I heard," came a voice from back in the line, presumably LuLu's.

"Of course she did," said Rollo. "Now please, Diva, draw again, and this time you keep whatever name and you say nothing. Just show it to Dear Lovey."

"I see. Well, fine then," she said huffily, but this time she drew out a name and smiled when she checked it.

"Next!" said Rollo, trying to keep the line moving.

Unfortunately, it was a very long day for Rollo and Dear Lovey. A few of the elves stepped up, drew their name, and moved right along, but more often they were like Diva. They took their time, pulling one out of the hat and then threw it back in, usually for the same reason as Diva – they either wanted a girl or a boy. A couple elves right away, immediately after stepping off the podium after telling Dear Lovey who they drew, told someone else and had to get in line again to redraw a name.

Finally, it got down to just a few names left. Sandra made sure she was the last person to draw a name.

"Saved the best name for last for you, Sandra," Rollo kindly said, looking very tired but keeping positive clear to the end.

"Thank you, Rollo," she said as she put her arm into the hat clear to the bottom and found the last slip of paper. She opened it with excitement to see who she was going to get to dote on this year and spoil even, from time to time, as the object of her Secret Pal affections.

No way! No way would she somehow get the Texas Longhorn who had just Santanapped her a month earlier! That was her thought as the blood rushed from her head and her feeling of excitement turned to annoyance. She double-checked the paper twice to make absolutely certain that was the name listed, but sure enough, no matter how many times she was going to read it, that piece of paper read "Gunny." Of all the names at the whole of the North or South or Equator Poles she managed to get Gunny's. Her good humor was returning and she had to laugh out loud! What else could she do? It was ironic, even annoying, but it was pretty funny. One way or another, she was going to have to be nice to him. It seemed even the magic of the North Pole had lined up to be sure of that.

After the craziness of the drawing, havoc had ensued for the next couple of weeks as the elves learned how to be good Secret Pals. The first week, there were a lot of cocoa coupons delivered everywhere and big bags of Hopping Frogs and Giganto Bubble Gum. They all gave each other things they themselves liked. On the plus side, that meant they all loved what they got! Week after week, it had gone pretty much the same way.

Sandra was pretty sure she too had an elf for her secret pal because she would find the coupons and candy treats on her office desk or sometimes placed sweetly outside her room at the hotel. There would often be a pile next to it for Birdie as well, with big tags with their names on them so they knew whose pile was whose. It was sweet. Literally too sweet, but also just so nice to have the little treats waiting.

For Gunny, Sandra was trying for a once-a-week secret pal act. So far, she had made him a picture frame that looked like a cutout of the state of Texas that he could put a photo in for his room. She had had his boots shined one night, which took some clever maneuvering to get them out of his room and nicely placed by his door for the morning. And just to make sure he didn't think she wasn't an elf, she too had left him cocoa coupons and favorite candies.

Once the program had been going on for a while, Sandra would sometimes see elves in the craft room holed away in a corner working on cards or projects for their secret persons. She loved that they were starting to get creative with what to give and what nice things to do as well.

The Secret Pal program promotion team had even got clever and developed creative signs around the Pole as reminders. They were bright but simple and kept you thinking about what you were going to do next.

The committee had also declared the seventh day of each month "Secret Pal Day." Everyone was encouraged to try to find some fun random act of kindness they could do for their pal on that day.

Sandra had come to love those days because the elves loved them so much. They loved the giving as much as the receiving. Everyone seemed happier on the seventh of each month now.

Elves were cool that way, Sandra thought to herself as she bebopped down Main Street with a happy step and a big smile to herself. She was off to go tell Dear Lovey thanks again for coming up with the great idea to make everyone a Secret Pal.

CHAPTER 25

An Unexpected Arrival

Location: North Pole Village

"Sandra!" Breezy had rushed into her office with Zinga, Alexander, LuLu, and Toasty right behind her, all looking rather pale for elves. "Sandra, we just received a post from the Esteemed High Council of the Magical Realm," she said, waving a gold sheet of paper in her hand. "They're coming!" She said the last part almost whispering as she handed the gold paper to Sandra to read. As Sandra took it, the elves huddled together hugging each other. "Well that's a little unnerving," Sandra said under her breath as she unfolded the paper and read it out loud.

"We, the Council of the Esteemed High Council of the Magical Realm and all that reside and practice within, do hereby notify you of the imminent arrival of our representatives at the North Pole at the stroke of noon, North Pole time. Please stand ready at the realm portal for our arrival," Sandra finished and looked up, completely confused.

"That's in less than two hours," she said to no one in particular. "Who are these people? And where is this 'realm portal' they are talking about?"

None of the elves said anything until finally Zinga spoke up in a whisper. "The Esteemed High Council of the Magical Realm rules over all of the magic realm, including the elves and elfins. They are the Council, in fact, that long ago created the position of Santa Claus. They felt the non-magical world of humans, particularly children, deserved to have at least a touch of magic in their lives each year, so they interviewed and selected Santa in much the same sort of way you were selected by Santa to be South Pole Santa. Then they established all of us here and determined how we could be of the best service to the seen world."

"Wow," said Sandra. "I never really thought about how Santa became Santa."

"While it may seem like an exciting thing to have the Esteemed Magical Council visit, it usually is a meeting tinged with tension even when the reason is a positive one that has brought them to us," Zinga continued. "Once, they awarded Campy – our outdoor specialist elf – with a medal of bravery for saving a gnome's life from a charging polar bear and even that visit made us all nervous. They're just so," she paused, searching for a word.

"So intimidating!" said Toasty. "And big and scary and really, really serious. They're not like Santa at all."

The other elves nodded their heads in agreement.

"And now they're coming because they must have heard somehow that Santa is missing," Sandra said, beginning to understand.

"They'll care about that, Sandra," Zinga said.

"We don't want you to go away!" Alexander exclaimed.

"Oh, Alexander, I'm not going away," Sandra said, scooping the elves up into a big group elf hug. Despite what she was saying to them all, she was not feeling all that confident. This Council visit did feel a little big and scary – and done without warning.

"Alright, we have no time to waste," she said, letting them go. "Run and go tell the others to get things cleaned up the best they can and to be on their best behaviors. Zinga, tell me where to find this secret 'realm portal' so we can get there, and then I better dash off and get ready."

With no time to lose, Sandra had hurried back to her room at the hotel to change her clothes and get ready for this big visit. She decided on a quick shower to help calm her nerves and when she stepped out, wrapped in a big fuzzy towel, there, scribbled on the foggy bathroom mirror that ran above the long vanity, was a message for her.

Darling, do not fear – daol

Daol? Who was "daol" and why had he or she come into her bathroom and written on her mirror? Kind of creepy, she thought. Until she realized what it really said.

It wasn't "daol," it was "dad!" The steam had caused the message to run making the "d" look like an "o" and an "l."

When she looked at it again, it clearly said "dad." "Dad!" she said, grabbing for a towel for her hair and opening the door to her room. No one was there. She had expected that would be the case, but she always hoped. Nevertheless, she spoke to the room.

"Dad? Mom?" she said, feeling slightly silly but connected to them at the same time. She could feel their presence. She felt a cool breeze blow over her. "I love you," she said and the breeze came again. "I'll be strong." She waited for another breeze but when none came, she knew they were gone just as she knew they had been there.

If she had needed any more proof than the note and her own feelings, she got it back in the bathroom. Added to the note on the mirror, drawn below the word "dad" was now, very clearly, a heart.

CHAPTER 26

A Group full of Surprises

Location: North Pole Village

Sandra stood at the secret Realm Portal located deep within the basement of the hotel of all places. Next to her was Mrs. Claus. She had wanted to include some of the elves, but none of them wanted to join her (except Em, of course, but Sandra had decided against that). Making it even more difficult, Mrs. Claus and Zinga felt it was better if Gunny stayed out of sight and away from the Esteemed Council representatives while they were there. The Magical Realm cared, in their way, for humans, but they were generally not keen about spending any real time with non-magical folk. Sandra, being human and not particularly magical herself, knew this time together was likely to be challenging.

As they appeared, one by one, promptly at noon, from the glowing portal that had just looked like a custodial room door a moment before, Mrs. Claus stepped up to do the greeting.

"Your most royal highness, ruler of the magical realm and elfins everywhere, Calivon," she said with a glance back at Sandra to see how she was doing, "welcome again to the North Pole." He nodded and stepped forward as Mrs. Claus greeted the next council member. Calivon was clearly elfin. He was thin and tall with sharp features and piercing green eyes. *It's ironic how completely different elfin and elves are*, Sandra found herself thinking as she prepared to meet one of the first full elfin she had ever personally met, though her own mother was mostly elfin and she herself looked very elfin. The two races were frequently believed to be related, when in truth, the only real things they had in common were the letters "elf" and that they were both from the magical realm.

"Grosson, leader of the granites, welcome." The biggest being Sandra had ever met emerged at that moment from the portal. He looked much like a giant muscular rock with large arms, legs, and torso. His skin was sort of speckled, like granite, and he had a big bald head with no neck. Strangely, he wasn't unattractive really. More menacing than anything.

"Laile! Royal larn of the Moonrakers," Mrs. Claus said with cheer in her voice. Sandra quickly deduced that a larn must be like a queen for other species. "How nice to see you, my friend! It has been far too long." The two women briefly hugged as Mrs. Claus moved on. Laile, like most Moonrakers, was of short stature, a bit plump with a round face and very large eyes. Though it was bright in the room, her skin gave off a soft glow.

"Zeentar!" A tall, striking wizard heard his name called as he stepped from the portal, but this time not from Mrs. Claus, but from Sandra as she stepped up to hug the ruler – proper or not. "I'm so glad to see you," she said to him. Smiling with true affection and getting a warm smile back, at least for a water wizard anyway. Sandra could feel that his clothes were damp as they always were. He was a being of the water. "Your daughter is here! Birdie is going to be so glad to see you!" she said.

"I cannot wait," he said in the deep methodical, almost hypnotic, voice that all male water wizards had.

"Reesa, Ruler-Apparent of the Supreme Realm of Fairies," said Mrs. Claus as the portal door closed behind this last guest. Sandra turned from Zeentar as she heard the name called. She had met a Reesa once, and as she looked that direction, she realized she had met this Reesa who gave a slight nod of recognition in her direction. With her striking white hair and regal stance, she looked as knock-out gorgeous as Sandra remembered her.

"This is a true surprise," Mrs. Claus said. "I did not realize that the fairies had taken a place on the Esteemed Council again."

"We have," said Reesa in what Sandra thought was a tone tinged in condensation. She offered no additional explanation.

"Esteemed High Council Members, allow me to introduce to you, Sandra Claus," Mrs. Claus was saying. She left off the dot dot dots and Sandra wasn't sure if she had forgot or it was deliberate.

"Yes," said Calivon, reaching out to take her hand. He held it tighter than was comfortable and looked Sandra directly in the eyes. "You are elfin? Is that correct? And who were your parents?"

Strangely at that moment, both her ring and her locket gave her a jolt, and despite his hold on her she knew it was not from Calivon, but from her parents. There was a sense to Sandra of not just uncomfortableness in the room, but danger. She heeded the warning.

"My parents were lost when I was young and my full background is a mystery even to me," she replied in a surprisingly even voice despite her sense of trepidation. The answer was true if not full. "Welcome to the North Pole to you all. It is my honor to meet you."

Zeentar had stepped up closer to her again and Calivon finally let go of her hand. "Sandra, Mrs. Claus," he said. "Would it be possible for us to see a bit of the Pole before we sit down to business? Particularly, I would like to see my very beautiful daughter, Princess Ambyrdena."

"Of course!" Sandra said, smiling, always thrilled to hear Birdie referred to by her title. Birdie's father was this regal water wizard but her actual royal title came from her mother, a princess with an African tribe. Birdie, she knew, was going to be so surprised to see her dad.

As the royal group came out of the elevator, they surprised a group of fairies gathered in the lobby talking and laughing. The fairies nodded at Sandra and then immediately bowed and changed to their orb selves when they saw Reesa. Sandra could tell it was a complete shock to them and wished she had been able to share that the royal fairy was coming to visit to avoid the surprise. She hoped the tense look on her own face helped them understand that she couldn't share what she didn't know.

"Your Grace," was all they said to Reesa, as the Council group walked by. She paid the fairies no more attention than she did any other group. They were Shanelles, and for Reesa that was only slightly better than if they had been, well, say, elves.

Elves, it should be known, did not get the level of respect they should have had by many in the magical realm. Elves had no real interest in royalty or politics or how things looked or what was proper. Elves were workers. Special, amazing, producers of toys that no beings in any realm could come close to matching. Elves were light-hearted with serving others and toy making as their two passions in life. Mixed with having fun. That combination was surprisingly not highly regarded by some. Sandra did not understand it, but Shan fairies were one of the worst about deciding who and what was "cool" and who and what was not. The granites were very similar. As were wizards, as well, although Sandra had always found them more "reserved" than judgmental.

"Daddy!" Zeentar turned at the sound of the happy voice to see his daughter running across the lobby smiling. Squawk was with her.

" . . . *squawk*! . . . Hi to you! . . . *squawk*!"

"Hi to you as well, Squawk," said the regal wizard. "And hi to this beautiful girl most of all."

The whole of the visiting council group paused to smile at Birdie and her father. "Join us please," Calivon said generously to Birdie, with a nod to Zeentar. "We are taking a tour of your factory here. Sandra, will you lead us forward?"

"Of course. The entrance to the toy factory is straight ahead and our lead elf over production, Tack, is going to join us for the, inspection, that is to say, the tour," she grimaced at her slip of the tongue. It was officially just a tour, though she knew it was really an inspection.

Sandra could take no credit for how wonderfully the factory ran. That was all about the elves with Tack at the top. She knew that even if neither she, or Santa, or any other official leader of the Pole was there, the elves would get their toy-making done. They might fret and stir on some things, but on toy-making the elves were the best of the best and it showed in every room the group toured. Sandra found herself, as she usually did, beaming with pride in room after room. In fact, it wasn't until the very last room of the factory that disaster struck.

In the main toy production room, things were running like a clock and the whole area was spotless and clean. It was like that all the time, not just cleaned up for this visit. Tack liked to run the factory efficiently and the benefits showed in the quality of the toys the hard-working crew produced.

It was in the finishing room, which is a big room full of paints and glitters and waxes and glosses – every kind of thing you could expect for putting last touches on the toys built at the Pole – that things turned crazy. The tour group quietly entered the room and found a tall stack of elves – by Sandra's quick count there were nine of them – standing on each other's shoulders, working together to get something from the very top shelf. They were giggling and laughing, swaying and arguing, all in the way of elves but managing to get themselves to the right place on the shelf and grab the can they needed. It seemed to all be going well, until the elf "totem pole" turned around, completely flabbergasted to see the Council members, including the bottom elf who leaned too far to one side, and got the stack swaying wildly out of balance. They tried mightily to steady themselves, but their efforts weren't coordinated and it got worse rather than better, resulting in them all being tossed in the air. The big can flew out of the top elf's hands, and as it did, the lid flew off, sending pink glitter out to the room, covering everyone in the Council party! It felt like the world had slipped into slow motion, Sandra thought, watching horrified as it happened. Everyone, from elves to the Council members, looked stunned for an instant. And then Sandra started laughing. She couldn't help herself. It was too funny. It was just glitter, after all, and they were elves. Things happen. The elves had all started laughing, too. It simply was too funny not to laugh at! Unless, it seems, you were a granite, a Shan fairy, or the highest ruling elfin of the magical realm. Then, it seems, it wasn't funny at all.

CHAPTER 27

Sparkle and Shine

Location: North Pole Village

All the clatter, and the glitter now floating dreamily into the hall, had brought elves from all over the factory running to see what had happened, and some who were not elves. Specifically, one Gunny Holiday, who had been pretty close to ordered to stay out of sight away from the Council, accompanied by one small green delgin, who Sandra had asked Gunny to keep occupied.

Now a pile of elves covered with glitter might spell disaster to some beings but not to other elves. That combination screamed fun – no matter who was visiting and what kind of best behavior they were supposed to be on! To be covered in glitter is an elf's best kind of accident. It means being able to tell grand and wonderful stories for days and days, laughing and tittering about how it happened and how fun it was.

Finding pieces of it still in your ears, caught in your hair, even hiding in your socks for days. That is the very essence of being an elf. If the Council members weren't standing there, and if Santa wasn't missing from the Pole, this might have gone down as one of the funniest things ever to happen at the factory.

Gunny assessed the situation quickly when he got there and went into full Gunny mode on how he could help. He started flattering the ladies.

"My, my, my, well who do we have here?" he said, drawing out his Texan drawl. Both Reesa and Laile looked at him. "Ladies, might I just say that you are both as beautiful as the sun is bright, but covered in glitter, well, you're an extra delight." He grinned, hoping his improvised poem added a little extra something.

Laile actually was already smiling. As a moonraker, she wasn't that different from an elf. One difference between them was that moonrakers preferred to do all of their work by night. Glitter, Laile knew, looked lovely under full moonlight.

Reesa, though, was less than happy and maybe even more intensely so now that this good-looking cowboy was on the scene. Gunny was genuine when he said specifically to her, "Your highness, truly glitter is your color." The glitter on the stunningly beautiful fairy just enhanced her looks in every way.

Zeentar had somehow not been hit by much and the little that had landed on him, Birdie had helped to brush off. Cavilon and Grosson, however, had received a full hit as had Sandra and Mrs. Claus. Squawk too had been hit hard and was sputtering and flying about trying to remove it from his wings, which wasn't helping anything since he just kept stirring it up in the room with each swoop he took. Em made it worse when she said he looked like a "Christmas tree ornament."

" . . . *squawk*! . . . not an ornament . . . *squawk*!"

"Yes you are," said Em, all over it now that she knew he didn't like it.

" . . . *squawk*! . . . am not! . . . *squawk*!" He zipped and fluttered about, keeping the air stirred up and Gunny realized he too was getting covered. He smiled at the full-on North Pole moment they were experiencing as Sandra tried again to get control.

"Council members, my huge apologies for this mini fiasco we have experienced here this afternoon," she said. "Please, may I offer you a place to get cleaned up?"

"We will pass on that offer as we have limited time, no clothes to change into, and I'm highly doubtful of how effective one round of cleaning up would be at removing this amount of glitter," said Calivon with as much dignity as he could muster covered as he was in mini points of pink sparkling light. He felt he looked like a fairy, which made him actually shudder at the thought. "We need to spend the rest of our time here with you in chambers," he said curtly to her as Grosson nodded his agreement. "Please lead the way expeditiously to a private room where we can meet and discuss the pressing matter at hand."

Sandra assumed the "pressing matter at hand" meant Santa missing. It seemed her theory that "glitter always made everything more fun" was about to be tested.

CHAPTER 28

Glitter-Covered Chatter on a Serious Matter

Location: North Pole Village

Sandra had directed them to the room where the Claus Council regularly met, and they each took a seat at the table. On the way there, Gunny had pulled Sandra to the back of the crowd for a quick, quiet talk.

"A little uptight I'd say," he said, worried about how things might be going. "The elfin guy seems too stern. The fairy chick is, well, you know, hot," Sandra rolled her eyes as Gunny smiled, "but tense. And that granite guy seems to have as much personality as his namesake rock."

"Shhhhhhh!" Sandra said. "Granites are also known to have superb hearing and they're really smart."

"That may be so," Gunny said, not talking much softer. "But that does not make him likable. He's my first granite to meet and I'm hoping my last. Kind of gives me the shakes. Like an earthquake would." He grinned at her, but he meant it.

"I kind of like him. He's the first granite I've ever met too," said Sandra.

Zinga had scrambled to bring in bowls of candy and steaming cups of cocoa, but they were both largely ignored by all. Besides the Esteemed Council members, Sandra and Mrs. Claus, Birdie had also stayed and Sandra had asked Gunny to sit in the back of the room as well. Birdie and Zinga sat with him there. There was no small talk or laughing in the room at all by anyone but Mrs. Claus, who worked to act as a cordial host. She was nervous. Sandra patted her hand and indicated she too should go ahead and sit down. She looked longingly at the extra seat by Birdie along the wall but sat instead next to Sandra, as she should. Sandra had insisted Em and Squawk and all the other elves stay out. In fact, she had told them they needed to have the glitter room mess cleaned up prior to dinner, which didn't sit well with any of them – bird, delgin, or elf – but she had stayed firm about it.

"Your Esteemed Magical Council Chair," Sandra said to begin the discussion. "I assume you have come not to check on our production as much as to check on what is happening here at the Pole with Santa missing. Am I correct in this assumption?"

She was bold and to the point, thought Calivon. Normally he admired those qualities, but the possibility she was a Leezle made her a threat to his rule. She also had the intelligence and the radiant beauty of the elfin race. All of that kept him from liking her. While she denied who some suspected she was, and avoided his inquiry as to her parents, he was suspicious. And yet, there were no true signs of the royal line she was said to be descended from. Most notably, her hair did not sparkle as it most surely would, as the hair of all Leezles did. Not to mention, he could not "read" her as being royal as he most certainly would be able to if she was a Leezle. She was a puzzle and Calivon hated puzzles. Almost as much as he hated glitter. For now, however, her threat to his rule was not the matter at hand. Santa missing was the crisis they were here to address.

"Yes, that is what has brought us here and our disappointment that you didn't contact us about this situation," he said this directly to Mrs. Claus.

"I, that is, we, felt the Sherlocks, our elf security force here at the Pole, were our best source of finding him," Mrs. Claus said, her voice shaking. "And, to be quite honest, we can't be sure who took him, so we didn't feel confident pulling in others until we had to — not even the Esteemed Council." She tried very hard not to glance at Grosson. She personally felt the granites could be involved since, long ago, they had championed for one of their own to be Santa Claus but she didn't want to imply that in any way, even through something as small as a glance. Besides, she had no proof and there were many others who could have taken him.

"There is protocol to follow, Mrs. Claus," Calivon continued carefully, not wanting to be rude. The Council actually found themselves in an uncomfortable position with this situation since they largely only dealt with Santa Claus regarding Pole business. Therefore, it was difficult to be firm with either Mrs. Claus or Sandra Claus... as neither had been counseled by them in the past. This meeting was largely to correct that and put the two women on notice of their expectations. In a firm, but kind manner, at least kind by Esteemed Council standards. That was also part of why Zeentar had requested to come.

"Sandra, Mrs. Claus," Zeentar said in his usual polite way with a slight bow of his head, as he addressed them both. "We wish to be sure word of Santa Claus missing does not reach the human world. We must take precautions."

"We agree," Sandra said. "It has been our worry that they would find out. The children would be so worried! That is part of why we have kept this news so hushed. I fear, though, with your arrival here, it says that more of the magic world is beginning to know, and if they know, well, it really only takes one brownie knowing and the secret will be out!"

Every person in the room nodded their head to the statement about brownies. They were such gossips!

"I, and the full Esteemed Council, will work to address the rumors of him missing," said Calivon. "Laile, in fact, has a bit of a plan that is quite out of my realm of comfort but these drastic times do call for some drastic action. Having met your human friend there, Gunny," he said his name with a bit of a pinched face which made Gunny feel quite uncomfortable. "I think her plan may actually be possible."

Gunny squirmed in his seat. He wasn't sure he was comfortable about something this group had planned that involved him.

"We do wish to be given a full report on what your security force – these Sherlocks – have uncovered so far. You understand that, while we are concerned word will leak out about Santa missing, we are most concerned about where he is and who took him. This could be a threat to the whole of the magic world or just a devious plot against Santa and Christmas. This is our primary concern," Calivon said.

"Yes, of course," Sandra said. "I can arrange for the Sherlocks to meet with you immediately."

"Calivon, would you mind if we stayed through dinner?" Zeentar asked unexpectedly. "I would like this bit of time to visit with my daughter."

"And I would welcome the chance to catch up with Laile as well," Mrs. Claus said quickly to Laile, who nodded agreement.

"Grosson, would this be acceptable to you?" Calivon asked.

"I will stay and listen to the Sherlock report. I have many questions," he said in the gruff and rumbling speech of a granite.

"And, for you, Reesa? Is staying acceptable?" Calivon asked.

"It is," she responded. "I have wished a word with Sandra Claus. Alone."

Sandra nodded. This did not surprise her that much.

It didn't surprise Gunny either. Reesa was supermodel stunning, but she was snake-in-the-grass cunning, too. Private meetings without him never suited him at all. What if something happened like it did the last time Sandra spent time with Reesa on their world tour and she got so badly hurt? He wanted to be there in case she needed help.

"I'd sure like to sit in with you ladies," he said, doubting the success of that proposal as he said it.

"Of course, Gunny!" But the lady who answered wasn't one of the ones he was talking to. It was Laile, who thought he was talking to her and Mrs. Claus. "I so want to share my idea with you."

Oh giddy-up, he thought. Now he was the one who needed help!

CHAPTER 29

Laile's Plan

Location: North Pole Village

"Hold still, Gunny," Sandra snapped at him. "Diva has to get this on just right or it's not going to look perfect, and if it doesn't look perfect, then the jig is up."

"I told you from the beginning that I didn't think I could pull this off," Gunny snapped back, not enjoying his morning at all. They had been at this almost three hours now. He thought he had never looked worse!

Laile's idea had been a wild one alright – and just creative and clever enough, that if done right, it just might work. They all had agreed that word getting out about Santa missing to the children of the world he served would be the worst outcome. No one wanted to make the children worry, of course. They had another good reason as well. They didn't want bad behavior to increase! If the children knew Santa was missing and thought he might not be coming back, well, there was a good chance that bad behavior would increase.

For the Esteemed Council and the magical realm in general, Santa represented one of their few remaining connections to the human world. The human world and the magical realm had fallen apart thousands of years ago, but true affection still carried throughout each realm for the other. In some ways, the magical realm felt like they were charged with being guardians of the human world. That was part of why they had appointed Santa to his important role. They had a vested interest in his success and grave concern over the situation.

All of that was the reason Gunny had spent the past three hours getting dressed up as . . . Santa! Ho Ho Ho! Laile's idea was to dress someone up as Santa - and as soon as she saw Gunny she selected him - and pass him off to Beatrice Carol, the reporter at World Wide News, who broke all the stories about the Pole to the world! They would invite her up, Gunny Santa would do his thing, sling around a few "Ho Ho Ho's" on camera, Beatrice Carol would show it to the world, and any possible rumors or doubts about what was going on with Santa would fade away. It wasn't a bad plan, but Sandra had no idea how they would really pull off tall Gunny as the much shorter Santa.

"Ouch!" Gunny said, swatting at Diva. "That's my hair you're pulling on!"

"Well we have to make sure this wig sticks on tight," Diva said.

"Gunny, you've been bucked off broncos in the past, you can handle a little hair pulling," Sandra said impatiently. She was still worried about whether they could carry this off or not. The Council members had left as fast as they had arrived and it was up to the rest of them at the North Pole now to successfully carry it off. "Beatrice Carol is due here in an hour. Practice your Santa voice some more."

"No, Sandra," he said but he did it in his Santa voice and she smiled. She knew this was hard for him too.

"Good, no trace of that Southern accent of yours," she said.

"Yeah, and no trace of my trim and fit figure either," he noted, patting on the fake belly the elves had strapped to him.

"There, you're ready," Diva said, stepping back and looking at her work. "I did a good job. See for yourself in the mirror." She spun him around in his chair to get a full look.

He couldn't see himself in the mirror at all. He had completely disappeared. There, instead, was jolly ole St. Nick. The big guy in the red suit. The man of the hour. The guy who put smiles on kids' faces. The man Gunny would have liked to have been for the South Pole. It was a bit of a melancholy moment for him.

"I look," he paused, looking at himself from side to side. "Quite chubby," he said and the room all laughed with him.

"Thank you, Diva," Sandra said sincerely, pleased with how real Gunny looked. "I know many people help Santa every year around the world by dressing as him as well, but this is surely the best duplicate Santa I've ever seen – and it needed to be."

"Thanks to you both," Diva said humbly, for her, as she left.

Sandra turned to Gunny again. "Can we really do this?" she asked him again.

"We can because we really have to. I promise you that I'll do my very best," said Gunny.

"She's here!" Barney came running in. "She's early but she's here."

"It's show time then," Gunny said and he reached over and squeezed Sandra's hand, trying to erase the worried look from her face. "Smiles on everyone and let's go."

The idea was that they would have "Santa" make an announcement from the stage in Happiness Hall. They had set it up so that Gunny would stand in a kind of "hole" behind the podium so he would look shorter. The two rushed to get him all set up before Beatrice and her cameraman made it to the hall as well.

Besides the preparations around getting Gunny "show" ready, they had also had to make sure the elves and the few Shanelle fairies at the Pole also agreed to say nothing. The fairies weren't really a worry since they almost always disappeared if there was a reporter around. They liked their quiet life. Shans loved publicity and adoration; Shanelles loved quiet and anonymity. Lastly, Sandra and Breezy had checked, and checked again, to make sure there were no posters still up showing Santa missing. That would have been the worst mistake of all.

"Okay," Sandra said to Zinga when they had Gunny Santa in place on stage. "Let her in."

Gunny purposefully fussed with something on the podium so he wouldn't have to have any kind of conversation with the reporter directly. They had invited several *North Pole Times* reporters there too so that it would be more of a formal "announcement."

Once Beatrice Carol and her cameraman were set up, Zinga stood up. "Today, Santa Claus and Sandra Claus dot dot dot will both be speaking to you about exciting developments at the two Poles. They will accept questions after their presentations but will not be available for individual interviews afterward due to pressing schedules. Thank you and now . . . Santa Claus."

There was no applause as the meeting was a press conference just for reporters.

"I thank you for coming," Gunny said in his best rehearsed Santa voice. He had spent hours practicing and in the end had got a little magic help from some Shanelle fairy dust that altered how his voice sounded to mimic others – but just for a limited time. "Today, I am excited to share that we believe we will deliver gifts to our highest number of children ever. This makes having two Santas, perhaps still not essential, but very helpful for making sure we reach each child on that all-important night.

"I also wanted to let the children of the world know of two new, very exciting, gifts the elves are working on that children might want to consider putting on their Christmas list. The first is an all new kit for explorers complete with camping gear, explorer maps, a telescope and binoculars." Gunny Santa showed each piece of the kit as he shared the news, and each piece was done in a fun style and color. "The other gift is a bit of a stretch for this old elf," Gunny chuckled to himself at that remark, "but the children of today increasingly love electronic gifts so the elves have put together something they are very excited about. Tack here will demonstrate."

Hearing his cue, Tack came on stage with a remote control in his hand. When he pushed the start button, he was joined on stage by a remote-controlled elf almost his own height!

"Now children everywhere can have their own house elf all year round," Tack said, grinning. "This is our favorite new toy we've made here at the North Pole in years. Elfie comes in both a girl or boy model. Each one can say several expressions, roll about the house, play Christmas carols, show Christmas movies on their built-in screen, and comes pre-loaded with seven classic Christmas stories.

"We will have both models available for your closer inspection, along with the new explorer kit, at the back of the room after the conclusion of this announcement."

"Ho Ho Ho, thank you, Tack, thank you! Such exciting new offers for this Christmas season already available this early in the year," said Santa. "I'd like Sandra Claus dot dot dot to introduce our third offering since this is one developed under her careful eye."

"Thank you, Santa," Sandra said, stepping up next to him at the podium but keeping him there so his true height continued to be hidden carefully. She was dressed in her festive Santa suit, too, knowing that the news coverage would run around the world. It was important that the children saw them both in their roles.

"I am so excited about this, it is my pleasure to share with you my first offering as South Pole Santa. As many children have heard from me, I am a supporter, like Santa, of how important it is for us all to be kind to each other all year long. I believe kindness can help make our world a very special place indeed. So, with Santa's support, I have developed an activity for children to participate in all year long.

"Now children will be able to send us a list of the many kind things they do each month, and for each of those kind acts that they have completed, their name will be put in this giant 'Acts of Kindness' bag that I hold here." She held up a sparkling gold bag. "As you can see, the bag is empty right now. My greatest wish is that it be too full to even lift by the end of the year." She smiled at the thought.

"Then, on Christmas Eve, we will draw out twelve names, one for each month of the year, and those twelve children will join Santa, the elves and myself for two fun-filled days here at the North Pole, the most magical place in all of the topside world!"

"Oh, my goodness," Beatrice Carol exclaimed. "That is indeed a most special new opportunity for children!"

"It is indeed, Beatrice," Sandra said, smiling. "I know you know well how magical it is here, as you have had the great and rare privilege of visiting with us all in person. And now that very rare opportunity will be something every child can have a chance at as well each year.

"Children, these acts need to be done with sincerity and kindness in your heart. Just as Santa knows who is naughty and who is nice, we will be able to tell if any of the items sent in have not really been done, or not done with kind intentions.

"With that, I will step back and see if there are any questions for either of us."

Immediately, Beatrice had her hand in the air. "Yes, Miss Carol," Gunny Santa said.

"Sandra, will you be touring the world again this year like you did last year? To promote your new kindness contest perhaps? I'd love to feature you in one of my news features," Beatrice Carol asked, catching Sandra off guard. She hadn't really considered that idea. She loved visiting with children, but with everything going on at the Pole, there was so little time.

"Ho Ho Ho!" Gunny Santa said. "I am keeping her so busy this year, Miss Carol, that that likely will not be possible."

"I'd be happy to come do your show, Beatrice," Sandra said at about the same time as Gunny Santa looked at her. She knew he was trying to help her but it was important she get close to children this year and Beatrice Carol was one easy way to do that.

"Excellent! I can't wait. I have several more questions, most of them for Sandra on this very special new kindness action, but I have some for you, too, Santa," she stated. The two Santas worked through each question asked until finally Santa announced he would only take one more.

"Santa, you seem to have lost a few pounds," Beatrice Carol said, catching Gunny off guard. "Has that been intentional?"

"Ho Ho Ho, you know me, Beatrice, not at all, not at all," Gunny Santa said, feeling relieved the press conference was nearly done. "That's just having two women now here at the Pole trying to watch out for what I eat but at heart, I am, after all, an elf and we elves love our sugar. The only skinny Santa you will find hanging around here is our wonderful South Pole Santa, Sandra Claus dot dot dot." He reached over and hugged her tight as the cameraman zoomed in on a last shot.

"Thank you for coming! Safe travels home!" He waved as he backed off stage straight back from the podium. "Ho Ho Ho!"

Sandra waved too, equally relieved and followed him back "Oh Oh Oh!"

CHAPTER 30

Life at the Pole

Location: North Pole Village

The coverage from the press conference came out better than they had dared to hope! Thanks to Laile's great idea, Gunny practicing his best Santa, the elves' talents at costumes and make-up, and just a little bit of fairy dust, the team had successfully worked together to calm any rumors of Santa missing. That gave the Sherlocks time to keep looking for the real Santa and finding him hopefully. Reesa had made it clear to Sandra when they met privately that she was less concerned about the world finding out than the rest of the council was about it.

"I understand Calivon's concern," Reesa had told Sandra, "but the worries of humans are generally no concerns of the Shans. Still, we will do our part in keeping this secret."

"And we will have the Sherlocks working around the clock in the search for him. He will be found," Sandra said with conviction. Reesa just smiled in a way that suggested she found Sandra's statement to be "quaint." She had another matter on her mind.

"I have recently met someone you know, I believe," Reesa said nonchalantly.

"Really?" said Sandra, truly puzzled. She could not imagine who they might have in common except . . .

"Yes, his name is Jason Annalise."

Sandra just knew that was who she was going to name.

"You met Jason," Sandra said carefully, not wanting to share any emotions with this she-devil fairy who was flat-out gorgeous and had met her boyfriend. Funny, somehow he had forgotten to mention her on their calls.

"He presented himself to the Supreme Esteemed Council of Fairies as our new would-be king. Personally, I believe he is a masquerader, perhaps an imposter even. What would you have me believe?"

The question surprised Sandra because it seemed genuinely sincere. Reesa sounded almost afraid of Jason and at the same time puzzled by him.

"I fear, Reesa, that I don't know enough of your fairy ways to know what is truth and what is not," she said carefully and truthfully. "I do know that I don't believe he has expected or sought out what has happened to him, so that makes me believe that what he speaks of and what has changed with him is true."

Reesa looked at her for a full uncomfortable moment, during which Sandra wanted to blurt out that Jason was hers and for Reesa to leave him alone, but she managed to stay quiet. She didn't want Reesa to know how close they were. Despite the long silence, she managed to hold her tongue.

"Well," Reesa finally said. "We shall see, we shall see. It is a perplexing issue for us in the realm of fairies at present but all unpleasantries eventually pass.

"It is good to see you again, Sandra of St. Annalise. I am pleased you have healed since our walk through the woods."

And with that she turned from Sandra and headed to join Calivon and Grosson for the Sherlock report. Sandra shuddered even now thinking about the whole Esteemed Council visit and the happiness she felt when they all left through the portal.

Since their visit, time was passing quickly, maybe even faster than usual with Santa gone because of all the extra things there were to do at North Pole Village, and the calendar suddenly showed the first day of May was just a week away.

May! Zinga and her volunteer helpers were working on a May Day celebration to bring in the new month and celebrate the longer days. Since the inspiring talk from Dear Lovey in February, the village had rallied and found strength in facing their concern over Santa together. There was no more news about where he and the reindeer were being kept than there had been in February really. Hope had stayed alive thanks to a photo of Santa arriving on the twenty-fourth of each month. In each photo, Santa was holding a copy of a current world newspaper – the *New York Times,* the *Beijing Press*, the *Toronto News*. And he was posing with a different reindeer – Dasher,

Dancer and Comet most recently. Most assuring of all, he was smiling. In fact, it looked like each reindeer was smiling too. That helped everyone at the North Pole smile as well. Plus, each photo included the strange little "ho ho hoo" message scribbled in Santa's writing in bright red ink.

Sandra had posted a blown-up copy of each of the photos around the village. Santa was missing but he was alive and apparently receiving good care, and that was a comfort to them all. Sandra had taken a lot of other steps since the elves awoke as well. Santa missing had meant she needed to step up and fill his shoes while he was gone and she was determined not to let him down. Today was the weekly check-in meeting with the Claus Council members and committee chairpersons for updates on all the different things happening currently at the Pole. She had come to look forward to the meetings. She had strict rules about being on time for the meetings and she was practically running to get across the village into Happiness Hall on time.

As usual, when elves were gathered with not enough to do, there was madness about, and Sandra walked in to a room where paper planes were flying in an apparent impromptu "build the best flyer" competition. "Oh yeah!" Gunny shouted just as Sandra walked in and a plane soared over her head. "That's a winner!" *Sometimes Gunny seemed more elf than the elves,* she thought holding back a smile.

"Okay, everyone," Sandra said. "I can see I'm the last to arrive, but I'm still on time," she took a quick glance at her watch, "and we have lots to go over. Let's start with report-outs.

Who wants to go first? Zinga, how 'bout you? How are you and your team doing on the Merry May Day festival?"

The always efficient Zinga gave her succinct report. "I am pleased to share that we are ready to go. The May Pole and decorations have been made and are being kept in the storage room ready to bring out and surprise everyone. We have flowers to hand out to everyone that we grew in the greenhouse. I can't wait to show them to everyone! The polka dot daisies that we've been trying so hard to grow came out in every color combo! And we have a special surprise that I'll let Diva tell you about." She turned to the best dressed elf at the Pole - their one and only "fashionista."

Diva stood, clapped her hands twice, and in walked two elves dressed in high fashion with the most fun British-royalty-style fascinator hats clipped on that anyone had ever seen. One looked like a candy cane and one looked like a gift with a bow.

"Why tell you about our plans when I can just show you our plans!" said the glamorous elf. "This, my dear dear friends, are two of the stunning models we will be featuring in our first-ever 'May Day Diva Fashion Show Presented to You by Diva!'"

Truth be told, the "stunning" elves looked a little more like cute normal elves playing dress-up stumbling around in very tall high heels. But you could see they loved their big fascinators with their equally giant-sized smiles, and the room applauded as the two circled the table and headed back out.

"Thank you, really, thank you," said Diva to the applause as the two dressed-up elves left the room. Sandra was smiling as big as the models. She knew the elves were going to love the fashion shows and the hats would be in fast demand at Diva's shop afterward. She expected she'd see them being worn everywhere for at least a couple of weeks after the May Day party. It was a sensational addition to the event.

"Ellen and I are ready for the event, too," said the little elf known to all as Buddy. He was the town troubadour and coordinator of music events at the Pole. Sandra had asked him to keep the music happy and try for more events like karaoke parties, which the elves all loved. So far she had not been able to get any of the elves to move past singing Christmas carols at karaoke nights, but the good thing was that they all knew them really well. Plus, where there is music, it is a joy to have dancing. That's where Ellen came in. She already loved to dance anywhere and everywhere she went, but Sandra had asked her to put extra effort in trying to get the elves to participate more often. Twice in the past week, Sandra had joined an impulsive Bunny Hop that had ended up with the longest line of elves you had ever seen with Ellen at the front. It cracked Sandra up that each time they were Bunny Hopping, it was to "Rockin' Around the Christmas Tree." Ellen could get them dancing to anything!

"Em, what are you and Barney whispering loudly about back there?" Sandra asked the little delgin she hadn't had the chance to see much of in the last month and realized she needed to make a little more time for her.

"Barney says that horses are safer to ride than delgins and I was being sure he knew they are not," the annoyed little elf said with a delgin dragon huff.

"That's not exactly what I was saying," Barney said in his own defense. "I said that for the May Day party, horses would probably be safer for the elves to ride rather than offering delgin rides because sometimes the elves get scared when Em dives low. Horses don't dive bomb elves so I think it's a better way to go."

Em was sitting way back in her seat with her arms crossed. "Em," Sandra said. "Barney has a point. I know how much the elves enjoy the rides you give them but for the May Day party I would really love for you to join with your cousins Goldy, Ruby, Violet, and Periwinkle and give us the best Northern Lights show ever as the finale for the day. Would that be okay?"

"Yes," said the little delgin, feeling a little happier about having an important role. "I'll coordinate us all for high shine."

"I've been busy helping Zinga with the decorations for the party," Violet said from the other end of the table. "And I'm hosting a finger painting party at the arts and crafts booth but I'll be sure to finish up there in time to join Emaralda and the others for the finale show."

"Excellent, Violet. By the way, who's putting up the May Pole?" Sandra asked.

"That would be me," Gunny said. "I'm the only one tall enough. Really, it's me with some help from a big crane and elves giving directions. I anticipate mayhem at the May Pole," he grinned.

Sandra smiled too. "And we have enough ribbons for the May Pole dance so that everyone can hang on to one? You know how elves get if they think they are being left out."

"It's going to be very crowded," Zinga said. "But we believe we can fit everyone in."

"Excellent!" Sandra said, pleased with how all the plans were coming together. "Noelly, are you going to be doing another round of cooking demonstrations?"

"I am. I decided to skip the healthy food this time; it always cuts down on my audience. Instead I'm going to offer do-it-yourself s'mores. There'll be a bonfire for roasting marshmallows and I'll show them different toppings they can add instead of just the same ole s'more."

"I will be coming by your booth for sure," said Gunny. "Maybe more than once!"

"Me too!" said just about every elf in the room at once.

Sandra laughed. "I think you have a hit on your hands, Noelly. Okay, great job, everyone! I'm very excited about how it's all coming together. Anything else on the May Day event to cover today before we move on?" Nobody spoke up. "Hearing nothing else I'm going to turn to Breezy. How are sign-ups for book club coming?"

"Kind of slow still, Sandra. We elves tend to love Christmas movies more than we like reading but I'm getting a few more to join."

"Good," said Sandra. "So, what's next month's book?"

"*'Twas the Night Before Christmas* by *Clement Moore*," Breezy said with a smile.

"But we read that last month," said Sandra, confused.

"The club voted that they would like to read it again," said Breezy. "It's our favorite. We just never get tired of it."

How I love elves, Sandra thought, smiling again at the ways they surprised her.

"So, who have I missed for updates? Oh yeah, a couple of our most important coordinators. Sporty, how is our new 'Stay Active, Have Fun' program going?"

A tall – for an elf – and fit individual jumped up from his seat and passed around a paper handout to everyone in the room. "Everyone up, c'mon, let's get standing up. That's right, you know this is the stretch-and-move part of our agenda. So step back and give me twenty jumping jacks on my mark."

The group did as directed with a lot of laughing at the same time. "Good to see you all enjoying yourself through exercise," said Sporty as they continued to jump. "Now, what you have at your places is the schedule for this week's activities, including the rec center, the track, and the pool. We've been having an increased level of participation in all of our classes but I've yet to see some of you at any of them. I'll be looking for you this week." He looked especially at Diva, who made a point at looking at her nails. Getting sweaty was not her thing. Sporty seemed to know that. "Diva, I think you would really enjoy our beginning ice-skating class. Some of the fashions worn at the rink are quite striking."

Oh, he's good, thought Sandra, as the group finally finished jumping and sat back in their seats. "Birdie, how are things going with the Secret Pals program?" Her watch dinged a chime just then, alerting her to her next meeting. "I'm sorry, everyone, no time for anything else today. Birdie, can you catch me up tonight over dinner?" Birdie nodded and Sandra moved on, gathering her things. So much to do! "Gunny, can you walk and talk with me? I'd like an update on the Sherlocks."

"Nothing to tell there still, but I got some other things on my mind."

CHAPTER 31

Other Things

Location: North Pole Village

Gunny was at least eight inches taller than Sandra, but she was a fast walker and sometimes he found himself scrambling to keep up instead of the other way around. It was the elf side in her, she liked to quip.

"... *squawk* ... where we going? ... *squawk* ..."

"Our next meeting is across town for a North Pole Village Chamber of Commerce meeting. I'm the guest speaker giving an update on things happening at the South Pole, of which there are few, so it should be a short talk."

" ... *squawk* ... snacks I hope! ... oboy! ... *squawk* ..."

"Sandra, that happens to be one of the main things I need to talk with you about - the South Pole and the barge. We're almost in the fifth month of the year and you haven't assigned anyone to get back to St. Annalise and get back to work on the South Pole Village barge. There is no way it can be ready for this Christmas season if we don't get people back to building it."

"Ironically, I've been thinking on that same thing quite a bit lately and I think we have to face the fact that we won't be operating out of the South Pole Village barge again this year," Sandra said. "It's disappointing, but all those plans were made before Santa got Santanapped. We know we can just squeak through this year with one Santa if we have to, and how I hope we don't have to face that challenge.

"Let's talk about how we can get a small team down there, though, working on the barge soon. And, Gunny, thank you so much for thinking on this too," Sandra said sincerely, feeling warm and fuzzy for a moment about her guardian who was always working to watch out for her, keep things flowing at the Pole, and keeping an eye on their best interests. When she was honest with herself, she couldn't begin to imagine how she would possibly get everything done if he wasn't there helping her. The whole thought gave her a pause on how much she had come to value their friendship. He was her guardian and second in command, but even more than that he was her friend. One of her best. It was certainly complicated but it definitely was a friendship. She reached over, wrapped her arms around him, and hugged him. He was surprised but it was the kind of surprise he liked and he stood there enjoying it.

"Uh, Jason," he said, pulling away as Sandra lost her smile. She and Jason were going through tough times and she really had no idea where they stood. She did know, though, that it wasn't the ideal time to bring him up.

"Gunny, now is not the time to be bringing up Jason. I don't know what's going on with us. We're on a break I guess, and," she paused, now turning and seeing what Gunny was looking at, and not believing her eyes. "Jason?"

"Yeah, that was what I was trying to tell you," Gunny said, stepping back from her.

"Guess I didn't get the memo that we're 'on a break,'" Jason said. "I'd yell 'surprise' but it seems I'm the one who is the most surprised."

"Jason!" Sandra exclaimed, now coming around to the wonderful, completely huge, surprise of having her very good-looking boyfriend at the Pole. "You're here! Gunny, I'll see you later. Oh wait! Could you do my Chamber talk please?"

"Yeah, yeah, catch you later," Gunny said.

"See you, cowboy," Jason called after him, reaching out for Sandra as she ran toward him. He held a big bouquet of flowers in one hand.

"You too, fairy king," Gunny called back. "Squawk, that guy gets on my nerves." Squawk was flying along next to him instead of hanging back with Sandra.

". . . *squawk* . . . fairies . . . blech . . . *squawk*"

"Exactly," said Gunny, heading to the barn to see how Jason had got there without any of them knowing ahead of time.

No one was allowed to visit the North Pole right now without his approval or the Sherlocks' approval. That was his, and the Sherlocks' orders, and that meant no one. Most especially that meant island fairy boys whom he didn't trust at all.

CHAPTER 32

A Crowded Pole

Location: North Pole Village

"Jason, I can't believe you're here! You're really here!" Sandra exclaimed over and over as she jumped around him excitedly and he grinned from ear to ear. He was happy too. *Why the heck did it take me so long to do this?* he wondered, as he tried to take his eyes off his stunning girlfriend and look around at the Pole. The North Pole! He was at the North Pole. To him, it didn't seem possible that a guy from a dinghy could have this girlfriend and this trip. He said as much to Sandra as they walked along.

"Anything is possible, Jason, anything," Sandra said in response. "You and I, of all people, should know that. I grew up on a tugboat and now I'm South Pole Santa. You grew up on magical St. Annalise and now you're king of the fairies."

"Please for just a few minutes, don't remind me," Jason said. "For just a little bit, I'd like you not to be Santa and me not to be a fairy king and both of us just to be us – Sandra and Jason." With that he reached out and grabbed her. "And for you to hold still and let me tell you how much I have missed you." He kissed her right there in one of the corridors of Happiness Hall and the two heard giggling.

"Jason Annalise, I'd like you to meet some of the elves of the North Pole," Sandra said as she pulled away and before she even saw who was tittering at them. She recognized elf tittering and anything mushy tended to make them laugh. Sure enough, there behind her, peeking out from behind a cracked door were a whole bunch of elves who came tumbling out all at once in a big sprawl in front of them. Both Sandra and Jason now were the ones laughing, as the elves looked up sheepish at them.

"We saw you kissing," said an elf named Kadoodle.

"He's cute," added Goldie, who was in the pile. Jason smiled at her and she flashed her pretty gold color.

"Nice," he said sincerely.

"Thank you," Goldie blushed, flashing again.

"Now, off with all of you," Sandra said. "Yes, this is my boyfriend who is visiting. Go on and tell the others that they must be on their very best behavior for our guest." They all scrambled to their feet. They had big news and they all wanted to be the first to tell!

"Okay," she said as the group of elves ran around the hall corner. "I am fairly certain we are about to be mobbed by a whole bunch of curious elves, and it will be impossible to talk. So let's head for my office where Breezy will never let anyone get by her until we're ready."

"Sandra!"

"Gunny," she said with as flat a voice as she could muster as she heard him before actually seeing him. When she did look from Jason down the hall to Gunny, she went pale. Gunny was striding quickly toward them – with Crow and Ghost next to him! Ghost's eyes seemed to be blazing at her. Or so she felt. That's ridiculous, she thought, trying to clear the idea but it nagged at her. Jason tensed up next to her and she prepared for what was surely to come. Oboy.

"Kadoodle said you two were back here," Gunny said with a big smile that seemed a little over-friendly.

"Sandra, it's so good to see you," Crow said with clear sincerity, giving her a big hug. "And you must be the Jason she talks so much about," he added, reaching out to shake Jason's hand while Sandra looked at him with appreciation. "I'm Gunny's brother, Crow." Gunny was right; Crow always acted older than he was.

It would have been great if the same could have been said about Ghost, but Ghost seemed to chronically act younger than he was. He stood there glaring at Sandra saying nothing to Jason until it got awkward and Crow once again stepped up.

"And this abominable snowman, who has been cranky the entire trip from Texas, is my twin brother, Ghost," Crow said. Ghost just nodded at Jason without shaking his hand or anything. Jason chose to follow his lead, taking an instant dislike to him for reasons he didn't even completely understand but had a theory he thought he would test. With that thought in mind, he pulled his girlfriend closer and saw Ghost's eyes flare. Yep he was right, he thought. He couldn't really blame the guy but he would expect him to back off.

Sandra knew what was going on. She loved having Jason there – although presently things were a bit awkward – but she wouldn't be used by him or anyone else ever for even something as nonsensical as this.

"So, Gunny, you didn't tell me your brothers were coming up to the Pole," Sandra said politely, moving out of Jason's grasp. Normally, at almost any other time, having Crow and Ghost there would be a surprise she would have welcomed, but right now, the little village called the North Pole was starting to feel really crowded.

"Well, like Jason, they didn't exactly share that plan with me," Gunny said. "But I did tell them they could come anytime so it's good to have them here."

"Like Jason," Sandra added, but Gunny said nothing and the awkward moment hung on with Ghost and Jason in a stare-down.

"Jason!" The tense group turned to see who belonged to the voice this time and saw a smiling Birdie and Spence racing down the hall with Squawk. *Thank goodness for best friends*, Sandra thought as Jason caught Birdie up in a big hug and even hugged on Spence.

"Jason," Spence said. "I thought we'd never get you up here. This is great!"

"Thanks, Spence. So good to see you. And you too, Birdie," Jason said. "Since I couldn't get her to St. Annalise, I had to come see my girlfriend up here."

A little strong on the "my girlfriend," Sandra thought. She caught Gunny looking amused.

The little group made introductions all around. Crow seemed particularly happy to see Birdie again. They had met briefly last year during the world tour to stop The Protest and Sandra could see that neither of them had forgotten. That idea made her happy. In fact, with the addition of Birdie and Spence, the group now seemed to gel quickly. They were all friends of one sort or another, and topping that, they were the only seven humans – or mostly human – at the Pole.

"Hey, how 'bout we all go get an early dinner at the Eat, Drink & Be Merry diner?" Gunny said jovially.

Everyone in the group heartily agreed with the fun idea. Everyone but Sandra and Jason. They would have been happy to skip dinner for some time alone but that would have to wait for later.

Sometimes though, later can be so elusive.

## CHAPTER 33

Dinner Conversation

Location: North Pole Village

"You CAN'T tell him. He's a FAIRY!" Gunny was practically shouting it at her but in a whispering sort of way so the others wouldn't hear. He had pulled her back on the way to the diner to have a quick chat.

"Of course I understand that, Gunny, but I've told you before, that doesn't matter to us," Sandra said calmly in response. "I'm not keeping secrets from Jason. He can know about Santa missing. You're about to tell your brothers, aren't you? Why is that any different?"

"Because he's a FAIRY! It is totally different. He's one and they aren't Fairies can't be trusted. He could tell others and then the word could get out."

"We trust fairies every day around here," Sandra said calmly in return, as one, coincidentally, buzzed by just then. "The Pole has always had fairies in residence. They haven't told anyone."

"That's not the same. You know that all the Shan fairies left the Pole as soon as they heard the rumor of a new king. Who even knows why but they're not to be trusted," Gunny continued. "Not to mention, the Sherlocks think there's a real good chance it's the fairies who have taken Santa."

"That may or may not be true, Gunny, but what I know *for sure*, is that Jason didn't take him," she said adamantly. "And besides, even if it did get out, and it wouldn't be from Jason, maybe it's time it did." With that, she ran to catch up with the rest, leaving Gunny feeling frustrated as he lagged behind.

The group had fun laughing and eating through dinner, and Sandra waited until everyone was done with their desserts before she shared the news about Santa missing. She hated to bring them all down but it had to be done.

Crow and Jason both seemed a little angry about not knowing earlier. "I knew something important was going on at the ranch when you all were there," Crow said to Gunny. To both Sandra and Gunny, he added, "you could have trusted me and Ghost."

Ghost hadn't said much at all through the whole dinner. He had shrugged his shoulders at the Santa news. "He'll show up," he said to the news. "No one would hurt Santa." He waved down the waitress to order another dessert.

Jason was more like Crow – a little indignant about not being trusted. "You knew on Christmas?" he asked Sandra.

"I couldn't tell," she nodded miserably.

"I guess I get it but you could have trusted me."

"I one hundred percent believe that," Sandra said, giving a little look over at Gunny, who refused to look her way.

"You're a fairy." This didn't come from Gunny this time. It was Ghost who said it.

"Yeah, it seems pretty sure that I am," Jason replied, getting more comfortable all the time with the truth of who he was. "Why does that matter?"

"Not sure if it does or it doesn't. Just seems weird." Ghost shrugged in his way.

"Ghost!" both Sandra and Birdie burst out surprised by his outright rudeness.

"No, it's all right," Jason said in response. "Seems weird to me too. Honestly, I'm just learning to trust them too."

Now it was Gunny who was shrugging. He actually respected that answer.

"How about a cocoa toast?" he asked, raising his mug. "To finding our dear Santa Claus soon and holding the ones who took him responsible, whoever they are."

Everyone raised their glass but Ghost. Gunny looked over and raised an eyebrow at his little brother. He got that he didn't like Jason but it was time for him to play nice with the rest.

"What?" Ghost asked to his brother's look. He held up his glass, upside down. "What can I say? I drank all mine."

"To Santa!" said the rest, ignoring Ghost and his moodiness. "Let's catch the villains."

CHAPTER 34

Finally Some Time Alone

Location: North Pole Village

With all there had been to do to run the Pole and get ready for the big upcoming Merry May Day festival, there had been only stolen moments here and there for Sandra and Jason to spend alone together. He had hung out with her going to her meetings and presentations and was impressed by how busy she was and how good she just naturally was at what she did. It didn't surprise him at all. He had always known she could do whatever she wanted. That had been part of the problem when they were younger because he never felt like he was worth having her as a girlfriend. Thank goodness she had convinced him different. He had grown a lot since they started dating.

One annoying, unexpected reason for why they could get almost no time alone had not just been that the elves always seemed to be nearby. Or that their friends seemed to be around most the time. It was the fairies! Jason hadn't expected so many fairies to be at the Pole, and they followed him everywhere. Everywhere! The Pole was home to many Shanelles. That made sense when he thought about Wistle telling him that Shanelles tended to stay out of the limelight and away from any conflict. The North Pole was a great place to live for those reasons for sure. They were a nice and gentle kind of fairy in general, but that also made it harder for Jason to be firm with them. They always seemed so hurt when they were rebuffed.

But they buzzed around him everywhere! They were pretty shades of pastel – pink, silver, light blues, and light greens. He had learned the Shans glowed in colors that could be described as "fiery." Their colors were more reddish, shades of orange, and deep golds. In contrast, his orb was made up of shades of all colors, which was one of the ways the fairies knew for sure he was the king and that he was neither just Shanelle or just Shan, but both. While the Shans found that troubling, the Shanelles seemed to accept it as something not just possible but positive. Besides all of that, they were beside themselves with the chance to spend time with the new king. It was almost as if they couldn't resist the pull to be around him. Fairies, whether Shan or Shanelle, were tribe beings and preferred to spend time with other fairies rather than be alone.

They were so thick around Jason at times, however, that it was all he could do not to swat at them. They asked him frequently to orb and come visit with them at their United

Fairy Organization (UFO) headquarters building where fairies could only be present in their orb state. Jason deferred. While he was learning to accept what he was, the state of orbing was not yet one of his favorite things about being a fairy. It was too different right now from how he viewed himself. He expected that would change, but for now, it was one step at a time.

Sandra loved having him around despite all the "company" that came with him. She thought it was amusing and could hardly complain since the elves followed her in much the same kind of fashion. There were rarely so many, but most the time, she had several elves tagging along wherever she was, simply because they loved to be with her and loved her attention. She loved them in return.

It had taken Jason a while to get around to sharing one of the main reasons he had come, but one evening when they found themselves alone at the cocoa stand, he spoke up.

"I wanted to see you, Sandra. That was my main reason for coming, but there were some other reasons too," he said, looking around at the quiet square. Elves liked to turn in early most nights and it was late for them. He was thankful for that. Even the fairies, this evening, seemed to have turned in.

Sandra looked at him curiously. "I'm not just a fairy," Jason said. "In fact, I'm not just the king even."

Now she was really curious. "It seems this 'divine mark', as it is called in the fairy world, is unique in its design as well as my orb color and who knows what else to come. I'm a Shanelle fairy, which the Shanelles find wonderful but the Shan's can barely tolerate. The Shan line has ruled for a very long time."

Sandra was quiet just listening.

"It turns out that I've learned from Wistle, of all people, that there's even more to it than that," he continued. "I'm also Shan. This mark indicates a combined house. Something that has been told in tales for years but apparently most have never believed it could be true because of the big division between the two fairy lines."

"That is a lot to take in," Sandra said. "I think I can relate to it more than most people can. I've been wanting to share something big about me with you as well." She felt this was the right time to finally get to share her own heritage with him. "You know I'm elfin," she said, reaching out to him across the table and unconsciously tracing the outline of the mark on his arm. "But I'm more than that. Like you, it seems I'm roy-"

"Owwwwwwww!" he hollered out. "Holy knife and daggers!" He was waving his arm in the air as if to cool it off. Suddenly, fairy orbs were coming from everywhere, responding to his cries of pain.

He quickly rolled his coat sleeve down again. Despite the excruciating pain, he didn't want to involve any of the fairies in whatever this new dilemma was.

"We're fine here," he said as reassuringly as he could. "Just you know, hot cocoa and me being loud with my girlfriend. Now, please, off with you all. Tonight, we are enjoying our time alone."

None of them were convinced though. They could see the pain in his eyes and in Sandra's.

"Your highness," one started to express the concern of all.

"Please, not another word tonight," Jason said as calmly as he could. "I appreciate the concern, I really do, but sometimes two people need to be just two people. I'm safe here. You all know that. Neither Sandra, or anyone else here," he had the briefest thought of Ghost before he finished, "would ever hurt me. Now, to bed with you all. Please consider that an order from your king."

Though reluctant, they would never defy such a command and they flew off.

As soon as they did, Sandra reached for him but Jason was reluctant to put his arm out for her. She insisted and he finally pushed his sleeve up to show her – to show them both – that where she had traced the divine mark on his arm was red and oozing like a severe burn.

"Jason! We have to get this looked at!" Sandra cried out. "We have to get you to the North Pole medical unit."

And then she asked what neither of them wanted to voice. "Did I do this?"

She reached out to him for some kind of assurance that she did not and that he understood she would never hurt him. He wanted to give that to her and would have, if her hand hadn't brushed the divine mark again and the pain that blazed up his arm was so intense it was all he could do not to cry out again, even louder, and risk waking up the whole Pole.

He had not cried out or answered her question but the pain on his face and the swell of his arm told them both more than they wanted to know.

CHAPTER 35

A Not So Merry Last Day in April

Location: North Pole Village

The rest of the week leading up to the ironically titled Merry May Day event was fairly somber for Jason and Sandra. Jason had gone into the clinic the evening his arm was mysteriously injured, and they had treated it immediately as a severe burn as the two of them had suspected. Jason asked the medical team to not speak of the injury with anyone and it being still cool in April at the village, he was able to keep the incident between them by wearing long sleeves.

Spencer and Birdie, though, both knew. Jason was bunking with Spence so he likely would have found out just by sharing a room, but Jason had been more deliberate about telling him than that. He had held out his bandaged arm to Spence and asked him to touch the mark.

"I know this is a very funky request, but I sure could use the help if you wouldn't mind going along with me here," Jason had said, telling him nothing else.

Spence gave him a weird look but as a guy interested in all kinds of experiments, in his book, this request didn't seem all that strange. He reached out to the uncovered part and grabbed it solidly with his hand as Jason braced for the pain. And he got . . . nothing. Just a normal squeeze on the arm.

"So you want to share why you needed me to do that and who did that number on your arm?" he asked. "It's cool if you can't. I mean I know there's a lot going on with you, but if you want to talk, I'm happy to listen."

Jason caught him up on it all and then they went next door to the girls' room, where Sandra had just been telling Birdie all about it. Jason asked Birdie to do the same thing as he'd asked Spence with the same outcome: no pain.

Except the pain that winced through Sandra's eyes. Her boyfriend was allergic to her. Not just allergic in the sense of some watery eyes that you could take allergy pills for. More in the sense of a so-allergic-that-you'd-like-to-saw-off-your-arm-rather-than-let-her-touch-it-again kind of way.

"I know why this is happening, Jason. I don't want to be-lieve it, but I know it's what is," Sandra said to him miserably.

"It's what I was trying to tell you last night. Birdie and Spence already know and clearly it is past time for you to know." She took a deep breath and blurted out the rest. "I'm not just elfin. Like you, I'm from a royal bloodline. They're, we're, called the Leezles. They're more than royal elfins. They are the ruling party of all of the magical realm – even over fairies. I didn't tell you before because it seemed so unlikely it could be me and I didn't want you to treat me any different. Very few people know this about me because there are some, actually many it seems, who would like to hurt me because of it. My mother protected me with my locket," she saw a flash of understanding in his eyes remembering what happened when he had taken it off and now realizing the reason, "which is why I must wear it at all times. It's the night you removed it that I found out about who I truly was and finally believed it."

"Okay," said Jason slowly, taking it all in. "For some reason, maybe because I have always known you were special, Sandra, this doesn't really surprise me. Other than again, I wish you trusted me more. Still, I don't understand what that has to do with this." He held up his injured arm.

"It's something Gunny told me, and as much as I hate it when he's right, this time it seems he is right," Sandra said. "He said that elfins and fairies – especially the Shans – do not get along. That the feud of sorts goes back for centuries and it was toxic between the royals. Now we know what 'toxic' looks like."

None of them spoke. What was there to say on this not so very merry day before May?

CHAPTER 36

Pole Pong!

Location: North Pole Village

The last meeting of the day had kept him late so Gunny found himself practically running to the big Santadome. It was on the other side of North Pole Central Park and he was determined not to be late. He had been looking forward to this evening since the minute Jason had suggested they compete in a game of Pole Pong.

As far as Gunny was concerned, ole Fairy King might be a surfing champion, he might be Sandra's chosen one, and he might think he was an all-around natural at pretty much any sport, but Pole Pong wasn't just any sport. It took time to get good at it. And, through a whole bunch of playing, Gunny had gotten good at it. This night was a chance for Gunny to shine and he didn't want to miss a minute of it.

Sandra, individually, had tried to talk both of them out of this game of "nonsense" as she described it. She knew it was some kind of strange competition they both felt with each other. She particularly tried to stress the craziness of what he was doing to Jason from just about the minute he had suggested the challenge to Gunny.

"You don't mean playing against him while you are here this trip, right?" she had said, thinking she hadn't understood what she thought she had heard. Jason had never even seen Pole Pong played. He had only heard about it from her. Granted, he had been completely interested in it as he was most sports, but it was ridiculous for him to think he could take on an accomplished Paddler like Gunny. But he refused to back down. He'd made the commitment and he was going to see it through. Since that time, he had managed to get a couple of lessons on it and a couple of games in with Crow, but even he knew he could have used more practice.

Pole Pong was unique to the North Pole and was played on a floor-to-arena high ceiling on what was called a board that looked a lot like a pinball game. The board was set at a steep angle, like a ski slope with big posts positioned down the playing area. Each post had a number on it like 20, 10, 5 and -10.

At the top of the board, elves in oversized inner tubes, would line up in four slots – two for each side. They were called the "pongers." At the bottom of the board was one more team player for each side called "the paddler" who controlled three large paddles each, all located at the along the bottom of the board. Teams could have two paddlers per team and up to eight pongers, all who traded off time playing.

The paddles could move about 180 degrees and there was three feet across between each paddle – just enough for an inner tube to slide through. When the buzzer sounded, the inner tubes would drop down from the top and the pongers would pong around the board hitting the posts to score – or lose – points. The game was truly madcap because the posts also acted as springs and sent the inner tubes careening in all directions and against each other as well. Plus, there were two round dots on the board that were lit up and kept changing color. If a ponger ran over them when the color was red, the inner tube would deflate and the player would slide down the board to the bottom.

Players lost points by hitting any minus post or by using his hands outside of the inner tube. They made their way around the board by using the middle wheel inside the tube space that let them steer and by flinging their weight from side to side. As a player would drop to the bottom, the paddler could work the paddles to fling him back high on to the board to score more points and head again to the bottom. Eventually, as the pongers would miss the posts and the paddles and slip through one of the gaps, a loud bell would ring and the referee would shout "pong!" Then the next ponger, ready to go at the top, would start his way down to "drop and pong" until one team hit 300 points. The final score would flash on the reader board and the round would go to that team. The team with the three out of five rounds won the match.

The little elves were lightweight and would fling around the pong board, trying to get as many points as possible before they hit the bottom, and then scream with gusto as the paddlers would send them flying back up for more. It was fast and wild fun, and the elves loved it!

On this night, Ghost was helping out Gunny on his team and Crow had agreed to be second for Jason on his team. Sandra and Birdie and much of the Pole had come out to see the game. Pole Pong was the national sport at the Pole. Elves talked about the games for days after a big tournament. The elves that played got a lot of attention too since it took quite a bit of bravery to be a "ponger" and typically elves were not known for courage. The elves that played set trepidation aside because the sport was so much fun.

Not surprisingly, Gunny and Ghost came out strong and Jason and Crow didn't have much of a chance. The first and second rounds went by at lightning speed with a clearly frustrated Jason trying too hard. Crow seemed more laid back about it all, smiling and watching Birdie more than he was watching the Pole Pong board. Jason, on the other hand, hadn't looked over at Sandra once. For him, it was all about the game. Sandra, being competitive herself, understood.

The third round, Jason seemed to better understand that Pole Pong was not so much a game of strength but more a game of timing. *When* you pulled back the paddle was more important for most moves than how strongly you pulled it back. Once he figured that out, his team came screaming back and outscored Gunny's team just about as fast as Gunny's team had been doing to Jason's the first two rounds.

The goalie announced the win and Jason and Crow jumped around with hands in the air cheering. Jason finally took a minute to look around and smile at Sandra before he turned back to the task at hand and win another. There were two more wins to be had if he was to take the tournament, and he was determined. The tides had turned and Gunny and Ghost were going down.

Gunny felt equally strong about it. This was his turf and his sport and it was going to be his win. He had Ghost sit it out and he ran the game on his own, slinging the elves all around the big Pole Pong board and dazzling the audience with his finesse. Elves loved a skilled paddler and Gunny was one of the best. Before Jason could say "tropical island sunset," the game had been won and the winning team announced.

Crow headed to the stands to talk with Birdie while the rest of the players headed to the podium for the official recognition of the winners. Gunny and Ghost were grinning smugly, while Jason stood on the podium with a sour expression, clearly unhappy about the score and their gloating. Until, that is, Sandra went skipping up to the stage and kissed her sweaty boyfriend on the cheek. Showing a bit of his Shan fairy side, Jason cast a challenging look at Gunny and kissed Sandra back full on the lips while the crowd cheered. Gunny had won the game but Jason had the girl. By the looks on their faces, that realization seemed to dawn on both Gunny and Ghost at the same time as they stared over at Jason.

Despite what the scoreboard read, everyone in the arena knew the real score for the evening: Score one for Gunny and one for Jason.

CHAPTER 37

A Merry Merry Morning in May

Location: North Pole Village

The elves woke up beyond excited. Joy was in the air on this first day of May at the Pole. Normally, it always was, but with Santa missing, the days were bright but not always as merry as usual. On this day, however, all sadness had been set aside. It was Merry May Day, a brand-new festival, and everyone was excited!

In the square, Zinga, true to her word, had worked tirelessly the night before with Gunny, Ghost, Crow, Spence and even Jason to stand up the giant May Pole and set up the booths for the fair vendors. Birdie, Breezy, and Sandra had helped with all the decorating touches under Zinga and Violet's careful direction, setting out beautiful pots of spectacular flowers Zinga had lovingly grown in the Pole's greenhouses. By just after two a.m., they had pronounced it finished and headed to bed to get a little bit of sleep before the big morning arrived.

Elves generally rise early — none of them ever want to miss a thing — but on this day they were up earlier than ever. Zinga had suspected as much and had cinnamon rolls waiting at three different fair booths with one of those booths staffed by Cappie and Thomas!

"Surprise!" the two called out when they saw the look on Sandra's face as she had followed her nose to their booth.

"I knew it was your cinnamon rolls, Cappie! I knew it! I would know that combination of special ingredients anywhere!" Sandra threw herself in her guardian's arms and squeezed her hard. She was so happy to see her. Until that moment, she hadn't even let herself realize how very much she had been missing her.

"And Thomas, I'm so glad you're here, too," Sandra said.

"I am too," said Cappie, shyly reaching over and giving him a little squeeze as he grinned.

"Cappie!" Sandra said, looking at her quizzically to be sure she understood what that squeeze had meant as the two of them grinned. Sandra grinned really big too. Above everything else in all the world, besides seeing her parents again, she wanted her guardian, whom she loved through and through, to be happy.

" . . . *squawk* . . . cinnamon rolls! . . . *squawk* . . . hooray!"

"Squawk! I'm so pleased to see you too and, of course, I have a cinnamon roll set aside for you," said Cappie, nudging on the big guy as he landed on her arm.

" . . . so happy . . . *squawk* . . ."

"Oh, my goodness," said Sandra, still grinning over Thomas and Cappie's "news" that they were now officially dating. "Look at how many elves are waiting for your treats, Cappie! You better get serving. Nothing is more dangerous than a long line of elves wanting their sweets!

"Besides, I have so much to do. I love you and I'll see you tonight!" She waved to them as she skipped away. Yes, skipped, she thought, because skipping was happy walking.

It was still early but the hubbub of the event was all around. The cocoa booths were bustling, other elves were setting up their booths for selling and showing that day. Still others were reporting to duty to Diva for the first round of fashion shows, and the always ambitious and talented music duo of Buddy and Ellen already had a Bunny Hop going through the crowd.

Sandra stood back for a moment all on her own and realized the deep level of happiness she felt. Everyone she loved and really cared the most about was here except for Christina, who she counted as part of her family. And her parents, of course, but they were always in her heart. There was nothing but sounds of laughter and fun coming from every direction, and despite the gnaw of Santa being gone, she even felt that he too was here in spirit, cheering them on to have fun on this day.

"You've done a good thing here today, Sandra," Gunny said, coming up to stand beside her with a big cup of cocoa for both of them. "Got you your favorite – peppermint mocha with extra whip."

She smiled and took a big swipe of the whipped cream with her finger, which made them both smile.

"I feel happy this morning, Gunny," she said with a touch of melancholy. "I think until right now, I didn't realize that I haven't been as happy as I used to be since Santa went missing. I've been so busy worrying about keeping the elves feeling happy and safe I haven't realized how changed I've been. Too serious and not as much fun I fear."

"Understandably, Sandra. Don't ever apologize for that," Gunny said, being surprisingly serious himself. "If I were you, I'd be so proud of myself for the job I was doing being two Santas and keeping it all together while he's gone and everyone is so worried. I don't think you fully realize how big that is and how proud all of the rest of your team are of you."

She grinned at him. "All of them?" she teased. "Even your brother?" She didn't have to name which one for him to know who she was talking about.

"Ghost is just his own worst enemy," Gunny said. "You surely have noticed he's got a crush on you. I'm pretty sure that's part of what is making him so sullen – all grumped out that you've got a boyfriend. Honestly, he's usually much more happy-go-lucky."

Sandra said nothing but she did suspect it and, if she was honest, she had conflicted feelings about Ghost as well. He had a strange kind of magnetism for her that she found herself having to fight. He wasn't like anyone else she knew. He could be super charming and funny. Then, out of the blue, and more often, he seemed more of a loner. A little bit secretive and miserable at the same time. As she thought about it, she realized in a lot of ways, he was a cowboy version of Jason.

"Well that explains a lot," she said quietly to herself, realizing that it made sense that if she was pulled toward all those traits in Jason, she would likely find Ghost interesting as well. Gunny heard her statement and responded, not knowing her inner thinking.

"It really does explain a lot when you also remember he started out totally not liking you simply because you beat me out for the South Pole Santa gig. When you look at it that way, he's come a long way. He's actually nice to you some days." He grinned his cowboy grin at her, which she couldn't resist returning. This day was a day for smiling.

She changed the subject. "Did you see Cappie and Thomas are here?" He nodded. "And that they are now officially 'a couple?'" She made air marks around "a couple" as Gunny's eyes widened with surprise.

"No kidding?" he said. "Well I'll be a tumbling tumbleweed, I did not see that coming."

"Well I did," Sandra said. "And I am beyond happy about it. Okay, so what needs to be done around here, Mr. Holiday, my very trusty second-in-command? Point me in a direction of where I'm needed."

"Sandra, on this beautiful day in May, you get a day off. Go on and grab your guy and have a fun day at the festival."

Sandra looked at him, thought about objecting, and then decided to do exactly what he said. She grinned and ran off, then doubled back, hugged him big, and ran off again to go find Jason, Birdie, and Spence for a day filled with fun.

CHAPTER 38

A Very Merry Day in May

Location: North Pole Village

Sandra dodged elves all along her path to the hotel to collect her friends, but wasn't able to dodge Ghost. Being wherever she was going was like his super power, she thought to herself as he approached, wearing of all things, an elf hat and a smile. On this merry day, it seemed even Ghost had decided to be happy.

"You know," she said as he got closer, "you look really good wearing that."

"Well, now that is kind of you to say on this happy day, Miss Clausmonetsiamlydelaterra dot dot dot," he said, sweeping off the hat and putting it back on. "Maybe I should forget about my cowboy hat and put this one on more often."

"Well I am all for that," Sandra said, taking delight in hearing her full last name spoken, which didn't happen all that often, and having some fun with him. "But I wasn't talking about the hat. I'm talking about that big smile you actually are wearing today. You really look good with it. Truly, you should wear it more often."

She actually thought she saw him blush. "Yeah, about how I've been lately," he said to her, catching her off guard with his sincerity. "I'm not usually the way I've been. I think, I hope, I'm better than I've been. I just sometimes act and then think or think something dumb and then act or maybe its--"

Sandra laughed at the spin he had put himself in. "You know what?" she said. "Whatever it is, it's okay. I've got to run," she said, getting ready to head out.

"Sandra," Ghost held her back. "I, well, you should know--"

" . . . *squawk*! . . . there you are . . . *squawk*! . . ."

"Hey, here you are," said Spence, catching up to Squawk and waving at Birdie and Jason to join them.

"Hey, Squawk, hey, Spence," Ghost tipped his elf hat at them. "Have a great day at the festival. I'll catch you later, Sandra." And in the way that he did, he somehow just disappeared into the crowd.

You should know . . . know what? she thought as he left and Birdie and Jason joined them. The famous - very annoying - words of the Holiday boys!

"What should we do first?" Birdie asked. Jason had on a nice long-sleeved shirt so Sandra dared to grab her guy by the arm.

"Well, since it's just about to pass by us here, let's start with the bunny hop. Hop hop hop!"

They hopped their way all around the village before finally bumping off in the center of the festival where they joined every villager at the Pole in enjoying a day off for nothing but pure fun.

The three fashion shows put on by Diva were huge hits, despite things going wrong that nearly made Diva faint, but made all the elves love the shows even more. The models simply could not walk well in their high heels and teetered and tottered down the runaway laughing all the way. Diva had asked them all to be "somber like a supermodel" so she kept making somber faces at them as they walked, which made them giggle even more. Elves could barely be serious for occasions that called for somber, let alone on a day filled with merry. Sandra loved that one of the three shows featured "tropical wear for working at the Equator Pole." How her heart soared!

In fact, all around the event, there were elves wearing the festive tropical shirts they had embraced wearing while working on the South Pole barge at St. Annalise. None of them had wanted to go to St. Annalise at first, but once they got there, they had adapted well. They had particularly embraced the fun clothes, glittery sunglasses, and their favorite part of all, the sno-cones! There were booths set up at the festival selling tropical shirts and sno-cones. And even a booth recruiting elves to work with Sandra on the South Pole Village barge.

"How are sign-ups coming, Naters?" Spencer asked his friend, the chief IT consultant to the South Pole. The two of them had become good friends and were working together now on developing a teleporter for getting things and people from pole to pole fast. Sandra liked the idea, but had no plans to be one of the first to try it out!

"Well, kind of slow, actually," Naters said. "I think the topic is just a little too serious for this crowd. I plan to close early."

"Just close now, Naters," Sandra said to the hard-working elf. "We'll get sign-ups later."

"Okay," said Naters, actually flashing a rare smile as he folded up his sign-up sheet and took off.

"That's actually the best conversation I think we've ever had," quipped Sandra teasingly about Naters as he zipped off.

The foursome grabbed sno-cones as they strolled (Sandra shared hers with Squawk) and had all sorts of fun trying on fascinators and old English court hats at Diva's Hat-a-dashery. She was selling the creations featured in her shows. They also sat in on some rounds of karaoke where even Spence got up and sang a number with Sandra and Birdie. They clapped for Em every time she flew low over them, with elves having a blast on board the *Mistletoe 2*, but hanging on for dear life. They were impressed with the very long line at Dear Lovey's booth where any elf could get a three-minute meeting with Dear Lovey to discuss their problem and receive an answer. Three minutes might sound very short for problem-solving but not when you considered that most elf problems were along the lines of:

Q: "Dear Lovey, Is it okay if I like blue more than red or green?"

A: Of course! All colors are beautiful.

Q: "Dear Lovey, Can you ever have too many shoes?"

(Lovey would never say so but she was pretty sure this one came from Diva.)

A: Well, in my case, yes, you can. (The elves all loved her ironic sense of humor. She never seemed to let not having any feet or legs bother her.)

Q: Dear Lovey, Help! I've been thinking about travelling but I like it here at home, what should I do?

A: Go! Home, and all of us, will be here when you get back from a grand adventure. Write and tell me how it went!

At the next booth, they found Noelly dealing with an equally long line of elves waiting to get in to the "Build Your Own S'mores" bar. They also found the Holiday boys at the front of the line!

"You gotta try these," Crow said, smiling at Birdie with chocolate all over his face and fingers. "I'm serious. C'mon, Birdie, Noelly won't care if I share mine, will you, Noelly?"

Birdie checked with the elf, who nodded her okay, and then she slipped in next to Crow for a big bite of his s'more. "I'll catch up with you guys," she said to Sandra and Jason and Spence.

"Great," Spence said. "Now I'm third man. Not cool. I'm going to double back and visit with Cappie and Thomas if you don't mind." And off he went, leaving just Jason and Sandra – and Squawk and a couple dozen fairy balls floating along with them. Sandra just smiled at the joy of it all.

After a while, Ellen and Buddy happened by, collecting everyone for yet another bunny hop, this time to the May Pole, and everyone at the whole of the Pole grabbed on. Sandra was glad to see that Gunny had thoughtfully gone by Dear Lovey's booth and wheeled her into the line so she'd get in on the fun too. Right behind her, Sandra could see Cappie and Thomas and even Mrs. Claus. No one wanted to miss out on the May Pole.

Zinga and Breezy were waiting for them all at the May Pole, handing every elf a long, colored ribbon that was hooked to the top of the pole. Once they all had one, Ellen was going to lead them off in a May Pole dance to Buddy's music. Then, Clicker, the "official photographer of the North Pole," was set to ride by on Em and take their picture from above. If everything went right, it was going to look like a giant, beautiful flower from the air and make for a beautiful Merry May Day photo to present to Santa when he got home. Sandra thought it was a beautiful sentiment and perfect welcome home gift.

"Are you ready?" shouted Zinga to be heard over the crowd.

"Wait just a minute," Gunny called out, stepping over to Zinga. "Go on now, you and Breezy, you go grab ribbons too. I know we need Buddy for the music but Santa will want to see your pretty faces in the photo too."

The two little elves seemed so pleased to be included and Sandra was distressed with herself that she hadn't thought of it. Thank goodness for Gunny, she thought, and then she smiled realizing it wasn't that long ago that she never would have thought that.

"Alright then," Gunny hardly had to yell to get attention with his deep Texan voice. He sort of commanded attention with the elves. "As Zinga said, are you ready?" he asked them again, getting them excited.

"YES!" they all yelled in unison and Sandra smiled even bigger if that was possible. She loved how excited elves could get.

"Clicker and Em," he shouted down the street. "Are you ready?"

"Yes!" Clicker yelled back.

"Okay then, Buddy, begin the music, and, elves, at Ellen's first step, begin to prance your way around the Merry May Pole!"

Sandra, Mrs. Claus, and the rest of the big people stood back admiring Buddy's music and the pretty movement of the elves prancing around the May Pole with the brightly colored ribbons.

"Santa is going to love this photo," Mrs. Claus said just as Em and Clicker came into view with Clicker leaning precariously over the side, which worried Sandra a bit, but she knew it wouldn't last long and then he could sit back safely.

The problem occurred when Em, being Em and being a very big delgin, miscalculated her distance above the May Pole. Elves had said many times that she often flew too low over the village but she generally ignored their remarks since she felt well in control of her flying. In this case again, she was very low. Not so low as to crash, but actually positioned at a perfect height and angle for Clicker to get a perfect picture. The problem was she hadn't calculated her speed. So when she came in low to the May Pole, the draft she created picked up the light-weight elves and sent them swirling and swirling and swirling around the pole as they hung onto their ribbons for dear life! As they became a tangled up mess, the spinning and screaming stopped. There was nothing but silence.

"Oh, my goodness!" cried Mrs. Claus at this unexpected outcome. Sandra and the others ran forward to help. "Oh, dear little elves. Are you hurt? Can you move?"

A collective sigh seemed to come from the mess piled up at the bottom of the May Pole and then laughing like you just rarely hear! Laughing from the heart and the belly. The kind that gets snorted out the nose because it's just so fun. They were tangled up, wrapped, up, upside down, and dangling. And every one of them – including even Zinga who had worked so hard to make it so perfect – was laughing the hardest they had since way before the Christmas season when things get too busy and fun can get forgotten. And certainly way before Santa went missing and joy became hard to find.

It was the very best sound Sandra thought she had ever heard.

CHAPTER 39

And a Very Merry Ending

Location: North Pole Village

It was dark by the time they were able to get every elf untied from the May Pole and the Northern Lights elves had to scramble. They had promised everyone their best show ever and even the elusive Rudy, with his lovely red color, was joining them that night. As the colorful elves ran out to get set up for their show, the rest of the festival goers gathered in the square for hot cups of cocoa and a sing-along of Christmas songs, of course.

Sandra and Jason were looking for seats by their friends, when Barney came running up, breathless, waving an envelope in his hand. "Sandra! Mrs. Claus! Another letter came in!" The letter had arrived like the others, through magical post, the same way many children's letters came as well.

"But it's not May 24th," Mrs. Claus said slowly, a little afraid to even open the envelope. Every post they had received from the Santanappers so far had come on the twenty-fourth of each preceding month. One of the Sherlocks stepped up, all business now, with the other Sherlocks close by at attention. Mrs. Claus had insisted they join in on the fun this day. All of them had somber faces now, in place of the smiles they had been wearing just moments before.

"Your Clausness," one of the Sherlocks said to Sandra, "may we assist?"

Sandra looked to Mrs. Claus to be sure that would be okay before nodding her agreement.

The little Sherlock pulled out the thin gloves she kept in her pocket and carefully opened the envelope. Inside was another photo of Santa, this time smiling and posed with Comet and Vixen. Instead of a newspaper, though, he held a sign on it that read:

MERRY MAY DAY, EVERYONE!

They all just stared at it a minute. Santa knew about the new Merry May Day festival?

Santa knew about the Merry May Day festival! Hooray! Shouts and cheers went up around the square as they all realized what that meant. Santa was still fine and somehow, he knew and was happy about what they were doing.

"How on earth could he possibly know about this?" Gunny was whispering beneath his breath to Sandra and the others so the elves and the fairies flying about wouldn't hear. Both elves and fairies have extraordinarily good hearing. If you want to keep any kind of secret when they are around, you have to talk very, very, low.

"Was this really the first one of these festivals?" Crow asked, not aware of that until right then.

Gunny nodded as he continued. "Seriously, Sandra, even you have to agree at this point. We clearly have some fairy chatter going on." He moved on quickly before she could object. "I'm not talking your boyfriend here, specifically." Jason just rolled his eyes. "I'm talking more broadly," he added, not entirely convincingly.

Sandra knew there was a good chance he was right this time, but on this day it didn't matter. "You know what, Gunny," she said, smiling a genuine, heartfelt smile. "I'm so glad to receive this photo tonight for the elves – and for all of us too – that I don't care how he found out. I'm just thankful that he did and that his Santanappers sent this to us. Tomorrow, first thing, we'll meet with the Sherlocks since this does appear to be an exciting possible lead to finding Santa."

"Agreed," Gunny said, just as the first flashes of the Northern Lights appeared in the dark North Pole sky.

Sandra leaned back against her boyfriend, who wrapped his arms around her. She looked over to see that Thomas had his arms wrapped around Cappie and she could swear she saw Crow reach out and hold Birdie's hand. She smiled, still feeling exceptionally happy. Jason held her tighter as the colors got bigger and brighter, ending a close-to-perfect Merry May Day Festival.

CHAPTER 40

The Day After Merry

Location: North Pole Village

A rare occurrence happened the next morning at the Pole: they all slept in. Every single elf, human, fairy, and visiting being of any kind, slept in. That usually only happened on Christmas morning ironically. While children all around the world woke their parents bright and early scrambling to see what Santa brought and what got tucked under the tree and in their stockings, everyone at the North Pole enjoyed what they too wanted most – some sleep.

Sandra was up as late as the others. She actually had woke up early, brushed her teeth and washed her face to wake up a bit but decided to not fight a little more sleep and had crawled back under the covers. She only woke a couple hours later when she heard knocking at her door. She could hear that Birdie was in the shower, so she got up and trudged to the door, swiping at her wild mop of hair.

"Jason!" she said, very surprised to see her boyfriend that early and knowing she looked a total mess. "I'm just waking up. What time is it?"

"Almost 8:30," he said. "I know it's early, but can I come in? I need to talk to you before I go."

"Go!" Sandra repeated, completely surprised by what he was saying and wondering if she just wasn't understanding it clearly since she had just woke up. "Of course, sure, come on in." She opened the door and felt self-conscious about how she looked. She plopped on the bed and pulled a pillow around her. After looking around a minute, Jason walked over and carefully sat next to her.

"Even this early, you look beautiful," he said quietly to her, reaching out and holding her hand. Sandra just sat there saying nothing, feeling like she wasn't going to like what he was going to say next.

"I've had such a great time here this week. It makes it really hard to go," he started.

"So don't, Jason," she jumped in. "Christina will understand. You know she will. She knows about Santa missing. She knows we can use the help up here and you know we have plenty of room for you."

"It's not about Christina, Sand," he said. "It's--"

"It's that my touch burns you, huh?" she said with sudden insight.

He looked at her with eyes begging for her to understand. "Sort of," he said. "That is part of it. I love you, Sandra, but if –"

Who cares what he is going to say next? Sandra thought.

"You love me?" she said, smiling.

He nodded his head. "For a very long time."

"Jason! I love you, too! I tried to tell you on our birthday for your gift but all the fairy king stuff happened and you wouldn't let me and now this is really so much better." She leaned over, smiling. Jason couldn't help but smile too, even though he didn't feel that happy. He knew she wouldn't like his news and this wasn't helping. Now he knew he was about to break her heart as well. He started again.

"I can't even believe you could love me," he said sincerely. "My girlfriend is South Pole Santa and she loves me."

"Yes I do, Jason Annalise. And I'm very pleased about having such a handsome fairy king who loves me back," she said, grinning.

"So, that's the thing, Sandra," he said, looking away from her now. "I'm not really Jason Annalise. I don't know who I am. I only just found out what I really am."

"That changes nothing," Sandra said, almost desperately, as she felt him pulling away from her.

Now he stood up, pacing. "That changes everything," he said, looking desolately at her. "Everything, Sand. Even you and me.

"I have to know who I am and I have to learn what it is to be a fairy. You know who you are and what you want. You are, through and through, South Pole Santa as if you were born to the role. You will soar simply because it's what you want, and who you are, so you live it with passion, and dedication, and from the depth of your heart.

"I've seen that this week. I want that, Sandra. I feel it calling to me. I think part of the reason I came up here, if I'm being honest, was not just to see you, but it was also an attempt to hide from my own truth. To try to get lost in your truth and away from my own path. The weird thing is that seeing you in action has made it impossible for me not to find my own.

"I have to go this morning, Sand, because if I don't, I won't."

Sandra sat there taking it in and understanding as much as she wanted to on what he was telling her.

"Okay, then I'll come visit you more often," she said. "We can make this long-distance thing work, Jason. We have so far and you know I love visiting St. Annalise as often as I can."

"I won't be there," he said quietly from across the room now, already putting distance between them. "That's not where I'm going."

"What do you mean? Where are you going? Are you moving? Then I'll go there." She was trying not to panic now as she realized what kind of goodbye this was – the worst kind.

"I don't know where I'm going," he said. "That's the truth. I've been to the fairy realm only once, so far. I don't exactly know how they got me there but I have an idea, and I know as king they will take me back. That's where my future is at, Sandra. The truth is, you're a royal elfin and I'm the king of fairies and the two don't go well together," he said, holding up his arm. "And, unfortunately, we know that for sure."

Maybe Sandra was part elfin and part elf but she was also human, and at that moment she was a girl whose human heart was breaking.

"Oh, Jason, no, really, we can make this work. Just give it time. I'm willing to be patient and see what happens next," she said, wiping away tears.

Jason was crying, too. This was just as hard for him. Harder though, he somehow knew, would be living a life as "Mr. Claus" and not knowing or following his own destiny. He walked across the room and folded her in his arms.

"It would just be either harder later or meaner later, Sandra, because one of us would end up resenting the other. I want to leave us in a place of love," he whispered it to her as she sobbed. He glanced at his watch. "I have to go. I love you. For all of time, no matter how things change or who comes into our lives, my love for you will be part of who I am." He kissed the top of her head, wiping at his own tears, pulled away from her arms and walked straight to the door without looking back.

"Noooooooooooo," he heard from behind the door but he headed down the hall. He loved her enough to do that.

CHAPTER 41

Heartbreak Hotel

Location: North Pole Village

Sandra didn't get out of bed the rest of that day or the next. Birdie had heard much of what had been said from the bathroom as she got out of the shower. When she heard the door shut, she ran to her friend's side to comfort her. But Sandra couldn't be comforted. Jason was her first love and her first heartbreak and only time was going to help heal the wound.

The first day no one at the Pole was that surprised not to see her out and about. It was unusual for her, but everyone needed a break. The elves had all come to love Sandra in the same way they loved Santa so they were happy she was getting some rest.

By the second day, though, they were all beginning to worry and Birdie was having a harder time of convincing them she was okay. "She's just feeling a little low," she said over and over. "I'm sure she'll be doing better soon." She had shared the news only with Cappie and Thomas, who were worried sick about her but understood Jason's decision. It was just a horrible situation. Cappie took up vigil in Sandra's room, taking turns with Birdie, while Sandra just slept hour after hour.

The third day came and Sandra still showed no sign of being willing or even able to get up. She didn't think she cared about anything anymore. Even being South Pole Santa didn't sound important enough to find the strength to get out of bed. Nothing mattered.

"Sandra," Birdie said, attempting again to coax her out of bed. "Em and Squawk are here and they're being nice to each other." Birdie gave them both a look to make sure they were and that they behaved. "They want to say 'hi' and see how you're doing."

"I'm too tired, Bird," Sandra mumbled. "Tell them to come back please."

" . . . *squawk*! . . . not going to leave . . . *squawk*! . . ." Squawk said, planting himself firmly on her headboard.

"Me neither," said Em, stubbornly setting herself down at the foot of her bed.

Now it was not just Sandra missing from the Pole, but Em and Squawk and Jason and mostly Cappie and Birdie too. By the fifth day, the elves were starting to worry – and cry. Gunny too was worried and he had had it. Whether Birdie liked it or not, he was going in that room.

"Birdie, with all due respect, I can pretty much figure out what is going on here, seeing's how fairy boy catches an express coach outta town without a word to any of us and Sandra takes to her room," Gunny said, talking to her outside Sandra's room in the hotel hallway. "I've had my heart broken before. I know what that is like. It sucks but you've gotta pick yourself up and move on. I'm going in."

"Fine," said Birdie, willing to try anything by anyone at that point to help her best friend in the world. They were all feeling helpless. "But I'm going in first to tell her. You wait here."

She opened the door and let herself in. Much to her annoyance, Gunny ignored her order and followed her right into the dark space, flipping on the light as he did.

"Sandra? Sandra, honey," Birdie said, shaking her friend a little bit. "Sandra, Gunny is--"

"Gunny is right here," Gunny said, moving to the bed. "I'm your wake-up call, here to help you get up and out." He was talking loud and shaking her.

"Go away, Gunny!" Sandra said, flinging her arm at him to make him quit shaking her. "I'm not feeling good."

"You are feeling lousy, horrible, like nothing matters anymore. I get that. I understand it," Gunny said, surprisingly supportive. "I'm really sorry," he added in a soft tone just for her. Tears ran down her face, which tugged at his heart. *That no-good fairy king*. But there was no time for thinking on Jason right now. Now was "Operation Save Sandra" and she wasn't going to like it.

"Birdie, would you run on in there and turn on the shower?"

"What?" Birdie said, then understanding and heading for the bathroom.

"Cappie, she's going to need your help once she's in there so if you wouldn't mind staying close that would be good, too," Gunny continued.

Cappie nodded, understanding that the situation called for some drastic action. In this case, drastic action involved Gunny reaching down and scooping up Sandra out of the bed, blankets and all, with her trying to squirm away and shouting at him the whole time.

"I know, baby girl, I know," he said softly to her, over and over, as he stalwartly walked, step by step, to the shower and stood her up in it. Pajamas, blanket and all.

She stood there, protesting and then slid down the wall to the floor, sobbing.

"Cry it out, sweetheart, cry it out," Gunny said. "Birdie, Cappie, she's all yours. I know she's fragile right now, but we also all know she's strong, too. No letting her get back into that bed. I expect to see her at the diner for dinner or I'll come on back."

The two nodded, agreeing with him, but none of them, not even Gunny as he left, was sure that was possible. He did know, though, what would help and he headed out to make that happen.

The power of a shower, sometimes, can be underappreciated and, very slowly, Sandra started to wake back up to herself. Birdie and Cappie helped her get cleaned up and dressed, and even Em and Squawk helped by cleaning up the room. She was not interested in getting dinner but when a knock came later for room service, Cappie opened the door to Gunny and his North Pole specialty - a cart full of cookies and cocoas. Cappie turned to let him in, and as he wheeled in the cart, he was followed by almost every elf at the Pole, starting with Breezy and Zinga, both looking pale and worried.

"Sandra!" they cried out when they saw their lovely South Pole Santa looking worn and exhausted and something they had never seen – deeply sad. They both ran to hug on her, followed by all the others who piled on.

"Breezy! Zinga! Everyone!" Sandra said, showing the first smile she had had in a week. "Hello, hello!" Seeing them, with their worry and their joy of seeing her, was exactly the medicine she needed.

"Now, now, everyone. I'm so sorry I've worried you. Yes, I've missed you, too. Gunny, can we get some more trays of cookies and cocoa in here?" she asked her friend with gratefulness in her eyes. "We have a lot to catch up on."

"Coming right up!" he said, feeling such a wave of relief. She was smiling. She was laughing even. She would be okay.

For the first time in almost a week, Sandra was thinking the same thing. She would be okay. Thanks to her wonderful friends and elves, she would be okay. Different now, but strong and okay.

CHAPTER 42

Heading South

Location: North Pole Village

Sandra made it through the next month, but it was more like going through the motions of her life then actually living. She shared with those closest to her that she and Jason had broken up and let the rest just believe she hadn't been feeling good. Elves hate anything sad, so none of them really pushed for an answer, and most were satisfied to know what they knew. What they liked most was that Sandra was now doing better, and that made them happy.

Her close friends, though, were keeping a close watch on her, especially since she had started doing some things they weren't used to her doing. For instance, almost every evening, no matter what time she was done with her day, she went and swam some laps at the pool. The shallow end of the pool was just two feet deep and the "deep" end was just five feet since it was designed for elves. Still, it was deep enough for her to swim in and the water was soothing to her. Swimming was something she had known how to do pretty much her whole life and she felt she could "swim away" her feelings of sadness. She didn't have to think, just swim. It was a bonus too that Dear Lovey was often there since she had dealt with many a heartbreak letter. In her own insightful way, she was able to offer snippets of guidance and consolation to Sandra. The two had grown quite fond of each other, and, after a bit, Sandra found she was going to the pool as much to meet up with her new elf friend as to swim away her troubles. It was one of the first signs of a turning point.

For Dear Lovey it was great too because wherever Sandra went, elves tended to follow. Soon she found herself with all sorts of people taking swim classes at the pool and joining her for laps. She was making all sorts of new friends. A sad time had turned into a happy time, and Sandra felt grateful as her heart began to heal.

Something else was helping to cheer Sandra up too. She had been spending time alone each day going through the piles of acts of kindness examples that children were sending in! Sandra could hardly believe how the idea had taken off. The sheer number of examples being sent in made her heart soar. It was clearly an idea the world was ready for and she loved that the children -- and even adults -- were enjoying it so much.

Being a resourceful reporter, Beatrice Carol had apparently recognized a good idea when she heard one too. She had started a weekly feature called "Being Kind with Beatrice" where she showcased some of the kind actions and good deeds children around the world were doing as a result of Sandra's request.

Sandra and Cappie were watching the show one evening together. Beatrice was covering kind actions by children in Belgium. Sandra was thinking that people often said English was the international language but, really, it was kindness. She smiled at the thought.

"It's lovely to see you smiling, sweetheart," Cappie said, reaching over and squeezing her hand. "You've had us all worried you know. You seem to have withdrawn a lot."

"I know, Cappie, but I've needed to have time to be by myself and just think for a bit. It's been the only way I've known to move forward. I had to retreat a bit to see ahead. I'm doing better though now. Thanks to you and Squawk and the elves and my friends. Everything is looking better again." She smiled a genuine smile at her guardian.

"Telina, Sandra, you know that," Cappie told her cherished charge, using the elfin language to say "I love you."

"Telina, too," Sandra said, loving the reminder to use the pretty language. Of all the languages Sandra knew, and there were a lot, she loved the elfin language the most.

"If you need anything at all, you send for me and I'll be right back. Or you come home to the *Mistletoe* and do your retreating there," Cappie said. She was leaving in the morning for St. Annalise and still wasn't sure she should. She wanted to say something comforting again about Jason but she didn't want to make Sandra sad by bringing him up. Besides, there was nothing really to say. She just stayed quiet about it.

"Cappie, truly, I am much better. I have so much to do that I don't have any time to be sad anymore! You must not worry about me. I'm glad you're headed home. Rio has to be missing us! And I know Thomas is missing you," Sandra said mischievously, smiling. "Besides, you know Squawk and Em won't let me be sad." They both smiled, thinking about the two who always liked to be with her but now seemed determined to be with her 27 hours each Pole day!

"You're in good hands," Cappie said, getting up to go. "I'm proud of you every day in every way."

" . . . *and I want to extend again an invitation to be on our show to my very good friend, Sandra Claus dot dot dot,*" Beatrice Carol's show had been running all along as the two had talked, but upon hearing her name, it captured Sandra's attention again. "Very good friend," she said to Cappie. "That might be stretching it a bit! But I do think I'll take some time and do her show sometime soon. I'd love to see some of these extra kind children."

In no time, it was June 24, the halfway point to Christmas Eve, and another photo had arrived. They had received one, as expected, on May 24, of Santa standing with Blitzen and holding the *Seattle Times*. With still no clues of where he was, the team had discussed, at length, finally telling Beatrice Carol, and, consequently, the world, the truth so that they could help look for Santa too, but had decided to give it one more month.

As June arrived, they were no farther along and believed they were just putting off, and putting off, the inevitable. They began to discuss their strategy around the announcement to the world and then the June photo arrived. Santa was with Cupid this time and holding a copy of a Brazilian newspaper. Someone, and Mrs. Claus believed it looked like Santa's writing, had written in big red letters across the front of the newspaper, "Please do not tell the children I'm missing."

So things continued along, with the Sherlocks running down every clue, and rumor, of Santa's possible location, while the rest of the Pole occupants, worked to keep everything else moving forward. Sandra had called for a Claus Council meeting to review next steps.

"Who wants to go first?" she asked.

"Sandra," said Gunny, not waiting to see if anyone else was hoping to go first. "We have to get the South Pole barge building going at St. Annalise. Equator Pole needs to be activated again! We don't have the same problem we had when we started down there with no elves who wanted to move. Now they're all willing to go back. We just haven't sent them, while we sorted out finding Santa.

"Here's the thing though, and I know no one in this room wants to say it or even think it, but we're having a tough time finding him. You heard the Sherlocks this morning after the newspaper arrived, the search is in a stall. And Christmas is still going to come. In just six short months, it's going to be here! We can squeak through this Christmas with one Santa if we have to, but we still have to plan for next year and all the ones that come after that."

The protests around the very hint that might Santa not be coming back began around the table until Gunny held up his hands with his own protest. "Hey now, I said 'if we have to' and face it, even if we had Santa back this afternoon, there is just no way we could have the South Pole Village barge finished and ready to go on time. Sandra will be accompanying Santa this year again as long as he's back. Are we agreed on that fact?"

Everyone around the table nodded their head yes, including Sandra, who didn't mind a bit. She loved going out on Christmas Eve with Santa.

"What we're talking about here then is making sure that, no matter what, the barge will be ready for next Christmas because, by then, my friends, we better have our act together or some children aren't going to be visited by either Santa. All because of us. The fact is, we've had enough time; we just didn't make it happen."

Gunny knew he was laying it on thick but he felt like he had to in order to get the group to take action. The elves were all reaching for tissues to dab their eyes. The very idea of sad children always made them sad too.

His words seemed to confirm Sandra's thinking as well. "You're right, Gunny. I've been thinking on this too. It's time to get back into action. We know Santa was completely supportive of building the barge and he would want us to continue. So let's get that underway! Birdie, would you and Squawk be willing to oversee the barge building for a while? I think I can get Spence to relocate to the island too without too much trouble. He is usually able to work on his technology updates from almost anywhere," she said, smiling, knowing that Spence, like her and Birdie, always enjoyed time at home on St. Annalise.

"Of course, Sandra," said Birdie.

" . . . *squawk* . . . I'll help . . . *squawk* . . ."

"Thank you both," she said, now firming up the plans she had been considering. "It's been too long since I've been home to St. Annalise myself and Cappie is hoping I'll visit so I'm going to go down with the first group for a few days to oversee getting the elves settled in and visit with Cappie and Rio." She didn't add Jason. He wasn't there anymore.

"Mind if I tag along on that trip?" It was Ghost who asked this. He had been quiet and respectful and had been a huge help, along with Crow, over the past month when Sandra had not done quite as much as she usually did and it was left to Gunny to fill in. Gunny had never complained, he just did it, but he had been grateful for the help of his brothers.

Ghost's question surprised both Sandra and Gunny. "Um, yeah, sure, I guess you could come along," Sandra said, surprised he had asked, but warming to the idea.

"Yeah, that is a no," said Gunny at about the same time as Sandra was saying he could go. Both Sandra and Ghost looked at him. He floundered with his answer because the truth was he just really didn't want his little brother, who had an obvious crush on South Pole Santa, hanging out with her. He'd just be a nuisance to her at a time when she was still recovering from heart break.

"Because, you know, with you gone, Sandra, that leaves a lot here to do and I'm going to be needing the help," Gunny said firmly.

"More than Sandra will?" Ghost asked rather nicely, aware of what his brother's real concerns might be and wanting to avoid a conflict.

"Actually, if anyone should be going to help at the Equator Pole, it should be me," said Crow. "Hey, it's my girlfriend who just got the assignment." He looked over at Birdie who smiled shyly. They had become an official "item" during the last month.

"Which means you probably wouldn't get anything done," Ghost said.

"Which means I'd probably get lots done to impress my girlfriend," Crow said in return.

"Okay, here's how I'm going to 'rule' on this, and I'm sorry if any of you feel like it's not fair," Sandra interrupted. "Ghost, you're going. I think it might be helpful for Birdie and me to have some muscle around. Crow, you're staying – for now. I totally understand you wanting to join Birdie there and get some sunshine but you are on point for finishing up the remodel on the main research and development lab and we have to get that done. Once you're finished with that, then you and Ghost can change places."

Gunny didn't like it. He just didn't think it was a good idea to send his wildly immature brother down to St. Annalise without some supervision, but he agreed with Sandra's reasoning. Still, he wasn't completely comfortable.

"I think I'm going to go with you," he said as casually as he could muster. "Before you can protest, Sandra, I mean for just a few days. Honestly, I could use a few days off in the sunshine and even though I'll be helping out, it'll feel like a vacation."

He didn't look over at his little brother, who he could tell was glaring at him.

Sandra could hardly object. Gunny had been working tirelessly for months, extra hard the last month or so, and had never complained or asked for any time off. He deserved a little time in the tropical sun.

"Alright, you get to go too, Gunny! You do deserve a little rest and relaxation," Sandra said. "That means Breezy, Zinga, Rollo, and Tack, you all will be up here watching over things with Crow for a few days on your own. Are you okay with that?"

"Of course, Sandra," said Tack. "We've handled the Pole on our own many times in the past while Santa was away for work, visiting children, or publicity appearances. We'll be fine."

"Okay then, let's gather up our South Pole barge builders and make plans to leave for St. Annalise in next week with the first group. Birdie, Squawk, and I will take them down and get things ready. Two days after that, Gunny, you and Ghost come with the rest." Everyone at the table nodded.

"It feels good to have a plan to move forward. Thanks, Gunny, for pushing us on this." He nodded as everyone got up to leave.

Ghost passed by his brother on the way out with, "Three's a crowd, brother of mine."

That was exactly why Gunny was going.

CHAPTER 43

Talking to Beatrice

Location: London, England

"So, Sandra Claus dot dot dot," Beatrice Carol said. "This is just such a pleasure to have you on my little show here. Children, don't you agree?"

The huge crowd gathered in the auditorium where the filming was taking place, full of children and their parents, cheered loudly as Sandra waved. She liked Beatrice Carol but she had come for the children. She had squeezed this appearance in before she had to head south to St. Annalise the next week. The children deserved to have her attention and take some time out from her regular duties, especially since Santa couldn't do any visiting this year. Not surprisingly, that was Beatrice Carol's first question.

"We adore having you here, Sandra," said the reporter. "I was wondering though, how is Santa Claus doing? We haven't seen much of him this year. Are we likely to see him later out on tour?"

Sandra stayed calm. She had anticipated these kinds of questions would come up.

"He will be so happy to hear you asked about him, Beatrice," she said. "This year, it's my turn to step up and get out to represent the North *and* the South Pole." She grinned. She loved having her own Pole. "Neither one of us, though, really has much time to spare, as you can imagine, since we do like to get out during the holiday season and visit more. That means we have to get a lot done during the rest of the year."

"Yes, yes, that does make a lot of sense and it's such a privilege to have you here today," Beatrice said. "I am so excited to talk more on your new kindness initiative. Tell me, were you at all worried that children would find it to be, well, boring?"

Sandra laughed out loud. "Kindness boring?" she said. "Why, it's the most wonderful, magical thing of all. I can't imagine anyone would ever find being kind to be boring." She meant every word of it. It had never occurred to her to think otherwise.

"The thing about being kind is that, while it is often a gift to the other person, or animal, or cause, or even toward our very planet here, it is also such a gift to ourselves when we reach out in a kind way. Don't you agree, Beatrice?" Sandra asked.

The reporter seemed a little surprised to be asked such a direct question. "Why, I guess I do agree. I know I always feel better when I'm kind than when I'm not."

"Exactly!" Sandra said. "That's the best thing about kindness." She turned now away from the reporter to address the children in the audience directly. "Being kind makes everything better. It can be small acts of kindnesses or large acts. They can be planned ahead or acted on in the moment. The important part is to decide you are going to be a kind person because then that starts helping you respond to all situations kindly.

"I know it's not always easy! Oh Oh Oh! Do I ever know!" She laughed out loud while the crowd smiled at her. "Let me give you an example. I have a very big delgin named Emaralda and my favorite bird in the whole world named Squawk. Have you all seen them?" She paused for a moment.

"YES!" the crowd roared.

"YES!" roared all the elves and her friends watching her appearance on the live TV feed at the Pole. They were so excited to see her again on TV. Only the Sherlocks had accompanied her on this trip. Everyone else stayed home. The Sherlocks had insisted on it.

"Well the two of them can be total sweethearts most of the time. Kind and thoughtful." Em and Squawk preened about a little hearing such nice words being said about them. Sandra continued. "But they can also argue like you can't believe. They can argue so much that I think about putting them on Santa's Naughty List!"

The crowd gasped.

" . . .*squawk*! . . . not fair . . . *squawk*! . . . your fault"

"It is not my fault," Em said, setting the two off on another argument and proving Sandra's point.

"Be quiet, you two," Birdie said. "We're trying to listen."

"Okay, not really, not really," Sandra was laughing and saying. "They are nice most of the time but still, when they get like that, I sometimes am not very nice about it either. And then I start to get grumpy and act not my best either. I start to act unkind as well. But I could have chosen to still be nice even though those two were grumpy. I made the choice to be part of the problem instead of trying to stay kind. It's just not always easy.

"So, I know being kind every day isn't always the easiest thing to do. That's part of why I have loved, so much, seeing all the many examples of how you are being kind that you are sending to the North Pole every single day. How my heart soars with your great acts of kindness, and watching your show about them, Beatrice."

"How nice to hear you that you watch it, Sandra," Beatrice said, beaming.

"All of us at the Pole do – we wouldn't miss it. It's the best show on every week because it's about being kind. There's nothing better. Kindness isn't boring, kindness is magical. Kindness can change the world and I'm so proud of the children of the world, who know it too. Children, you are making a difference for so many, and for yourselves, every day. If you find yourself having a down day, don't be down, be kind! It can help turn any frown into a smile."

The crowd in the auditorium, and at the Pole, jumped to their feet in applause. Sandra knew they thought it was for her, and it was certainly kind of them, but really it was for kindness itself and kindness deserved to be applauded.

She clapped the hardest and the longest.

CHAPTER 44

Homecoming

Location: St. Annalise

While she was over visiting London, Sandra managed to fit in a couple of stops to nearby cities she hadn't seen before. She swung by for a Christmas in July celebration in St. Petersburg, Russia, which she decided was a beautiful city with lovely children. She also made it to Reykjavik, Iceland. She could hardly wait to get back to that city and bring the elves with her. It turned out that elves lived in Iceland! She knew the North Pole elves would love to visit with them. At both cities, children had come out by the thousands to get a chance to meet her and personally hand her their lists of the kind things they had done recently. She loved every minute of it.

Between those stops, she only had one night back at North Pole Village before it was time to head south to Equator Pole on St. Annalise. The whole of the Pole came out to see them off. It was the beginning of July and a beautiful day at the Pole. Ellen and Buddy had rustled up the Pole's marching band, and Ellen led them at the front with a big baton. It made it extra festive when elves joined in behind the band just to march along. Elves all loved a parade! Even a parade that wasn't really a parade but just a band acting like a parade.

This group heading south was small since Sandra wanted a few days, and needed just a few elves, to help get things open, dust things off, get resupplied and be ready for the bigger group to arrive with Gunny and Ghost. The elves going with her, unlike the last time around, were smiling and happy, decked out in their tropical gear and wearing flip-flops, which cracked Sandra up since she had no idea where those had come from, though she suspected Diva's shop. On the job, close–toed shoes were required. She believed in safety over fashion. But for the trip, and off-hours, they could wear whatever they liked.

"Thanks for all the help again, elves," Sandra said loudly to be heard over the din and the marching band that was still playing off in the distance. "Be very good and good to each other. You can call me at the Equator Pole if you need anything, using the new pole-to-pole-to-pole phone system that Brainy, Naters, and Spence put together. For now, Gunny is in command. After he leaves, please report in each day with Zinga. Tack, Rollo, and Breezy will be assisting her.

"Alright then," she was hesitating, surprised at how hard it was to leave North Pole Village especially when she was going home for a little while. "I will see you all in a week!" She waved and got in the coach with Birdie, Spence, Squawk, and Em. All of her very best friends in the world. If Em and Squawk didn't fight the whole way, it promised to be a great trip.

And mostly it was. The two were on their best behavior for the two of them. Birdie, Spence, and Sandra hardly ever got time with just the three of them alone anymore, so they had fun being just best friends together for a few hours, and talking about news of their classmates and other people at St. Annalise. Birdie and Spence were careful not to bring up Jason or even Christina, and Sandra knew they were doing that for her. They all were happy about Cappie and Thomas and Birdie opened up about officially dating Crow. Spence had turned to a book by then, so the two girls had a chance to talk "girl talk" for a couple of fun hours. Before they knew it, they were coming in to land at St. Annalise. Sandra had asked the driver to set them down right at Equator Pole Village, which was on the opposite side of the island from the *Mistletoe* but an easy walk. The coach landed and Spence, Squawk, and Em bounded out, eager to be out of the cramped coach, but Sandra hesitated. Her best friend understood.

"It will be all right, Sandra," she said, patting her hand. "I know how hard this must be for you to come home to a place that reminds you of Jason everywhere. Just remember, though, this island is also your home. It's not just a place about him, it is a place full of all of us and our wonderful lives and experiences. Let's get out and make some more."

Sandra was so appreciative of Birdie always knowing the right thing to say. She squeezed her friend and hopped out of the coach. "Home!" she said to no one but herself, throwing her hands in the air and feeling good about it.

The other two coaches of elves had also landed and Sandra headed in their direction. "Okay, everyone, let's start with setting up one of the big bunk rooms for everyone tonight. Then we can figure out what we can get to eat."

"I smell something good," said LuLu.

"Me too," said Wicket. "It's coming from over there." He pointed across the way, and when Sandra turned, she could see it was her wonderful guardian, busy putting out a big picnic for everyone.

"Cappie!" she hollered, waving, always happy to see her. *Of course Cappie would be here to help me,* she thought. *She's always around to offer just what I need.* Next to Cappie, Sandra realized, setting things out on the table, was none other than Christina. Sandra's heart pulled a bit, but she knew she would need to face her ex-boyfriend's mom sooner or later. Sooner was as good as later.

The picnic helped things a lot because food was a great motivator for elves. "Okay, everyone, your attention here please," Sandra said and they all gathered around her. "There are three things that must be done before we can sit down to the dinner that smells so delicious. First, we'll unload the coaches and put away the supplies. Second, we'll go in and set up the beds in one of the bunk rooms for tonight. And third, we'll make a list of supplies that we'll need to get Equator Pole Village up and running again so that Birdie and I can go shopping tomorrow. Only when all three of those things are done do we get to eat. Agreed?"

"Agreed!" they all sang out. Elves don't mind hard work and they generally take direction very well.

Sandra helped with getting the coaches unloaded and then left the elves and the rest to get the other things on the list done while she walked over to hug on her guardian.

"Sandra, honey, it is so good to have you home! I can't even believe that you're here." Cappie unconsciously fiddled with Sandra's hair and looked deep in her eyes to check for her pain level. She knew it would be hard for her charge this first time at home without Jason in her life.

"I'm happy to be here, Cappie. Happier than I even thought I would be. There's no place like home. And I have a great home, thanks to you," she said, looking right at her guardian to make sure she knew she meant it.

Christina had hung back, uncertain whether she would be welcome or not but very glad to see Sandra. Christina loved her too and was heartbroken herself over the break-up. Jason had shared the news with his mom before he left. His departure had been very hard for her too. He was seeking out his "real" parents, which she understood in her head, but in her heart she was his real parent. Seeing her now, Sandra immediately realized how hard his leaving was for her too and hugged her extra hard.

"I'm sorry, Sandra," Christina said softly.

"I'm sorry for you, too," Sandra said back with true compassion.

"Sandra, we've made fish tacos for dinner with pineapple," Cappie said, trying to lighten things up.

"My favorites!" Sandra grinned as Birdie and Spence came up and hugged Cappie, but not before Em flung herself in her arms. "Cappie!" she cried. For the life of her, Sandra could not figure out why that little delgin loved Cappie so much, but she was happy that she did.

" . . . *squawk* . . . tacos . . . oboy . . ."

"Yes, Squawk. And a banana split bar for dessert, courtesy of your island host, who so generously is letting you all build this big bulky barge that Sandra and you all plan to call home part of each year," said Cappie.

"*squawk*! . . . skipping dinner . . . just dessert . . . *squawk* . . . joking . . ."

"Squawk," said Christina. "You've become quite funny!"

" . . . *squawk* . . . I know . . ."

That made all the rest of them laugh, mostly because he wasn't as funny as he thought he was. They all worked together to help Cappie and Christina get set up just in time as the elves came running across the grass, wearing their tropical shirts, big sunglasses, and floppy hats. It was another special moment for Sandra. No way would she choose to be anybody but South Pole Santa, she thought again, smiling.

"Hi, everyone," Cappie called out. "I think I've met all of you, but in case you haven't met her, this is Christina Annalise.

She's Jason's mom, the director of the St. Annalise Academy, and the owner of this island who is letting you all build your big barge here. Isn't that nice of her?"

"Yes!" they all shouted at once.

Then Wicket asked, "Where is Jason, Sandra? I haven't seen him around lately."

"Yeah," some of the elves said nodding. "Where is he?"

The topic was still just raw enough that, when it came up unexpectedly, Sandra always felt like she might cry, which was awful. She didn't want to feel that way. Christina kindly filled the awkward pause.

"How kind of you to notice he's not here," she said. "Jason has some new duties in his role as the king of fairies and will be away for quite a while. But I know how much he is going to miss seeing you all. Now, who would like to sit where at this big table?"

It took several hours to get everyone fed, the picnic area cleaned up, and the elves settled in, before they all got to head for their own homes. Spence would be staying with his folks. Sandra could tell he was looking forward to seeing them. Birdie's parents, though, lived in Africa and since she had graduated, she couldn't stay in St. Annalise Academy housing anymore. She would always be welcome with Cappie and Sandra on the *Mistletoe* and that's where she was going to be staying this trip and any other time she came to St. Annalise. She loved the *Mistletoe* and her best friend and Cappie.

Even though it was late, and they were all tired from trudging across the island, when they got close to the big tugboat,

Sandra took off at a run. "Rio!" she called. "Rio, we're home! Come out and play!"

"*Eeeee eeeee eeeeeeeeeeeeeee*" said the beautiful green dolphin, doing flips and turns when she heard her name being called. She loved Sandra as much as she was loved by Sandra.

"I'm coming in!" Sandra said as she dived in, grabbed hold of Rio's dorsal fin, and went for an evening swim in the warm St. Annalise waters.

"Do I hear a familiar voice over there?" Thomas called from his place a couple boat docks down the way.

"Hi, Thomas! Cappie says you're coming over in the morning for breakfast. We'll see you then," Sandra called to him as Rio pulled her by his boat and then out farther in the bay.

She let go of Rio for a few minutes, just to float on her back, look at the fading light and the beautiful stars of the Caribbean sky as they began to appear. Rio was playing around her and she marveled at how perfect the moment was – right up until she heard the all too familiar buzzing sound she had come to know was not a bee but a fairy orb approaching. Besides the buzzing noise, there were other similarities between them, Sandra thought. You needed to be cautious around them both and they both had stingers – bees had real stingers and fairies used their words as stingers. She smiled at her clever thought as the orb came into view and her feeling of dread that it was Wistle was made true. Her smile faded quickly.

"Honestly, Wistle, I've just been home a little while, I'm floating quite a ways from shore, enjoying this beautiful place, and you pick now to come visit me? Don't you generally avoid buzzing over water?"

"I do, but I made an exception tonight because I had something important to tell you and I didn't want the others to know I was speaking with you," Wistle said.

"Important how? In what way?" Sandra asked, now dog-paddling in place while she talked to Wistle, who kept darting about. "Could you hold still please?" Sandra finally asked.

"Our king has left," she said, sounding genuinely distressed about it. "He's gone to the fairy realm."

"I don't get it, Wistle. I would think you would like that," Sandra said. This was not surprising news to her.

"Not going by himself," she was sort of whispering this, while looking at the shore. "I just don't think as a Shanelle he's safe going there alone."

"He's not just a Shanelle, he's a Shan too," Sandra said, as Wistle looked surprised. "Yes, he told me. It doesn't make sense that they would want to hurt him,"

"The world of fairies is not as easy to negotiate as the simple world you live in," Wistle said haughtily.

"Be that as it may," Sandra said, looking around for Rio. "You got your wish and we broke up so there is very little I can do about any of it." She finished speaking just as a large wave came up and washed over her. It washed over Wistle too, who immediately changed to full size.

"I can't swim!" Wistle said as she flailed in the water going under quickly as Sandra tried not to panic at the quick turn of events.

"RIO!" she yelled for her dolphin friend whom she suspected had swum off when Wistle arrived. No one in Sandra's circle was real excited ever about spending any quality time with the fairy. "RIO!

"Wistle! Breathe!" Sandra pulled the water-logged fairy up above the water. "Orb, Wistle!"

"I can't!" she cried. "I'm wet! Fairies can't orb when they're wet!" She slid under the water again as Sandra tried to keep them both afloat.

She was worrying for nothing though because Rio was right there. She scooped the fairy up over her back and then swam back by so Sandra could grab on to her fin. Sandra helped Wistle hold on to Rio's fin as well, and then tucked in behind her to be sure the weakened and scared fairy wouldn't fall off. Rio got them back to the dock in record time and Sandra scurried to get Wistle out of the water and safe on the dock.

"Wistle, are you okay?" Sandra said as the disheveled fairy looked highly shaken. Sandra realized why none of the other fairies spent time by the water now, which she had always thought was ironic since they lived on an island. This was very likely the first time Wistle had ever been in water and very likely the last as well.

"I am beholden to you, Sandra," Wistle said, as humble as Sandra had ever heard her.

"Nonsense, Wistle!" said Sandra. "Anyone would have saved you. Not to mention, you are my friend, maybe not one of my best friends, but nonetheless a friend. I would never wish you any ill and could simply not bear the thought of you drowning."

The fairy looked at her and did something she had never seen another fairy do – she burst into tears.

"Never in my fairy life has anyone spoke such kind words to me," said Wistle. "It is not the way of fairies, even Shanelles, to speak of their feelings toward others or to express kindness. Shans pride ourselves on the ironic and the sarcastic views of life. But this kindness that you have shown in the water and now here, this is a new feeling for me. One that it will take me time to consider."

Sandra smiled. It was a special thing to watch, and understand, someone you knew and cared about, consider changing and growing.

"I am sorry, Wistle, for the unkindness I have shown you in the past," said Sandra, meaning it.

"Please promise me that you won't change," Wistle was almost pleading now. "I am a Shan fairy. I would have it no other way but, inside, in here," she was pointing to her heart, "things will be different."

"I understand," said Sandra as Wistle swiped at her tears and Sandra grabbed a towel from the side of the *Mistletoe*. "Now let's get you dried off so you can orb on home."

"I will take the towel but I prefer to walk tonight. The time will do me good."

"There you are, Sandra! Oh, Wistle, hello! What a love-ly surprise. Would you like to join us for an evening cocoa?" Cappie had come out on the deck.

"I'll pass on that but thank you, Cappie. It is late and I am needed elsewhere," Wistle said, sounding more like herself as she turned to walk down the dock.

"I am in your debt, Sandra. A fairy never forgets a favor owed," she said softly so only Sandra could hear. Ironically, Sandra had heard that before from a fairy. "Remember what I said about Jason." She used the name of their friend this time versus his title. "He too may need saving."

Sandra just nodded in return. Saving one fairy a day was all she had strength for.

CHAPTER 45

Home Sweet Island

Location: St. Annalise aka Equator Pole

Sandra took her time getting up the next morning. She didn't mention to anyone what had happened with Wistle the night before. That could stay between her and Wistle and Rio. She did her yoga stretches on the deck, had breakfast with Cappie, Birdie and Thomas, and finally headed over to Equator Pole Village with Birdie to see how things were going.

The two best friends relished the rare time alone at home and walked with their arms linked. They took the long way around the island along the water's edge.

"I miss him, Birdie," Sandra said as they passed by Jason's home. Birdie didn't have to ask who the "him" was.

"I'm so sorry, Sand," Birdie said, trying to squeeze even more love into her best friend for strength.

"It doesn't seem the same on St. Annalise without him. I think that must be how he felt when I was gone so much, which makes me feel terrible," she lamented. "I went off chasing my big dreams and expected him to be here whenever I could pop on home. Meanwhile, he was on St. Annalise, by himself, trying to figure out what to do next. I would have broken up with me too." Her voice broke on the last words.

"Nonsense!" Birdie said in a stronger voice than she usually used with her friend. "Jason was happy here, Sandra. Or as happy as he could be, for him. Truthfully, if you really think about it, he has always had the same kind of airs as a fairy."

Sandra looked surprised and prepared to defend him, until she realized her wise friend had given her an important insight. Jason had always been a bit of a loner, aloof, a little snobbish even and different than others. That had drawn her to him in the strange way that love can work. He tended to see life as a little jaded and full of irony, while she approached everything as possible and positively. She suspected that Jason, like Birdie just did, had seen this difference between them sooner than she had.

"I love you, Bird," she said, squeezing her. "You are by far the best friend anyone, ever, anywhere, in the whole of the world, has ever had."

"Hey, wait a minute, what about me?" Spence said, running up behind them and just catching the last of their conversation. These two were his best friends, too.

"Spence!" they both said at the same time, completely delighted to see him. "Of course you are the greatest best friend ever, too," said Sandra, meaning it. "Right, Birdie?"

"Times one hundred!" Birdie said with a smile. "Now, catch us up on what you'll be working on while we're all home on St. Annalise together for a change."

"I'm here actually to add new features to the communication tower for Equator Pole Village so all three of the Poles can link into systems together and talk easily," Spence said. "Network Naters and I are both pretty excited about it. I'm headed over to meet him in the village. Gotta run in fact."

With that, he sprinted off, gave a wave, and called back, "Bye, best friends ever!" flashing them both a big grin as they grinned back.

"Bird, I need a big favor again," Sandra said, back to being serious, as they got closer to Equator Village.

"Of course, anything at all," Birdie said without a speck of hesitation. She knew Sandra would never ask her to do something unreasonable.

"Can you run Equator Pole with Gunny?" she asked. "I haven't talked to him yet but I really need him here to oversee the construction and then I need you here for everything else, including making sure things go well between the elves and the islanders like you did before. And right now, particularly with Santa still gone, I'm needed most at the North Pole."

"Of course, I'll do it," Birdie said. "I would have been disappointed if you didn't ask me."

"Thanks so much," Sandra said. "I know I said I was going to take this week off to be here but that is a luxury right now. My to-do list is really long and I lost that whole week over Jason. But, I'm done with all that, I have things to do and I'm needed more than ever. Starting with," she took a deep breath, "flying out tomorrow to visit the elves at the South Pole."

"Sandra, really?" Birdie said. "With who?"

Sandra pointed at herself. "Just me and Em this time." She refused to look at her friend, knowing she wouldn't like that answer.

She was right. Birdie felt instantly concerned about Sandra going anywhere by herself. "The Santanappers are still out there."

"I need to go," Sandra said. "I haven't told anyone but you so there's no fear I'll be taken. It's my true second home and I need to see it for myself, not to mention, conducting a Santa check on how they are all doing. Besides, Em will be with me. She's on alert mode these days since the Santanapping so anyone should be scared to try something with her around." They both laughed at that thought.

"Okay, but I already know Gunny is going to be mad, mad, mad when he gets here tomorrow," Birdie said.

"I know. That's part of the reason I have to head out before he arrives," Sandra said. "And to avoid Ghost. I swear that brother of his turns up in the darndest places when I'm around. Although, I have noticed he's been going back and forth to the ranch a little more often now, so maybe he won't hang here for long either."

"Sandra, it's obvious to everyone, but you, that he has a huge crush on you," Birdie said. "Jason didn't like him at all and I'm sure that's why. Well, that, and he helped beat him at Pole Pong probably." She grinned thinking about it. "Now that Jason's gone, though, you need to start getting in the dating game again. We could date twins!"

"Noooo way, Bird! There's something just not right about that," Sandra said. "Maybe it's because he looks too much like Gunny or something. That alone would make it weird. Those three Holiday boys could be triplets!"

"It's true!" Birdie said, laughing. "Suit yourself, but now I'm going to have him mooning all over when he finds out you're not here."

"Put him to work!" Sandra said, laughing and waving at the elves who were running toward them excitedly. "Thanks for the talk, bestee."

# # #

Sandra treated herself and took most of that day off. She had checked on work at the village, which was well underway with the ever busy elves, and then she had handed oversight to Birdie. From there, she had headed to her favorite beach for the best therapy she knew: surfing.

She had spent hours in the water. Catching a wave, riding it in, thinking on things, going again. Catching a wave, riding it in, thinking on things, going again. By the time she came out of the water, she felt calmer – until she saw Mango come running up and her heart raced as she scanned the beach looking for him.

Instead, over the dunes came Christina out for a beach walk.

"He left Mango here?" Sandra said, for some reason feeling surprised.

"He did," Christina said. "You, me, and her. Tough on all of us." She bent down to pet Mango and throw her stick.

"Do you think he'll come back?" Sandra asked, trying to sound more nonchalant then she felt.

"I'm honestly not sure," Christina said. "I don't know if he even knows." Then after a moment, "I haven't heard anything from him since he left." Sandra could only imagine how hard that must be for a mother with her only child. Now seemed like a good time to share something with Christina she had thought about for months.

"Christina, thank you for taking care of me. I don't think I've ever told you that before, but thank you for being one of my unknown protectors for all of this time. I have felt safe on this island since the minute Cappie and I arrived on the *Mistletoe* all those years ago. That is a great gift you give to all of the academy students but none more than me and I could never thank you enough."

Christina looked at her with tears welling in her eyes and a big smile. "To see who you are and who you are becoming is more than thanks enough," Christina said.

The two spent time talking about the village and logistics with the elves and the academy until Sandra knew she needed to head for home and a visit with Cappie.

"Sandra," Christina said as she got ready to go. "I know it's my role to be concerned about you but I sense there is still more coming about this Santa business. Maybe it's just that I'm becoming a little jaded from the happenings the past few months and that Santa's still missing, but it seems like more than that. Just, everywhere you go, be careful. Keep people around. I don't think it's about you actually, but something doesn't feel right to me."

"Of course. Sure," Sandra said in return. She felt it wasn't the right time to tell her she was heading south tomorrow at sunbreak. Alone.

## CHAPTER 46

South Pole Ahead

Location: St. Annalise

Sandra did share her plans with Cappie but asked her not to share them with Thomas until after she was gone. Cappie reluctantly agreed, feeling in her own heart that Sandra was right and she would be safe. Em, of course, was going with her, since she was how Sandra would be getting there, but Sandra wanted Squawk to stay home.

" . . . *squawk*! . . . not fair . . ."

"Squawk, you know I always love having you with me, but it's too far for you to fly alone and I didn't bring your carrier because I hadn't planned to go. Besides, Birdie really needs you here to help with the barge building."

" . . . *squawk*! . . . not the same . . . *squawk*!"

"I'm going," Em said smugly.

"Only because you can get us there," Sandra said impatiently. "Otherwise, you would be staying home too."

"But I'm going," she said, smiling and looking at Squawk, who simply turned his tail feathers on her and walked out of the room as if he didn't hear her.

"I love you, Squawk," Sandra called to him, meaning it with all of her heart.

" . . . *squawk*! . . . I know . . . *squawk*!"

She smiled at her proud bird friend.

"I have to turn in, Cappie. I'm planning two nights there and then back," Sandra said. "No one but Birdie and you all know I'm going, not even the elves at the South Pole. I'm trying to be extra cautious since there is still no sense of where Santa is or who took him."

"Still nothing?" Cappie asked. Sandra just shook her head. It was too upsetting to think about, let alone talk about.

"Goodnight, Cap," she said, kissing her guardian affectionately on the cheek. "You coming, Em?

"In a few minutes," said the little green delgin. "Cappie is teaching me how to crochet."

"Really?" Sandra said smiling, knowing that would take a lot of patience from both of them. "Well, I'd like to put in my order now for a nice long Christmas scarf."

She found Squawk already asleep on his perch when she got to her berth. She tried to be quiet so she didn't disturb him.

"Good night, Squawk," she whispered.

" . . . *squawk* . . ." he managed quietly. " . . . love you . . . *squawk*"

Sandra smiled in the dark as she lay down on her bunk. No one had a better family than she did, she thought as she drifted off to sleep.

Very early the next morning, she woke up Em and gathered the few things she was taking with her. It was warm out already, but she dressed in layers, knowing that soon she would be quite cold even dressed in the layers. If she were riding in the *Mistletoe 2*, she would have been riding in comfort for sure. It even had a heater in it. This trip, however, was all going to be done bareback on Em. It would be challenging for Sandra since the trip was so long. The two were comfortable riding that way together, but they would be subjected to the weather come what may, which would be harder on Sandra then it would be on Em.

"Ready, Em?" she said to the little elf as they walked out on the deck and Em began to spin herself into her big size.

"Planning to go without this? Or me?"

The two startled early risers whipped their heads to the other side of the *Mistletoe* deck to see who else was up this early and talking to them. There stood Gunny looking a little stern.

"Gunny?" Sandra said, walking over to where he stood next to the *Mistletoe 2* saddle as Em began to spin.

"You really didn't think I'd let you go clear to the South Pole without me," he said.

"Well yes, especially since I hadn't mentioned it to you," Sandra said, now feeling a little annoyed at whoever had told him. She couldn't believe Cappie or Birdie would break her trust. He seemed to sense her concerns.

"Before you accuse anyone of telling me you were going, no one did," he said, shrugging and lugging the big saddle over toward the now full-size Em. "I could use a hand here," he said. The saddle was large for one person alone to load.

"How'd you get it here?" Sandra said, as she pulled it along with him.

"Had some help by some of the elves," he said, as they both pushed hard to get it on the wriggling-around delgin's back. "I figured in the long run it would be good to have a *Mistletoe 2* here on the South Pole Village barge and one at North Pole Village as well. And then I got to thinking on what I would do if I were you and down here for a while. So I had them help me bring it here to the *Mistletoe*. I figured I'd just wait around a bit and see if you were as much like me as I thought you might be. If you didn't get up, I would have just left it and met up with you later. But, here we are."

He could be maddening at times on how well he knew her, she thought as she snapped the saddle in place and straightened to go.

"Well, thank you, Gunny. Yes, I am heading to the South Pole as I understand you already deduced." He nodded.

"And I need to be going to catch as much sunlight as possible for the easiest and safest trip, so if you would just step aside--" she paused, motioning him back with her hands.

"Nope," he said not budging. "Not going to do that, Sandra."

"Gunny, this is not your decision."

"Now that's where you and I see it differently," he said, wrapping a scarf around his neck. "Cause I see it as I'm your friend and I'm going with you."

"Don't you mean, you're my guardian?" she said a little angrily, annoyed by this change to her plans, but doubting her wishes would prevail.

"No," he said, looking right at her. "I mean I'm your friend. That's why I want to go. All the rest is incidental. It's safer for you to have a friend along." He gave her a look that asked her to understand.

"Gunny," she said hesitantly, trying to figure out what she wanted and what to say to him.

"I'll take that as a 'yes!'" he said with his usual enthusiasm. "Now jump on up here. I'll let you drive."

"You'll let me?" she said, raising an eyebrow at his grinning face. Truth be known, she found herself welcoming the unexpected company and especially the gift he had brought of her saddle. Gunny just kept grinning at her and she finally grinned back.

"Fine, you get to go. But I mean it, Gunny. This is my trip so things need to go my way. Agreed?" she paused, blocking him from jumping up with her.

"Agreed. Now c'mon, let's get this big green delgin flying marvel in the air and fire up the cocoa maker," Gunny said, hopping on board.

Before he even sat down, Sandra snapped the reins, "To the South Pole, Em!" Gunny tumbled over the seat into the back. "Oh, riding coach class this trip, Mr. Holiday?" she said impishly, as he scrambled to get settled back up front with her and reached for the cocoa maker. "Make mine a tall with extra whip!" Sandra said as St. Annalise faded from view below.

# # #

Meanwhile, things weren't going well for Ghost. His brother had just left St. Annalise with the girl he wanted to know better, which would have been more than annoying if he had been there too. Instead, he had been called back to Happy Holiday Ranch. Nothing lately was going his way.

CHAPTER 47

Soath Pole!

Location: South Pole

"You said the elves helped you get the *Mistletoe 2* to St. Annalise," Sandra said. "Why not Ghost? Wasn't he coming too?"

"He got another one of his calls to get back to the ranch," Gunny said with a shrug. "I keep meaning to ask the Major what all of that is about, but I haven't had a chance to check in down there for a while. We've sort of been busy."

The two whiled away the many hours to the South Pole talking about all the things they'd been busy on, what all needed to happen next with the barge building, and hashing out any ideas they could think of on where Santa might be that they hadn't checked.

When they were just an hour away, Sandra finally radioed in to let the elves know she would soon be there.

"You'll be where?" Xylo said into the radio. "Over."

"To your South Pole outpost!" Sandra said smiling, knowing it was a big surprise. "Over."

"She's coming here!" Sandra heard Xylo shout before he got officially back to her more seriously. "Roger that, South Pole Santa. We've activated our South Pole tracking radar and picked up your location. Dervish and Periwinkle will be topside to wave you in. It's a good day for a visit, as visibility is clear. Over."

"Thanks, Xylo. We'll be there in forty-nine minutes according to my instruments. Over and out," said Sandra. She turned to her seat partner.

"I've never actually been here," she said excitedly. "I only flew by with Santa. I can't wait to see it.

"Gunny, thank you. This really was so much nicer in the *Mistletoe 2* and having your company made the time go by fast. Plus, the bonus was that we really got a lot of planning done!"

"I've never been down here either. I'm excited for the chance to visit too. Look," Gunny said pointing. "I think I see the outpost beacon."

Em landed them safely right at the beacon where Dervish and Periwinkle waited all bundled up against the cold of the Antarctica ice plain.

"Sandra!" exclaimed Periwinkle, as Sandra climbed down out of the *Mistletoe 2,* happy to be standing on land again even if it was cold and icy land. "We can't believe you're here!" She hugged on Sandra and then Em hard. "Em! Can you believe you're at the South Pole, cousin?"

Em gave a little huff. She didn't talk much when she was her full delgin size.

"Hey, how 'bout a big hug like that for me?" Gunny said as the little blue elf turned, smiling, happy to accommodate the request. The elves all loved Gunny. He liked to joke around and elves love to laugh. "Gunny!" she exclaimed. "I just can't believe three of my favorite people are here."

"Peri, let's not keep them out here," Dervish said in his practical way, directing them to the first of the four small, unobtrusive buildings.

While the outside of the buildings were plain to blend in better with the surroundings, the inside rooms were bright and cheery with the feeling of Christmas year-round. The whole group of South Pole elves were gathered to greet them and piled on the minute they got the outside door shut. As far as Sandra was concerned, there was nothing better in the world than an elf hug pile!

There wasn't a lot to see at the outpost really. The four buildings were each connected by a hall. The first building was for maintenance, equipment, transportation parking, and storage. The next building was the central workspace with some offices and a large communications control tower, which was the main function of the location – tracking Santa on Christmas Eve in the southern hemisphere. The third building was where the elves spent most their time. It was comprised of four rooms. One was a gym where Sporty kept them all busy, moving and playing; one was a big room that could be set up for things like bingo games and craft projects; one was set up with a giant-screen TV and comfortable chairs, and one was the most popular room of all - the dining room. Whatever Noelly was cooking up for that night smelled divine.

"We're having cinnamon roll bread pudding for dinner," said Noelly.

"Hooray!" some of the elves shouted.

"With coconut & fruit cocktail on the side," she added. There were no "hoorays" to fruit. The elves still didn't welcome healthy choices much.

"And cinnamon roll snicker-doodles for dessert," she said.

"HOORAY!" Now all the elves were shouting. Noelly smiled.

"Well I, for one, am ready to eat," said Sandra.

"Me too!"

"And me!"

"And me!"

And so it went until every elf said something. They all sat down to a long table together. Tea and Sugar, who helped Noelly as well as ran craft projects, games, and other activities at the South Pole, and put on sparkly silver and gold Southern Light shows, formally served the three guests first despite their objections.

"Now, now," Noelly said. "Let us have the fun of serving our guests."

It was late when they wrapped up the very fun meal and headed for the last building of the four where the dorm rooms were located. Most of the rooms were set up to house elves, but two of the rooms had been reserved for taller folks – with Santa and Mrs. Claus and any full-size guests in mind – so Sandra and Gunny found they had comfortable quarters to crash in. For once, Em chose to sleep away from Sandra and bunked in for cousin talk with Periwinkle.

As "good nights" rang down the hall, Sandra kicked off her shoes and crawled into bed without even changing. She was exhausted but it was her favorite kind of tired. The kind that came about from having too much fun.

CHAPTER 48

Round Trip

Location: South Pole

"Sandra. Sandra, wake up."

"What? No, too early," Sandra said groggily, rolling over.

"Sandra, we gotta go."

"What time is it?"

"Three fifty-five."

"In the morning?" she said incredulously, not believing she was being woke up. "Gunny! Go away!"

"I wish I could, but a storm is blowing in fast and we have to get out."

Sandra flipped over to see Gunny and Dervish standing there. "You really do have to go, Sandra," said Dervish. "The storm is too big. If you don't get out ahead of it, you could end up here for weeks and weeks."

She was wide awake now. This was going to be one quick trip.

"Is Em ready?" she asked.

"Network Naters is getting her up now," said Gunny.

"Try not to wake anyone else, please. They all need their sleep," she said, reaching for her shoes.

They headed quietly out to the hall – right into the rest of the barely awake elves looking sad and worried.

"Now, now," Sandra said, taking in the looks quickly and reaching down to hug them all. "We will be fine. You all know that. I have Gunny with me and Em is the very best delgin in the world at keeping this Santa safe."

Em flashed her green light, which set off Periwinkle's blue and Tea and Sugar's pretty silver & gold colors as well. Sandra didn't feel worried at all. She just felt happy.

"Okay, I'm so sorry I have to leave early and we can't do all the things we planned on today, but you know that I love you and I'll be back for more time in the future. For now, we all have this beautiful memory of fun, right?"

Her nice words made the tired elves tear up. Dervish and Network Naters, though, were all business. "Okay, that's it for this goodbye," Dervish said. "Em, are you ready to spin?"

"Yep," she said, heading for the far building with everyone right behind her.

Sandra and Gunny stopped only long enough to get their scarves and hats on, and with one last hug of everyone, they climbed onto the *Mistletoe 2*. "Raise the door please, Dervish," Sandra called out when they were all set.

"Wait, please, wait!" came a soft voice that Sandra almost missed. From a far corner of the room, in the very highest spot, hidden from view, came a pretty, very little fairy orb.

"It's Quisp," Sandra heard Tea tell Sugar. Sandra had heard there was a fairy at the Pole, but when she had asked about her the night before, Periwinkle had told her Quisp was too shy to come out and meet her. That was okay with Sandra. She knew some relationships took time.

"Sa-sa-sandra," the little fairy managed to stutter out, clearly battling against her extreme shyness.

"Well, Quisp," Sandra said warmly, wanting to be sure the tiny, brave fairy felt safe with her. "How nice of you to come see us off!"

The orb flickered a bit, zig-zagged about, and then darted off back to her corner. "Quisp," Sandra called out to her. "Thank you for visiting me. Ready, Em?"

"Ready, Sandra!" Em called.

"Ready, Gunny?" she asked, smiling at her seat mate.

"Ready, Sandra!" Gunny said, playing along.

The door began to open, and out flew the little fairy again. She dropped something in Sandra's lap, zipped away, and out the door they flew!

"Goodbye, everyone!" Sandra called as the door closed on the waving elves as quickly as it opened.

She looked in her lap to see that the shy little fairy had dropped her a note. "I love you, Sandra Claus..." it read in sparkle ink.

Everything about being South Pole Santa was better than she imagined, she thought again, wiping away a tear as the outpost fell away and they moved far above the threatening storm.

"No one would have loved me as much, island girl," Gunny said softly, using one of his affectionate terms for her, having read the note and understanding the tear. "Santa is a wise old guy."

They got back to St. Annalise in record time and set down just outside of Equator Pole Village. Em quickly changed to her elf self and ran off to tell the elves all about their adventure. Elves loved to have a story to tell.

"Gunny, thank you again. That was more fun than I thought it would be, even though it didn't last as long as planned! I know you say you didn't come along because you're my guardian. Would coming along to oversee me like a big brother be a better analogy?" she laughed, thinking he would find that entertaining.

He looked at her for a long minute across the *Mistletoe 2* they were carrying together before setting his side down and walking over to her. "I don't know, Sandra," he said, tilting her chin with his hand so she was looking up at his eyes. "Does this seem like a big brother thing?" With that, he leaned down and kissed her with both tenderness and meaning behind it and then jauntily walked away whistling.

CHAPTER 49

What to do? What to do?

Location: North Pole Village/St. Annalise

After the big kiss at St. Annalise, Sandra had tried her best to avoid Gunny for days. She needed time to think about her feelings and why she was always caught off-guard by how guys thought about her. She had been crazy about Jason for years, with never a sign from him that he cared for her at all, before that magical Christmas Eve when he had kissed her on the *Mistletoe*. In the end, he had dumped her and broken her heart and, just like when he kissed her the first time, she hadn't seen it coming. Then she got that wild hallway kiss from Ghost, which she chalked up to being just a Christmas mistletoe thing, but, more recently, it had come to seem, even to her, like he had a crush on her. And then there was Gunny.

During the South Pole Santa competition, despite being competitors, she had begun to get a crush on him. He was funny and strong and seemed to like her too. He had squashed those feelings, though, when he had taken off without so much as a "congratulations" when she was selected over him for South Pole Santa or a "goodbye" when he left. Not to mention, he had Santanapped her on top of it! She wasn't sure she could ever trust Gunny enough to return any feelings he might have for her.

One evening, despite her best efforts at avoiding him, Gunny had tracked her down and apologized. "I know you're not over Jason," he had said. "I can be very patient when I need to be, but I couldn't have you thinking that I think of you as my little sister. I *never* think of you as my little sister." He had grinned a sort of wicked grin at her.

"I do still have feelings for Jason even though I haven't heard anything from him since the day he left. But the feelings are a little less each day and I think my heart is healing. But you and me? I'm not sure." Sandra preferred to be honest with him, even if it was a little bit too direct.

He hadn't pressured her for more. "Hey, the heart loves who the heart loves," he said, trying to be lighthearted. "I won't push you."

And he hadn't. But somehow knowing how he felt had started to change her own feelings for him, and the idea of Gunny as a boyfriend wasn't something as awful as it had used to seem. It was a thought that, every now and then, actually made her smile.

Even if there had been strong feelings between them, there wouldn't have been time enough to pursue them anyway. The weeks and months had kept speeding along. Sandra divided her time between the North Pole and St. Annalise pretty equally. She marveled at how much life seemed fine, even happy most days, despite Santa still missing. Each month on the twenty fourth, a photo of Santa and one or two of the reindeer would arrive with Santa holding a recent newspaper and his "Ho Ho Hoo" note scribbled in the border. There had been no real clues other than the Sherlocks felt he was being held somewhere hot. Through the summer months, he had his coat and hat off in all of the photos and even the reindeer looked hot. That still left a whole lot of the world to search since much of the world was hot that time of the year.

With Santa still gone, every day Sandra had long to-do lists to complete. A typical week included:

- Meet with the Claus Council
- Presentation to the Elves Merry Makers group
- Swim session with Dear Lovey
- Send email to Esteemed Council with update on Santa
- Review toy supply with Tack
- Plan Secret Pal act of kindness
- Review Kindness List Reports

The last two items were her favorite things to do. Every month on the seventh for Secret Pal Day, fun just buzzed in the air. Sandra was proud of how well the elves were doing at keeping their secret pals a secret. That she knew of, there had only been three elves that had told, guessed, or discovered who their secret pals were and they all agreed to just forget they knew. Sandra still had no idea which elf was her secret pal, but she loved the little treats and nice things he or she kept doing for her. She found she looked forward to the seventh of each month as much as anyone else. In fact, being the secret pal for Gunny had been more fun since they had gone to the South Pole together. She looked forward to figuring out something unique for him each month.

The Kindness List Reports though – or the KLRs as they had become known -- were beyond fun for her to review! Every single day the kind things children were doing for their families, their friends, and best of all, as far as Sandra was concerned, for others they didn't even know, came in by the tens of thousands! Kind acts were happening everywhere! She especially loved reading the nice things children everywhere were doing for animals and their little brothers and sisters.

"Sandra, the number of kind acts being reported has doubled since you did your tour of those three cities and so many more requests keep coming in for visits from you. Not so many ask for Santa right now, which is unusual, but good, under the circumstances. They keep asking for you to talk on kindness," Breezy said as she worked her way through another bag packed full of kind acts. The multi-talented elf was now the official overseer of the "Kindness List."

"I'm sure they would love to have Santa too," Sandra said. "It's just that they've seen me more recently. I wish I had time to do more visits but you know that is really unlikely this year. At least until December.

"These stories are the best! The absolute best!" she said again out loud. Breezy just smiled. Sandra said pretty much the same thing after every letter she read.

The one letter Sandra never got, though, was one from Jason. From the minute he shut the door on their relationship in May, she hadn't heard anything from her old boyfriend. She knew she shouldn't have expected to really, but she still thought about him most days and wondered how he was doing. Every day, however, got a little easier and she had found she was happy again despite the heartbreak. Besides, she always had Ghost hanging around ready to help her get past Jason when she was ready. He seemed to be everywhere and, like his brother, had a keen sense on how he could help her, making him quite useful to her and the Pole. He was often immature, and could be totally rude at times, but he pulled at her in a way no one but Jason had in the past.

He looked uncannily like his older brother and had the same kind of intensity to him. His mood swings were far greater than Gunny's, though. Ghost could be light and happy one minute, and then get a call from the ranch about things that needed done there, and be stoic and sour the next. Sandra didn't like how he could change so quickly. When he was in a good mood, though, she enjoyed being around him. He enjoyed sports as much as she did, and the nights she could get away for a good game of racquetball or some Pole Pong were full of big laughs for her.

That was what was happening at the North Pole, but her work days at St. Annalise were just as busy. A typical day there included:

- Reviewing the progress of the barge building
- Meeting with the various planning committees. She enjoyed meeting with the interior design group the

most right now since the finishes for each room were fun to pick out.

- Meeting with Spence and sometimes Network Naters on new technology possibilities.
- Checking inventory supplies so they didn't run out of whatever they needed.
- Fixing the sno-cone machine. For some reason, the machine kept acting up and the elves had come to love the crunchy, cold treat.
- Surfing whenever she could get the chance!

She enjoyed being at St. Annalise every other week, but her days there tended to be even longer than her days at the Pole. One evening, late, Sandra sat on the beach, thinking about her great life on St. Annalise and now as South Pole Santa. She sat thinking about Santa, the elves, her friends, her parents, Cappie, the kiss from Gunny, and the complication of Ghost. If she wanted to date a Holiday brother, which one should she date? She pondered that thought a bit before moving on to think about someone else. In this case, that was still Jason, even as she began to consider a new relationship. As she thought his name, she heard him call her own.

"Saaaaaaandraaaaaa!"

It came to her on the wind and she jumped to her feet whipping around in every direction to see where the voice had come from.

"Jason!" she called out. "Jason? Was that you?"

Nothing. There was nothing more. Just sea birds passing by.

"Of course it wasn't him," she said out loud to herself, swatting sand off her legs. "You need to keep it together, Cassandra. Don't mix a sea bird up with an old boyfriend." She smiled to herself before saying out loud. "It's an insult to the sea bird." She thought she was funny as she picked up her stuff and headed home to the *Mistletoe*.

# # #

Time hummed along, but as the weeks crept closer to Christmas, a darkness was creeping into the edges of each day. A darkness related to Santa being gone. Where was he? What were they going to do? The questions were getting whispered more and more frequently as the concern grew. Then the photo of Santa and the newspaper came in October and everything changed again. A truly dark day indeed had arrived. Santa looked stressed in the photo and there was no reindeer at all with him. But that wasn't the worst of it. There in red pen was the "Ho Ho" note but this time it read, "Ho Ho Hoooo." Four o's! Santa's code for distress! Something now was terribly wrong.

CHAPTER 50

Say it Isn't Sooooo

Location: North Pole Village

"Hey, Zinga, how you doing?" Gunny said as the efficient elf came clipping along the hallway.

"Fine, Gunny. The newest photo of Santa just came in. Sandra asked me to get it back to the Sherlocks," she said.

"Mind if I take a look first?" Gunny asked. He was always interested in the most recent update. Like Sandra, Gunny had been splitting his time between the North Pole and St. Annalise and was very busy. He hadn't had a chance to talk with Sandra or any of the rest about this latest arrival yet. Like everyone, Gunny had a growing concern about it being well into fall and they still had not found Santa Claus.

Zinga handed him the envelope.

This time in the photo, Santa held a copy of the *Honolulu Times*. Gunny scanned the photo quickly and saw the four O's in the "ho ho hoooo" message. His heart dropped. He knew what that meant. Santa was in trouble. Unlike all the others sent before it, however, this photo had been shot from a slightly wider angle. It was just a little bit different with more of the background behind Santa showing. As Gunny looked at the scene, he realized he recognized something in the photo, and his heart began beating wildly.

Suddenly a lot of things from the past months became clear as an array of emotions flooded through him. Despair came first, which quickly changed to denial, and then full-on anger. An intensity of anger more than he could remember ever feeling before followed by a big dose of bewilderment. There was no time to try to understand the whys. There was only time for action because that photo made one thing crystal clear:

Santa, dear, wonderful, Santa Claus, beloved by the world and missing for so many months, was being held at Happy Holiday Ranch. His own home ranch and he knew just the guy to talk to about it.

"Zinga, how about I deliver this to the Sherlocks?" he tried to sound casual while his heart raced. "Have you happened to see Ghost?"

"I think he headed back to Texas again yesterday, Gunny," Zinga said. "I can check with Barney--" She stopped talking as she realized Gunny was already way down the hall heading in the direction of the stables.

CHAPTER 51

Gunny, Ghost & the Big Guy

Location: Happy Holiday Ranch (which wasn't feeling so happy)

"Ghost! GHOST! Ma, where's Ghost?"

"Well, hello to you too, Mr. Gunny Holiday," said Josie. "I don't see my handsome son for months and this is how you greet your mother? Screaming for your brother?"

"Sorry, mom," Gunny said, slowing down for a minute. The ride to the ranch had felt impossibly long even taking an express coach. It had given him time to study and think, however, and his conclusion had stayed the same as much as he hated it: Santa was being held on the ranch and Ghost knew where.

It explained why Ghost had come and gone so often back and forth to the ranch. It explained why it felt like there was an "insider" involved. They thought it was a fairy, but no, it was HIS OWN BROTHER! The words were shouting in his head.

It also explained why Ghost had seemed so wishy-washy the past months. Gunny had always been close to all his brothers but Ghost had been distant. It had concerned Gunny, but he'd assumed it was about Sandra. "Yeah, and wouldn't you know, in a weird way, it was," he said out loud to himself. What he couldn't figure out was why Ghost would take Santa. That part didn't make any sense and gave him the tiniest bit of hope that he could be wrong.

He walked over and gave his mother a big squeeze and a kiss on the cheek. "Sorry, ma," he said again. "Just lots going on and I need Ghost's help with something big."

"Well your moody brother has been coming and going with barely a word to anyone. What is it you all are working on anyway?" she said. "Oh, never mind, I know it's all secret North Pole stuff. Come in and say hello to the Major and your sisters."

While that sounded like a warm invitation, Gunny knew it really was an order wrapped up to look like an invitation. He couldn't blame his mom for it. He hadn't been there for months and then he comes storming in looking for his little brother with not so much as a nice "hello" to any of them.

"Absolutely," he said to his mom, realizing how much he had missed her and the others. "I would love to see them all." He held the door into the house for his mom and then stepped through himself to squeals from his youngest sister.

"Gunny!" Glory called out. "You're home!" She ran over to hug him as his sister Blue came out of the kitchen smiling and hugged the other side.

"Well, I'll be a wild turkey," the Major said, getting up out of his comfortable chair where he was working the crossword puzzle from the *Honolulu Times* Gunny noticed with a grimace. "I do have five sons after all. I was beginning to forget about this one." He clapped his son's shoulders affectionately and Gunny reached out and gave him a big Texan hug.

"So good to see you too, Major," Gunny said, feeling the happiest he had in hours. This family of theirs would get them through whatever was ahead.

"You're here just in time for lunch, brother of mine," Glory said, bringing out a big platter of sandwiches to the table. He was going to object and then thought better of it. He was hungry and could use a shower.

"Of course I am," he said, stealing a sandwich off the platter, grinning as he sat down at the table. "I know how good the food is around here."

After a quick but delicious lunch, made especially great by setting aside his worries and catching up with members of his family, Gunny grabbed one of the ranch trucks and went out to find his brother. Or Santa. He suspected he'd find both.

The building Santa was being held in had the Holiday Ranch brand burned into one of the wood slats on one of the walls. That's what Gunny had seen in the wider angle photo. It was just a little bit of it, but he'd recognize their ranch brand anywhere, even a small part of it, in a Santanapping photo.

There were actually several buildings like that on the ranch. If he needed to, he would check them all. But Gunny had a theory. The day he and Sandra had tried to find Santa using her locket they had been booted out into the middle of one of the most remote parts of the ranch – with a single outbuilding in the distance. That was where he was headed.

The dirt road he was using gave him the advantage of seeing the building before anyone at the location could see him. As he neared the spot, he could see Ghost's truck parked next to it and Ghost out waving his arms in the air talking to someone, though Gunny couldn't see anyone. His brother was either really losing it or there was magic afoot with this Santanapping. He parked the truck and decided to quietly walk his way in from there.

He didn't have to go too far before he could hear his brother. It wasn't that hard since he was yelling loudly.

"You are not moving him!" he was shouting. "Yes, this was my stupid idea. Very stupid idea, but it has gone on way too long! I wanted to let them all go MONTHS ago!" He kicked at the dirt around him. Gunny could finally see he was talking to two murky-colored fairy orbs. He'd never seen that color of orbs before and assumed the color didn't indicate anything good. He'd heard about fairies gone bad, and it was just like his brother to hook up with them.

Right then, out of the building, came two of the tallest beings Gunny had ever seen with very long thin legs and arms. He had no idea what species they were. Between them they held Santa like he was a ragdoll with a bag pulled over his head.

"Put him down!" Ghost was now shouting at the tall guys. "This ends right now!" He reached to grab Santa and one of them flicked a long finger at him as if he was an annoying insect of some sort. He went flying back, rolling end over end in the dirt until he stopped at last and lay there, not moving. Gunny ran back to the truck. He'd seen all he needed to see.

He barreled down the road, toward the outbuilding, revving his engine and blaring on his horn. The noise seemed to bother the tall beings since they both reached up and covered their ears, dropping Santa. Ghost managed to get up and limp his way over to Santa, pushing and pulling him over to his truck. Gunny stayed on the horn and the two giant dudes, after staring at him with menacing eyes, finally ran, hands over their ears, taking great strides. With their long legs they were soon out of sight, the murky-colored fairies flying right beside them.

"Gunny," Ghost said, sobbing, so glad to see his brother. He knew his brother would be extremely angry at him – he deserved the rage and more – but right at that moment he was just so thankful to see him. He had nearly lost Santa for good and the full despair of the situation came to him as he leaned Santa against the truck and fell to the ground totally dejected. Pain shot up his arm. He realized it must have been broken when the walking stick tossed him, along with a rib or two, judging by how much pain just breathing was causing him.

Gunny went right to Santa and pulled the bag from his head. "Santa! We've been waiting months for this day. I am so glad to see you," Gunny said, relief pouring over him as he reached over and hugged the beloved figure, who was blinking against the bright sunlight.

"Not as glad as I am to see you," Santa said, his eyes beginning to adjust. "Can you get my hands untied?" He turned so Gunny could get them undone.

"Are the reindeer inside?" Gunny asked as he undid the ties.

"Not anymore," Santa said, nodding behind Gunny. There they all were. Prancing about, out in the open for the first time in ten months!

"Guys!" Gunny said. "I'm so glad to see you. Everyone okay?"

One by one, they all nodded their heads. Then Dasher saw Ghost lying there and came, well, dashing over. Ghost was pretty sure he was going to stomp on him but he made no move to protect himself. He deserved it. Instead, the reindeer bent down and nudged him. Ghost just sat there. Dasher nudged him again. He knelt down with one of his front legs and Ghost finally realized he was trying to help him get up.

"Brother of mine, I could wring your neck right now but you went and got yourself hurt. I want to help you up but can you tell me first, what all is hurting?" Now that Santa was secure, Gunny had moved over to check on his brother and was offering him a hand to get up.

Ghost reached out with his good arm and Gunny pulled him up. A little bit hard – like a mad brother would. "Thanks," Ghost mumbled to both Gunny and Dasher. Then he turned to Santa.

"I am so so sorry, Santa," he wailed. "It was never supposed to go this way. I just wanted you to be gone for a little bit of time so you could see how Gunny would be as second Santa since he would need to fill in for you and then you would reconsider your choice. But then I met Sandra and right away, I mean right away, I knew how wrong I was and how right she was for the role. Sorry, brother." He paused and looked over at Gunny, who was just taking it all in and starting to understand it now.

"So I wanted to let you go right away. But these other guys - this 'Band of Baddies' I had hired out of the *Magic Times* want ads you had left in your room once from one of your visits, Gunny - they wouldn't let me. They put the building in some kind of a magic bubble so other magic folk wouldn't be able to use magic to find them, and Santa and the reindeer couldn't get out."

That must have been what happened to Sandra and me, Gunny thought, thinking of the many times he and Sandra kept bouncing out and away from Santa when they were trying to find him with the locket.

Ghost continued. "They kept saying, 'another month, just another month.' I kept looking for a way to break the magic spell so I could let Santa and the reindeer go. Sometimes that's how I used my time at the Pole - talking to the elves and fairies about magic spells.

"But then the Baddies started threatening to hurt people if I found a way to let Santa go. I thought at first it was just because they needed the money I was giving them, but after a while I realized they never meant to let him go from the very beginning. If I had taken Sandra too, as I had originally planned, they wouldn't have let her go either. I came early one day and overheard them scheming on how to get a new Santa in place from the other realm. One that wasn't as nice and that they could control better and that would fire Sandra. I threatened them that I'd go to the Esteemed Magical Council myself if they did, but then when I came back today I caught them planning to leave the reindeer and move Santa. It probably would have been to somewhere we never would have found them. And then you came, Gunny, just in the nick of time."

"The Saint Nick of time you mean," Santa joked, laughing to himself.

"I am so sorry, Santa," Ghost said again, not laughing at all, or even smiling. "Gunny, can you stop me back at the ranch to say goodbye to everyone before taking me to Sheriff Cody?"

Gunny just gave a nod. He hated it, but it had to be done.

"Now wait just a minute," Santa said. "From my perspective, I've just been rescued and I don't believe that I want to press any charges. Yes, I'm very disappointed in you, Ghost, but I believe you tried to make things right. You gave me regular updates on how things were going at the Pole, snuck out the update photos, and brought me all those letters from the children which helped me stay busy.

"Gunny, your brother, despite the trouble he created, kept us well fed and hydrated. He brought things to keep us comfortable and sometimes at great risk to himself, he stood up to those miserable magical beings. In different circumstances, you would have been proud of him."

Gunny looked at his brother with surprise. He was pleased that Ghost had managed to do the right thing in the middle of the wrong thing. It was a lot like how Ghost was every day, he realized.

"Good job on the letters from the children," was all he said. Ghost nodded somberly.

"They shouldn't have to suffer because I acted stupidly."

"As far as the reindeer and I are concerned," Santa said. "We just chose to work from a different location."

Ghost and Gunny were standing there now, looking at Santa with their mouths wide open, taking in the gist of what he was saying. Santa, the kind man of the North Pole, wasn't going to press charges. Ghost wouldn't go to jail!

There was still a lot to figure out but, understandably, Santa and the reindeer wanted to head home. Gunny went inside to get Santa's hat, collect the letters, and pick up anything else that had been left behind. He caught a glimpse of one of the mud-colored fairies as he walked out the door.

"Hey," he said waving Santa's hat at it. "Get outta here, you scumbag!" It buzzed toward him, flashing some kind of bright light, and then buzzed away.

The reindeer had managed to nudge, push, and pull Santa's sleigh out into the open and Ghost was working with Santa to get them tethered in. Gunny threw the letters into the sleigh and handed Santa his hat.

"One more thing, gentlemen, about this incident before I head back. You should know that I don't plan to tell anyone – not Sandra, not the Sherlocks, maybe not even Mrs. Claus – where I was. It will remain a North Pole mystery and myth eventually. It means you can't tell anyone that you rescued us either, I'm afraid, Gunny."

"Ah, Santa, are you kidding?" Gunny said feeling terrible that Santa would be worried about that.

"My own brother Santanapped you and kept you hidden for ten months! I don't want credit for anything. I just hope you'll allow me to be of service to you and the children of the world still, Santa. My family is now deeply in your debt."

"Because of me, sir. No one else knew, just me," Ghost said, speaking up. "I have a lot to be making up for that is going to take me a very long time."

"Very true, Ghost, very true," Santa said. "Gunny, this was not your fault. It is I who is in debt to you, for all you've helped Sandra with while I've been away, and for finding us today.

"And speaking of being away, boys, let's go home. What do you say?" Santa called out to his reindeer team.

The reindeer team, with Rudolph at the front, all nodded and snorted and pawed at the ground.

"All right then, up, up, and away!" Despite their months of not flying, the sleigh lifted off effortlessly. "See you at the Pole, boys!"

The two Holiday brothers watched the sky until Santa and the reindeer were long out of sight.

"If your arm wasn't broken, I'd be tempted to leave you out here right now without any truck keys," Gunny finally said.

"I wouldn't blame you," was all Ghost said in return. "You gonna tell her?"

"You mean am I going to tell Sandra you took Santa, which has made her sick with worry more than she lets on about where he's been, and if the kidnappers would be back for her next? Am I going to tell her that the reason I Santanapped her and she is STILL trying to forgive me for that was that my own brother took Santa?"

Ghost just listened knowing all of it was true.

"You can't make me hate myself more than I already do, Gunny," he said.

"You want to know the thing that is hardest for me in all of this?" Gunny said, looking at his little brother believing that he felt awful. "It's knowing in your own crazy way, you did this for me. For me! Ghost, you had to know I would never want to be Santa in this way." He was almost begging him for assurance that his little brother knew that about him. Ghost just sobbed and wiped at his face with his sleeve. Gunny continued, feeling so conflicted about the whole situation.

"I'm not going to tell her, and you aren't either. I never want her to know. You get that? She's just getting over Jason hurting her. It would hurt her too much to know this about someone she trusts. She trusts you, Ghost! We Holiday boys have a way of hurting her when we're not even trying." He kicked at the dirt out of frustration. He didn't want to think about it anymore.

"Grab your stuff and let's go. Can you drive with that arm?"

"I can."

"Then let's skip stopping at the ranch house and go get it set at Docs." Gunny said, turning to his own truck. "And, Ghost, no words to anyone ever on this and nothing like it ever again. You got me?"

"I got you. Never again. Thanks for somehow knowing where he was and rescuing Santa – and me."

"That's what big brothers are supposed to do. Sometimes you may make me mad - real mad this time – but you're my little brother. I love you, even when you screw up."

"I don't deserve it," Ghost said glumly. "But I'm sure glad you do."

Gunny climbed into his truck and just sat there a minute, the full implications of what had just happened fully hitting him. This was such a different ending to finding Santa than he had thought about so many times. In his dreams, he and Sandra and the Sherlocks always went storming in, overcame the bad guys, and saved Santa. Hooray! But there was no hooray moment when you were rescuing Santa from your own brother. Just disbelief and sorrow.

CHAPTER 52

The Overdue Homecoming

Location: North Pole Village

"Look! Look!" Elves everywhere were looking and pointing to the sky as Sandra wrapped up for the evening and was headed for her room at the hotel.

"IT'S SANTA!" It seemed the whole of the North Pole screamed those two words at once.

Sure enough, Santa and the reindeer were returning in grand style by looping and circling over North Pole Village so all would know of their return. Sandra, and every elf at the Pole, went running to the stables where they were getting ready to set down.

"SANTA!" The elves were all screaming at once as they scrambled to hug Santa and the reindeer, who normally pre-ferred not to participate in acts of overt affection but this time made a clear exception. Each reindeer was beaming back at the beaming elves.

"Ho Ho Ho!"

Sandra could hear Santa's jovial greeting as she ran to the stables herself. Santa was home! He was back! Just like that. Sandra released her own full inner elf as she too took her time squeezing hard on Santa and all of the reindeer. She finished her second round of hugs just as Mrs. Claus arrived, breathless.

"Make way! Make way!" Zinga was calling out.

"Kris!" Mrs. Claus said, tears flowing down her face.

"My darling, you are more beautiful than when I left," Santa said, hugging his wife to him. The two walked slowly, arm in arm the whole way, and the elves formed two lines for them to walk through, laughing and crying all along the way.

There were hundreds of questions but the answers could wait till later. Santa was home!

CHAPTER 53

Catching Up

Location: North Pole Village

Sandra hadn't been able to sleep that whole night. She tossed and turned as she thought back over the past two months and all that had happened.

Santa had returned with his story of being Santanapped by a Band of Baddies and finally escaping but not really knowing where they had kept them. Somewhere hot was all he would say. The Sherlocks found the answer very unsatisfying. Santa always knew where he was, they insisted. But Santa refused to discuss anything more about it except for talking on ways to increase the security around himself and Sandra. He wanted to put the question and experience behind him and focus on all there was to do to get ready for Christmas. Case closed.

While Santa had governance over the Sherlocks, he had no sway over the Esteemed High Council of the Magical Realm and they were not satisfied at all with Santa's answers or the outcome. As far as they were concerned, it was a wide open case and they had a full search on for the perpetrators. Every lead was being tracked down with particular attention on looking for the mud colored fairies. There were not many fairies that simply went completely bad, actually, so there was a small number to be looking for, and the Council had called for a full alert. A threat to any part of the magical world was a threat they would not tolerate.

Not surprisingly, Santa had called a Claus Council meeting the very next day after his return to get a full report on everything that had happened while he was gone. After hearing each of the elves give their updates, he sat for a moment, enjoying his sixth frosted sugar cookie and marveling at the creativity and innovation of his team under Sandra's leadership.

"Well maybe I should go away more often," he finally said.

"Nooooooo, Santa!" the whole group screamed out at once, none more loudly than Sandra. Technically, Mrs. Claus and the elves might be the happiest to see him, but Sandra felt she was definitely, without a doubt, the most relieved to see him. Christmas was getting too close.

"Dear Lovey," Santa said, turning to the smiling elf. "What marvelous advice and ideas you had for the elves during this stressful time. No wonder you are so good at your job. Thank you! I look forward to getting in on the Secret Pal drawing next year."

"I'll be your Secret Pal, Santa," said Em.

"Me too."

"And me."

"Not fair. I want to be his pal."

All the elves at the table piped up, not wanting to miss out on something so special.

"Now, now, elves, let's not worry on that this year. You all have secret pals and I have Mrs. Claus to be my official pal for this year," Santa said, enjoying the elf love coming his way.

"Well, okay, that's true," Em said. "I'll wait to be your secret pal next year, Santa."

"Not fair! You can't just decide that, Em," said Violet, giving her a glare.

"Yes, I can," said Em smugly, feeling glad she thought of it.

"No, you can't," said Toasty.

"Em, you remember that we draw names to decide our secret pals. I'm sure that's how we'll do it again next year," Sandra said, trying to head off another disagreement on the positive topic.

"Maybe I'll still get him," said the stubborn little delgin, crossing her arms and sitting back in her chair.

"Well, Santa, you'll at least be here for the big Secret Pal Reveal at this year's Christmas Cotillion dance," Zinga said. "I'm so excited. We weren't sure we would have the dance this year with you gone, but now that you're home we have even more to celebrate! I have to get our planning committee together. The dance is scheduled for December 7 on our normal monthly Secret Pal day."

"Oh, my goodness," said Breezy. "I have to get a dress."

"Me too," Birdie said. "I'm pretty sure Crow is going to ask me." She had a big smile on her face thinking about it.

Sandra would be going, but without Jason around, she doubted she would have a date. She hadn't seen Ghost in more than a week, and Gunny seemed to be just as invisible as Ghost the last few days. He didn't even know Santa was back, Sandra thought. He had sent a note that he was needed at the ranch and would be back as soon as possible. It wasn't like him, which made her feel that it must be something big to take up both Ghost and Gunny's time now. She hoped everything was okay and couldn't help but think how ironic it was that usually there was one too many Holiday boys around, and now, when she needed just one, they'd both disappeared.

"I'm excited to hear we have a Christmas Cotillion scheduled," boomed Santa over the many conversations that had broken out about it in the Council Room. "I always enjoy seeing Mrs. Claus in a new Christmas party dress.

"Now, one more thing, before we go," Santa said in a more serious tone. "I wish to thank all of you for running the Pole so well while I was kept away. You did an outstanding job and I could not be prouder of each of you." The little elves sniffled and reached for the tissue box.

"Sandra, those thanks go most to you," he continued. "You have shown us all how perfect a choice you are to be our South Pole Santa. You provided outstanding leadership in a time of great crisis and led this team with grace and commitment. Thank you."

When he finished, every person in the room – elf and human alike – jumped up and gave Sandra a standing ovation.

"Bravo! Bravo!"

She prepared to object, then thought better of it. She just grinned and bowed. It was a really great moment, after months of stress, and really great moments were meant to be enjoyed.

## CHAPTER 54

Ranch? Pole? Ranch? Pole!

Location: North Pole Village

Under orders from Gunny, even after he healed, Ghost wouldn't be returning to the North Pole this year. Or the South Pole or the Equator Pole. Ghost had objected, stating he had lots to make up for, but Gunny stayed firm. Ghost could start repaying his debt to Santa next year. For this year, Santa deserved a break from having to see him.

Gunny had stayed behind at the ranch himself. He needed time to think about whether or not he should return to the Pole that year too. Despite not knowing anything at all about Ghost's plans, Gunny still felt a sense of responsibility, and he couldn't help but wonder if Santa would feel the same way. It was Gunny's brother, after all, who had Santanapped Santa. That never would have happened if Gunny hadn't tried out for South Pole Santa and then complained about not getting it to his family. Ghost would have just stayed an anonymous, immature, teenage boy, working on the ranch, shooting at empty cans and breaking broncos, and still on Santa's Nice List, if Gunny hadn't pursued his dream of becoming South Pole Santa. Now that he knew it was Ghost who took Santa, he wasn't at all sure he could even face Sandra again.

He knew she would be excited Santa had returned and he was sure she would want to ponder with him over where Santa could have been. That thought alone kept Gunny at the ranch. Every time he made progress toward gaining her trust, something came up and pushed them even farther apart. He didn't want to lie to her, but he had promised Santa and Ghost that he would never tell what he knew. Not even to Sandra.

Soon, however, the decision of whether to stay at the ranch, or return to the Pole, was made for him when he received a note from Santa by North Pole express mail.

Gunny, we are in great need of your services here. When can we expect your return? Ho Ho Ho! Santa

If Santa wanted him back, as he clearly seemed to, then he was going back. Maybe he could just avoid seeing Sandra.

# # #

Ha!

Gunny thought about how he had actually considered he might be able to avoid seeing Sandra as he saw her smiling and waving at him as his coach landed. Normally, that was a sight he would have completely welcomed, but this time, well, he took a big breath before he climbed out of the coach.

"Gunny!" Sandra said, and actually came up and gave him a hug. Well, now, on the other hand, if staying a few days at the ranch got him this kind of welcome back, he thought, he'd be going home a lot more often.

"Well that is a mighty fine welcome back," he said to her, as she smiled a little shyly at him.

"I'm just so glad to see you," Sandra said sincerely. "It hasn't been the same up here without you and you heard that Santa is back, right? Some terrible fairies and tall creatures took him," she shivered. "Having him here again is even better than I had imagined! We've all been wearing our biggest smiles about it."

"I love seeing that smile on your face. It's already good to be back," Gunny said, still keeping an arm around her waist lightly, enjoying the close moment right up until Em came running up and threw herself in his arms, with Squawk following right behind her.

" . . . *squawk*! . . . welcome back . . . *squawk*!"

"Gunny!" Em squealed.

"Well, now, thank you very, very much, you three," he said, looking especially at Sandra. "This was a much better homecoming than I deserve." He grinned. It felt so good to be back at the Pole. The Ranch was his home of origin, but the North Pole was becoming his home of choice.

CHAPTER 55

Joke Telling

Location: St. Annalise

With Santa and Gunny back, Sandra had spent most of the next month overseeing things at Equator Pole herself. Big progress had been made on the South Pole Village barge and she was feeling good about how it was coming.

Sandra had got to the *Mistletoe* late every night. Most nights, Birdie and Cappie had already turned in, but when she got there that night, Cappie was sitting in one of the comfortable oversized deck chairs gazing at the clear night sky.

"Cappie, you're still up!" Sandra said, tired but so glad to see her. She went and snuggled in next to her and laid her tired head on her guardian's shoulder. Cappie loved these moments. "Is Squawk asleep already?" Sandra asked.

"Asleep and snoring. How was your day, my hard-working Santa girl?" Cappie said with concern and interest. Sandra worked too hard but Cappie knew she would have it no other way.

"Long, but good. Really good, actually, Cappie," Sandra said. "I'm feeling happy again." She knew Cappie had been worried about her after Jason left so she wanted to update her. "I love my job. It's hard, but so full of joy every day. I love the elves and you and Squawk and Rio and Em and Birdie and Spence and, well, just everyone really.

"And I especially love that everything worked out with Santa. It's strange that there are no answers about where he was, but the most important thing is that he's back.

"And I don't miss Jason like I did, and that is a really good thing too. And, Cap, Gunny kissed me and it wasn't an all bad thing."

She looked up and grinned at Cappie mischievously. Cappie was surprised at the declaration but couldn't help but grin back. She liked anyone who made her girl happy.

"Well, aren't the two of us just special as can be?" she said, still cradling Sandra. "Because, truth be told, Thomas kissed me – more than once – and it wasn't an all bad thing either." She grinned big as Sandra pulled back.

"Cappie! You should have told me immediately!" Sandra was completely happy about how that relationship was going for her guardian and their good friend.

Cappie decided to change the subject. "Okay, well besides gazing at this beautiful night sky and visiting with my Santa

girl, I had another reason for why I stayed up. To give you this."
She handed Sandra a big package in an oversized red and white
envelope clearly sent from the North Pole.

"A package for me? How nice," Sandra said. Most days
while she was there, the elves forwarded at least one bag of the
Kindness Acts children everywhere were sending in. She and
her elf team took time to be sure each one was read. Usually
they laughed and cried through the pile since acts of kindness
tend to be very emotional.

"So let's see what we have here," she said, ripping into the
envelope like an excited kid on Christmas. Inside she found a
big note in elf writing:

Happy, a little bit late, Birthday! Love, Your Secret Pal
Sandra's birthday had actually come and gone with little notice or fanfare this year. She had been adamant about it. Last
year, there had been such a big party and turnout for her and
Jason, whose birthday was the same day, so this year she had
just wanted something simple. She had spent her birthday
working, got lots of elf hugs, and got in some surfing. The
best thing that had happened is on her way home from surfing, she had found in her path, with no one around to explain
it, a large circle, drawn in the sand with three lines in it. Her
family symbol! When she was small, and her parents were
still with her, they had created the symbol to represent the
three of them in the world. Next to it there was a heart drawn,
and she knew with certainty in her own heart that both had
somehow been put there as a message to her from her parents

on her birthday. She did a happy dance right there in the sand as celebration.

That evening, Cappie had made dinner for the two of them and her close bunch of friends who were there on St. Annalise. Everyone had lingered and laughed till late on the back deck of the *Mistletoe*. As far as Sandra was concerned, the day had been perfect.

It was a couple days later now and Sandra thought it was very kind of her Secret Pal to remember her. She shook the envelope and out fell five photos. There was one of Squawk, one of Em, one of Santa, one of her with Cappie with both of them wearing funny hats, and one of her with Birdie and Spencer. She loved them all.

"Cap, remember this from the Merry May Day celebration? We were at Diva's hat shop. That was so fun! And this one was when Birdie, Spence, and I were watching the Bunny Hop line go by. How in the world did my Secret Pal get these without me noticing? These were perfect for today!"

Cappie knew Sandra was Gunny's secret pal. "What did you get your secret pal?" she asked. "I mean besides the kiss." She grinned, and Sandra swatted at her.

"That was a while ago now! See if I tell you anything anymore" Sandra said jokingly. "I know this sounds silly but he has seemed down so I got him a joke book. I think he liked it. He's been cracking the elves up with the bad jokes."

"Do you remember any?" Cappie asked.

"Of course! I'm part elf after all," Sandra said. "I remember the elf ones. Here you go, first one.

What do you call an elf who sits on a shelf?" She waited for Cappie to shrug.

"A shelfie!" Cappie groaned.

"What do you call an elf who has lots of money?" Sandra continued. "Welfy! What's an elf's favorite number? Twelfth!"

"Enough! Enough!" Cappie said. "We have got to go to bed."

"One more," Sandra said, laughing at her own jokes. "What do you call an elf who doesn't share?"

Cappie said nothing.

"Elfish!"

"Alright, my joke teller," Cappie said grinning despite herself. "Off to bed for us. Morning comes too early, and that is no joke."

"Lindigo, Cap," Sandra said, bidding her sweet dreams in elfin.

CHAPTER 56

Catching Up With Gunny

Location: North Pole Village

By the end of November, Sandra and all the elves working at Equator Pole had returned to North Pole Village for the push to Christmas. Even the South Pole elves returned for the busy month. Right away, Sandra could tell something was different with Gunny. She couldn't put her finger on what had changed, but something was definitely different. At this time of the year, the whole of the Pole was working long hours, so it wasn't just that he was putting in a lot of time at work. He seemed quieter to her. Almost sad at times. And he kept to himself more. Sandra rarely saw him, which was much different than how he normally acted. There were times the gang would gather at the cocoa stands for a double tall with extra whip cream after work, and Gunny wouldn't be there. Sandra missed him. At first she thought it was just her imagining he was different, but the elves had started to notice, too.

"Sandra, what's Gunny doing lately?" Toasty asked one evening over cocoa. "It seems like we hardly see him since he's got back from the ranch."

"Yeah, what's up with that?" Tack added. "He hasn't even been to Pole Pong and we could use him. We got whipped on by the Polarities last night!"

" . . . *squawk*! . . . he's quiet . . . *squawk*!"

When even Squawk noticed, Sandra decided it was time for a heart-to-heart with her friend. She planned to do it first thing in the morning, until she saw him heading for the factory on her way to her room at the hotel.

"Gunny! We missed you for cocoa tonight," she called out to him. She was sure he had seen her but he seemed to have picked up his pace as she called out. She had to run to catch up, until he finally slowed down.

"Hey, you're back up from St. Annalise already," he said. She had been gone for almost a month but she was sure he knew she had been back again for a couple of days. "I'm just heading back into the factory to run an inventory check on the bicycle horn supply. I'm thinking we're running short on those and – "

"It can wait, Gunny," Sandra said. "I promise I'll get one of the elves on the night shift to check it for you. That way, you and I have some time to talk. Right here, on this nice bench, would be good." She pointed to a private spot close to where they were standing.

Gunny hesitated, and then seemed to think better of it and moved toward the bench.

"Of course," he said. "What's up?"

"What's up is that I want to know what's up," Sandra said, facing him. "We miss you. *I* miss you. Since you got back from your visit to the ranch you haven't seemed the same and we're all worried about you. Did something happen there? Is everyone all right? Is Ghost all right? I know he broke his arm in that ranch accident so he's resting there, but is he recovering all right? Is it something else?"

Is it something else? Gunny thought to himself. It was so much of something else. He was still racked with guilt over what his little brother had done, but also full of loyalty to him. Ghost had messed up, big time, but he was still his little brother. But, at the same time, Gunny hated keeping anything from Sandra. He wanted to tell her, and since he couldn't, he felt it was better to simply stay away from her.

"Work, work, work, Sandra. That's the main thing. Yeah, there's some things going on at the ranch that I need to keep private, but mostly I'm just busy." He didn't lie and he hoped she would accept it without asking for more.

She looked at him for a long minute before finally taking his hand and saying something that in a million years Gunny felt he never, ever, would have guessed.

"Okay," she said. "I understand that some things need to stay private, but Santa and I clearly have you working too much. I have the perfect idea for a break." She stood up and faced him on the bench taking both his hands.

"Gunny Holiday," she said solemnly. "I would be honored if you would escort me to this year's Christmas Cotillion dance and Secret Pal Reveal party."

So many emotions flashed through the thunderstruck cowboy. The most beautiful girl, inside and out, he had ever met had just asked him to the biggest event at the Pole. She was asking despite his abysmal performance when he had walked out on her two years before. She was trusting him. He knew he should say no, but there was no way that was going to happen.

"You're making me nervous," Sandra said, trying to be lighthearted. He was taking so long to answer that he was making her worry. Maybe she had just thoroughly embarrassed herself.

"I'm making you nervous?" Gunny said standing now. "Because I didn't answer right away, you mean? Because I'm floored that the most beautiful girl that I have ever met would give this rough-cut guy a second chance at something he blew so badly the first time.

"Cassandra Clausmonetsiamlydelaterra dot dot dot," he grinned at her. She was grinning back. After all, he had just said she was pretty. Beautiful, actually, she thought to herself extraordinarily pleased that he thought so. "There is nothing I would rather do on any night than escort you to that event, or any other event you would like me to be at with you." He was standing very close to her now, still holding her hands.

"Really?" she whisper-talked, now feeling weirdly shy about it.

"Really," he whisper-talked back, lifting her chin up with his hand so she could see the sincerity in his eyes. *Oh ginger-snaps, he's going to kiss me again*, Sandra thought, surprised by the idea of how much that pleased her.

But he didn't. Instead, he broke the moment, released her hands, and stepped back. The magic moment was broken. "But for now, I need to do that inventory," he said, back to business.

Sandra shook her head as if to clear it. "Of course, sure," she said. "It's late though, Gunny. You need sleep like the rest of us." She had to call it out to him as he was already heading down the sidewalk.

A good night of sleep had eluded him since he'd found out about Ghost. "I know," he called back and then he stopped and took a few steps back to be sure she could hear him.

"Seriously, Sandra, you just asked me to the Cotillion, right?" he said. She nodded her head.

"I knew you liked me." He grinned the biggest smile he had worn in weeks. Sandra was pretty sure she heard him whistling. Best sound ever, she thought, smiling too.

## CHAPTER 57

The Cotillion and the Big Reveal

Location: North Pole Village

It was December 7 and all the elves were gathered at the North Pole. The Equator Pole workers were back through January, and the South Pole elves were up until they returned to the South Pole right before Christmas Eve.

Since she had come to the Pole, Sandra could not remember any occasion that had created more excitement than the upcoming Christmas Cotillion. The North Pole had celebrated the event for more time than anyone could remember, except for Santa himself and Mrs. Claus. Two years ago, when Sandra had been named South Pole Santa, it had been a really big occasion, but this year there seemed to be even more excitement about it. Sandra broke it down to three reasons:

First, they had been through a crisis this past year, but all of them, down to the smallest fairy and elf, had gotten through it together. They had joined forces to be sure the children of the world had not been worried about Santa missing and they had kept the secret, which was a huge accomplishment for elves and fairies. Joy to the world!

Second, the elves were beyond excited about finding out who was their secret pal.

The third reason was all about fashion. It was definitely going to be the year of the fascinator! All of the girls, including even Em, who rarely liked getting dressed up, were excited about wearing one of the headpieces. The most popular style seemed to be the ones that looked like wrapped gifts, and the elves were busy adding their own glittery touches to make them each their own. Even Sandra and Birdie had decided to get in on the fascinator fun.

"So how do I look?" Birdie said, turning to Sandra with her fascinator headpiece fully in place. She had selected one that looked like a holly sprig.

"Uh, hello!" said Sandra. "You are too stunning! I thought those were supposed to make you look goofy, but you look fabulous." The red and green in the hat matched Birdie's dress perfect.

Birdie grinned. "I hope Crow thinks so too," she said. "Okay, now let's see yours."

Sandra pinned it in place and turned to her best friend. She had selected a shooting star shape that matched her gold and silver dress. "Whoa, Gunny won't be able to look away."

"So, are we ready to go stun our dates and have a ball at the ball?" Sandra linked her arm with her best friend's, and they headed to the lobby where the guys were waiting.

They might have been born and raised on a ranch, and looked good in boots and chaps, but the Holiday brothers also could bring their best to a tuxedo. Both Birdie and Sandra drew in their breath as they sighted their dates. The brothers, in return, both felt weak in the knees. The two young women were stunning alone, but coming into the lobby area together, big smiles on their faces, fascinators in place and perfectly fitted gowns on, they were breathtaking.

Going into the merrily decorated Happiness Hall with Buddy and his band playing cheerful Christmas tunes, the gorgeous foursome was barely noticed. Everyone was having too much fun to even look their way!

"I'm so happy," Sandra said as Gunny whisked her around the big dance hall to a Christmas waltz.

"There is no way you could possibly be as happy as I am right now," Gunny said. "After all, you are not holding South Pole Santa in your arms, knowing you are the luckiest man in the whole of the world. Very likely the luckiest man in the whole of the Universe." The thought crossed his mind briefly that, ironically, while he didn't like the guy, he had Jason to thank for how happy he was at that moment. If Jason hadn't left and not looked back, Gunny doubted he would have ever gotten a second chance with Sandra. Now that he was gone, though, Gunny had no intention of blowing it. Sandra was trusting him again and he was not going to mess it up.

The big crowd mingled and mixed, dined and danced, before Santa stepped up to the podium to make announcements.

"Ho Ho Ho! So are you all ready for the big Secret Pal unveiling?" he said, playing to a crowd he knew were anxious to tell.

"YES!" It seemed the whole hall yelled, including Sandra and Gunny playing along.

"Well then," Santa said. "Let me bring out our lovely Dear Lovey, who started it all, to share her Secret Pal first and then we'll let you all figure out your own." He went off to the left side of the stage to wheel in Dear Lovey, who was dazzling in a sparkling blue dress and big bow fascinator.

"Merry Christmas, everyone!" Dear Lovey called out. She too knew how to work a crowd. This was a group that loved to say "Merry Christmas."

"MERRY CHRISTMAS!" It seemed they all shouted it while giggling so the noise level was like a sonic boom and echoed through the hall.

"It's at last time to share who our secret pals are. Isn't it exciting?"

"YES!"

"Who did you get, Dear Lovey?" someone shouted out.

"Well, here's how we'll tell. I'll start and tell who I was the secret pal for and then that person will tell who they got and then the next one will tell and the next until all of us know. Got it?"

"YES!" They were all abuzz about this good way to share. Santa was on stage with Mrs. Claus, nodding in agreement for what a smart way that was to share. This way everyone got to share in the surprise of finding out everyone else's secret pal.

"Okay then, without any further ado, I will share that I was the Secret Pal for," she paused. "I was the secret pal for Breezy!"

Everyone clapped. Breezy went up and hugged Dear Lovey and then announced to the group. "I was the secret pal for Barney!" He too was excited and round and round the hall it went until it got to Clicker.

"I was the secret pal for Sandra! I was very excited about it," the normally shy elf assigned to taking pictures at the Pole announced. No wonder she got such beautiful photos from her secret pal for her birthday, Sandra thought. She gave Clicker a hug and a big thanks.

"And I, was the secret pal for," she deliberately paused as she knew elves loved and hated big pauses. "I was the secret pal for . . . Gunny!"

"What?" Gunny exclaimed. "No way! You did good."

"Why, thank you," Sandra said and curtsied to him, playing up the fun.

On and on it went, around the room, until every elf and fairy and human had found out their secret pal. Santa went to the podium again.

"Ho Ho Ho! Well, that was a lot of fun. A lot of fun," Santa boomed in his big Santa voice. He never really needed a microphone. "Sandra, can you join me on stage?

"As she makes her way up here, I want to thank all of you again. I believe this is our very best Christmas Cotillion ever. The reindeer and I are particularly thankful to be here this year." He hastened to add as he heard sniffles, "now, now, no crying. This is a joyful occasion and a true celebration. We had a close call, but I am so proud of all of you and thankful to be in this role of Santa still."

Sandra reached the podium then and gave her mentor a big hug that really came from everyone in the hall.

"We love you, Santa!"

"We're lucky to have you!"

"We love you, too, Sandra!" Both Santas were grinning as some of the elves were hauling big bags onto the stage as Sandra came up.

"One of the great surprises I came back to from my time away," Santa now continued. "Was coming back to the incredible idea that Sandra had for children to practice regular acts of kindness and then share those acts with all of us here at the Pole. Sandra, truly, I am humbled by the thoughtfulness of this inspiring idea. And, if the idea itself didn't humble me, then all of these bags packed full of examples of kindness, from children all around the world, certainly would. We have almost as many bags of acts of kindness as we do letters to Santa, and a lot of those letters are addressed to you."

Santa stepped back and applauded for Sandra, while the hall joined him. Sandra saw, and heard Gunny especially cheering loudly, until he seemed distracted by a couple of the Sherlocks. The Sherlocks were there enjoying the evening, except the few assigned to be on security, which in the past was never the case but the Santanapping had changed several things. The two Sherlocks Gunny was talking with were both in uniform. Sandra turned her attention back to Santa as he continued.

"Sandra, this truly was a spectacular idea that will add caring and goodness to our world. Thank you for showing us all such leadership. I understand we'll draw the names of the twelve lucky children on Christmas Day and they'll get to come visit us next year."

"That's exactly right, Santa, and thank you for your support. The children all seemed excited about the chance to win a trip to this special place, but even more than that, to step up and demonstrate the ways they are kind. I'm already excited to meet the twelve who will be selected to visit us here," Sandra said. She turned to the elves fully now, not seeing Gunny at all in the back of the room. "I believe all of you are excited too, right?"

"YES!" came the thundering response.

"Okay, well thank you again, all of you," Santa said, hugging on Sandra. "This has been a magical night but tomorrow, however, is a work day so Mrs. Claus and I are going to head for home. I bid you all a good night!" He walked off stage with Mrs. Claus and just like that, they were gone.

And so was Gunny it seemed. "Sandra!" Breezy came running up to her looking pretty in a red and white gown with a candy cane fascinator. It took a minute before Sandra realized she was upset.

"What is it, Breezy?" she asked.

"The Sherlocks arrested Gunny!" the little elf said, very distraught.

"What?" Sandra said, feeling wide awake instantly. "For what?"

"For this," Breezy said, handing her a photo. In the photo was a fuzzy picture of Gunny walking out of a building with Santa's hat, a big bag of letters, and a *Honolulu Gazette* clearly strewn about on the ground in front of him.

"He took Santa, Sandra!" Breezy said. "Gunny took Santa! The Esteemed Magical Council got this photo sent to them and demanded the Sherlocks arrest him."

"Are they sure?" Sandra said, feeling sick.

"Gunny said to tell you not to worry. He said it wasn't true and he believed in you not to believe it."

Not to believe it? The proof was right in front of her. She looked again at the photo she held in her badly shaking hand and headed to see Santa. He would know what she should believe.

"Breezy, don't tell anyone else," she said. "I don't want to take away from the fun of tonight's party - including your fun. No sad faces. I'm sure it will all be fine." She wished she meant it. Something didn't feel right, but a feeling served no real purpose at that minute. "I'm going to go find Santa and get it sorted out."

The little elf nodded her head as Sandra took the photo and slipped out the back just about as fast as Santa had earlier.

This Christmas Cotillion started out great and had ended just like her first, she thought ironically. Gunny was gone and her trust had been shattered into tiny little pieces.

In spite of heading straight to find Santa, Sandra found he too had heard the news of Gunny and had already left with the Esteemed Council Representative, the Sherlocks, and Gunny. Sandra had no way of knowing where they had gone and no way to follow.

CHAPTER 58

December 23

Location: North Pole Village

Just as things had started to brighten up at the Pole, Gunny's arrest put a veil of gray over the happiest month of the year. Santa had returned the next day from wherever the Esteemed Magical Realm Council meetings were held, but he had returned alone. He had pulled everyone at the Pole together to review the situation. Gunny, he explained, despite his objections, would be held with the Council while they conducted their own investigation.

"I feel confident, however, that he could be released at any time. I personally, of course, know that he is innocent," Santa said. "The important thing for all of us to remember right now, and what Gunny wanted me to emphasize with all of you, is that we must put our focus on serving the children. We have toys to be built and a Christmas Eve coming now only days away! So back to work with you all!"

What he hadn't shared with them was that the Council meeting had not gone as smoothly as he had believed it would. He had expected to share that he knew Gunny had nothing to do with his Santanapping and that statement would then end the proceeding, with the two of them able to return to the Pole.

Instead, they had grilled him with questions. Questions he wasn't necessarily ready to answer as well as he should have anticipated. He had been used to answering the same kinds of questions from the Sherlocks, but Santa could be more controlling of that group since they worked for him. He had asked the Sherlocks not to focus on where he had been but instead to focus on being sure it could never happen again to either him or Sandra. In his mind, that had been the end of it and, like Gunny, he had simply chose not to talk about the incident anymore, thereby not having to be deceitful. And when he did speak of it, he was very careful not to lie to anyone. He especially did not want to lie or mislead the Sherlocks or the Council. So when the Council had asked him to explain the photo they had and why Gunny was pictured in it, he did not have an answer. Finally he had sputtered something about "people being able to manipulate any photo on computers these days." It was after that question and non-answer from Santa that the Council had ruled to keep Gunny until they could determine his involvement level.

Santa had contacted the Council every day since then, and finally on December 23 he received the good news that there was not enough evidence against Gunny to continue to hold him and he would be released. In time for Christmas Eve! The news put extra pep in the step of every elf who could hardly wait to have him back.

For Sandra the news was both a relief and a quandary. She wanted him home. She had found herself missing him and thinking of him often. On the other hand, fair or not, the incident hadn't helped at all with her trust issues with him. She had Santa's assurances that Gunny was not guilty of what they were charging him with, but her Santa senses told her there was more to the story than either Santa or Gunny was sharing with her. She couldn't put her finger on it, but she believed both of them knew more than they were telling. Part of her wanted to press them, and part of her was learning to accept that, even if she was right, sometimes it was important to simply let things be. That choice made her feel the best about his return, so she put her focus there and looked forward to seeing his smiling face. After the cotillion, she had begun to suspect which of the Holiday boys would likely be playing a closer role in her life. She smiled to herself thinking about it.

The thought surprised her and quickly gave her twinges of guilt about Jason, which she knew were ridiculous at this point. He had been so important to her and she had felt adamant that they could have overcome the challenges they faced from the fairy and elfin conflict. But he hadn't felt the same way, and after month after month of not even a postcard, or call - not even on their birthday - she had accepted it was time to let that dream go and move on.

"That time in your life is over," Sandra said out loud to herself firmly as she turned to the village to see if she could find a fun Secret Pal gift to give Gunny for Christmas. Something special that would help show she was starting to think of him as more than just a pal. Gunny was helping her say goodbye to the past and welcome the magic of the future.

CHAPTER 58

The Most Magical Night of the Year!

Location: All Around the World

"Are you ready, Em?" Sandra said lovingly, checking again that Em was comfortable and ready for the biggest night of the year. Em had never felt better – or more impatient. She was ready to fly. She gave out an impatient delgin huff in response. Sandra laughed. With her merry Christmas Eve Santa suit on, her hair in its true sparkling state, and the big smile on her face, she had never looked more the part of South Pole Santa. She had grown so much already in just the two short years since she had been selected for the role.

" . . . *squawk*! . . . me too . . . *squawk*!"

Sandra's favorite bird anywhere called out from his perch on the *Mistletoe 2* saddle. After her disappearance on this night, last year, Squawk wasn't about to let her go without him.

"Squawk, I am so happy you are going with us this year," Sandra said, feeling joy flood through her. "We're ready over here, Santa," she called over to her mentor, as she climbed up next to Squawk into the *Mistletoe 2*.

Plunking down in place, she looked out at the whole population of the Pole, who always came out to see them off. It was, without doubt, one of the best moments of any year. It was only dimmed for her, by not seeing Gunny's face amongst them. While he had been released from the Council's detainment, there seemed to have been some kind of additional delay. In the mega busy hubbub of the busiest days of the year, Santa had not been able to check in to get an update. She would miss seeing Gunny before Christmas, but it came along with having the best job in the world. Personal Christmas activities came after Christmas deliveries.

"Alright, reindeer!" Santa called out. "Let's ride!"

"Bye, Santa! Bye, Sandra!" the elves called out. "See you tomorrow, Santa! Have fun at St. Annalise, Sandra and Squawk and Em!"

"Merry Christmas!" Sandra called back.

". . . *squawk*! . . . Merry Christmas! . . . *squawk*!" Even Squawk was jolly on this magical day of the year.

This time, like a normal Christmas Eve, there were no surprises and no Santanappings in the works. Even if there had been, with the new tracking devices the Sherlocks had installed and secret security measures that they refused to discuss with anybody, there was almost no chance either of the Santas could ever be taken again.

Sandra and Em had become much more efficient at deliveries and had become valued assistants for Santa. Next year, they would be completely on their own for deliveries to much of the world so Santa was pleased to see the progress. Both Sandra and Em were naturals at the role and Squawk too found ways to help. He was able to read off the Nice List to Sandra about what deliveries were next and, once, even warned her about a child he saw through a window still awake.

Despite it taking twenty-four hours of nonstop work to get the whole world done, they finished up with three minutes to spare, feeling energetic and wonderful. This time, Santa insisted on seeing Sandra, Em, and Squawk to St. Annalise, where he stopped for just long enough to wish Cappie and Thomas a Merry Christmas before heading off to home at the North Pole.

"We'll see you soon, Santa," Sandra called out to him. "Thank you again for believing in me and giving me the best job in the world." Thomas and Cappie came over and hugged her as she waved to her jolly mentor. Em had already switched to her small elf self and there was Christmas magic in the air.

"eeeeee eeeeee,"

"Rio! You love Christmas, too! Thanks for staying up!" Sandra called out to the beautiful green dolphin.

"Ho Ho Ho! Merry Christmas!" Santa called back, still easily heard though the sleigh was now quite a distance from the tugboat.

"Merry Christmas!" The group on the *Mistletoe* called back to him in response.

"Oh Oh Oh!" Sandra said as she turned around for a big Christmas hug. It was wonderful to be South Pole Santa and wonderful to be home for the holiday!

EPILOGUE

"Santa, this is a surprise!" Sandra said a few days later. She was doing a little dreaming about the future while she walked the completed decks on the South Pole Village barge. There was still more to be done, but it was beginning to look and feel like a place she could call home. "Are you bringing me a late gift?" She couldn't imagine what else would bring Santa back to St. Annalise at this time of year. He should be home getting ready for Slumber Month like the rest of the North Pole.

"I wish that was it, Sandra," Santa said. "Instead I am bringing news about Gunny."

"Gunny?" Sandra said, going from teasing about a gift to a high state of concern quickly. She hadn't talked to the cowboy since he returned from where the Council had been holding him, but she had assumed that was because he was busy catching up with his own family. She expected to see him soon.

"Yes," Santa said, nodding his head and looking far from jolly. "It seems the Esteemed High Council of the Magical Realm released Gunny as they had agreed to do, but before he could get back to the topside world, the Supreme Esteemed High Fairy Council, led by Reesa, who was appointed to the chair position in place of Juna recently, took him. She, and the majority of the Supreme Fairy Council members, are demanding a swap."

"A swap?" Sandra said total confused.

"For Jason," Santa said.

"For Jason?" Now Sandra was completely confused. *"They* have Jason."

"Not according to them. They say the last time anyone saw Jason Annalise was when he visited you at the North Pole. They believe you have hidden him away to keep him from being the fairy king. They demand to have their fairy king back before they will release Gunny."

Sandra struggled to keep on her feet and finally leaned back against one of the big deck rails of the South Pole Village barge. Jason wasn't with the fairies?

Where was he?

# # #

Today is New Year's Eve, Jason thought. He hoped they had found Santa in time for the big night and that whether they did or they didn't, Sandra had enjoyed Christmas Eve. He realized that day was already a week ago now. It felt like it had been even longer ago than that, but time moved slowly where he was at.

"Here's your New Year's Eve dinner, *your highness.*" The last two words were said with a great deal of mockery as the same meal Jason had been given every day for the last seven months was slid under the cage door.

He had been sure he knew the way back to the fairy realm when he had set out on his own through the cave opening he had discovered on Cassandra's Cay during the big storm. Turned out he'd been wrong. It was indeed an entrance to inner earth, but an entrance guarded by the drags, a species that had no regard for fairies – or most any other species either.

He had said goodbye to the topside world and never told the inner world he was coming. So there he had sat. Missed by many but not missing. Before he could stop himself, he cried out again, as he had done before, more grief and despair than he could keep in.

"Saaaaaaanndraaaaaa!"

Hot Cocoa Brownies

An elf favorite! Recipe by Betsy Chan, Bloomington, MN

½ cup unsweetened cocoa
½ cup all-purpose flour
½ teaspoon baking powder
1 teaspoon kosher salt*
1 stick (1/2 cup) unsalted butter**
1 cup mini marshmallows
¾ cup brown sugar, packed
1 tablespoon milk
1 teaspoon pure vanilla extract
2 eggs
½ - 2/3 cup mini chocolate chips

Preheat oven to 350 degrees F. Line an 8-inch square pan with parchment paper and spray lightly with non-stick spray, or grease and flour pan.

In a small bowl, use a spoon or fork to mix the cocoa, flour, baking powder and salt. Set aside.

In a large microwaveable bowl, microwave the butter on medium power until most is melted (watch it carefully so butter doesn't overheat and splatter.) Add marshmallows and microwave on high for 45-60 seconds or until marshmallow puffs up. Stir until smooth. With and electric mixer (or vigorously by hand) stir in the sugar, milk and vanilla then add eggs and beat for 2 minutes. Add dry ingredients from the small bowl, scraping the sides of the bowl while blending the batter. Stir in chocolate chips. Spread batter evenly into the prepared pan.

Bake in preheated oven for 23-25 minutes, or until a toothpick inserted into the center of the pan comes out with the brownie slightly clinging to it. Remove pan from oven; cool on rack. It's best to wait at least an hour before cutting.

*Can substitute with table salt

** If using salted butter, add only ½ tsp of salt

Enjoy this yummy Hot Cocoa Brownie as is or top with your favorite frosting! Extra mini marshmallows can also be added. Just stir in ¼ cup mini marshmallows to the batter.

Acknowledgements

My life overflows with wonderful family and friends at every turn. Huge thanks from my heart go out to:

Brie Vennard for coaching me again through another of Sandra's adventures.

The uber-talented **Tina Fischer Mitchell** my wonderful cover artist.

Diana Kwong a genius with placing commas.

Betsy Chan my friend who works magic in the kitchen.

And also to **Wendy Parris, Carolyn Pinard, Krysta Rasmussen** and my top readers **Ryan** and **Leonie**. Girls, you keep me writing!

Thanks most of all to my guy, **Glen**, who believes in me every day.

Don't miss!

Other books by JingleBelle Jackson available

Book 1: The Search for South Pole Santa - A Christmas Adventure

Book 2: Sandra Claus… - A South Pole Santa Adventure

Book 3: The Santanapping – A South Pole Santa Adventure

Book 4: Coming Christmas Season 2015!

For updates, insights and some madcap elf fun year-round, stop by www.JingleBelleJackson.com

If you enjoyed this book, I would welcome your review. Thanks so much!

About the Author

JingleBelle Jackson resides in the Pacific Northwest with her husband, family and many friends. She was born on the 4th of July and besides holidays, loves parades, laughing, celebrating, wearing funny hats and fun! She believes in the power of kindness to make the world a better place.

Made in the USA
Lexington, KY
08 December 2014